THE EVENTS IN THIS BOOK ARE REAL.

NAMES AND PLACES HAVE BEEN CHANGED
TO PROTECT THE LORIEN,
WHO REMAIN IN HIDING.

OTHER CIVILIZATIONS DO EXIST.

SOME OF THEM SEEK TO DESTROY YOU.

THE LORIEN ▭ LEGACIES

BY PITTACUS LORE

Novels

I AM NUMBER FOUR

THE POWER OF SIX

THE RISE OF NINE

THE FALL OF FIVE

THE REVENGE OF SEVEN

Novellas

I AM NUMBER FOUR: THE LOST FILES #1: SIX'S LEGACY

I AM NUMBER FOUR: THE LOST FILES #2: NINE'S LEGACY

I AM NUMBER FOUR: THE LOST FILES #3: THE FALLEN LEGACIES

I AM NUMBER FOUR: THE LOST FILES #4: THE SEARCH FOR SAM

I AM NUMBER FOUR: THE LOST FILES #5: THE LAST DAYS OF LORIEN

I AM NUMBER FOUR: THE LOST FILES #6: THE FORGOTTEN ONES

I AM NUMBER FOUR: THE LOST FILES #7: FIVE'S LEGACY

I AM NUMBER FOUR: THE LOST FILES #8: RETURN TO PARADISE

I AM NUMBER FOUR: THE LOST FILES #9: FIVE'S BETRAYAL

Novella Collections

I AM NUMBER FOUR: THE LOST FILES: THE LEGACIES

(Contains novellas #1–#3)

I AM NUMBER FOUR: THE LOST FILES: SECRET HISTORIES

(Contains novellas #4–#6)

I AM NUMBER FOUR: THE LOST FILES: HIDDEN ENEMY

(Contains novellas #7–#9)

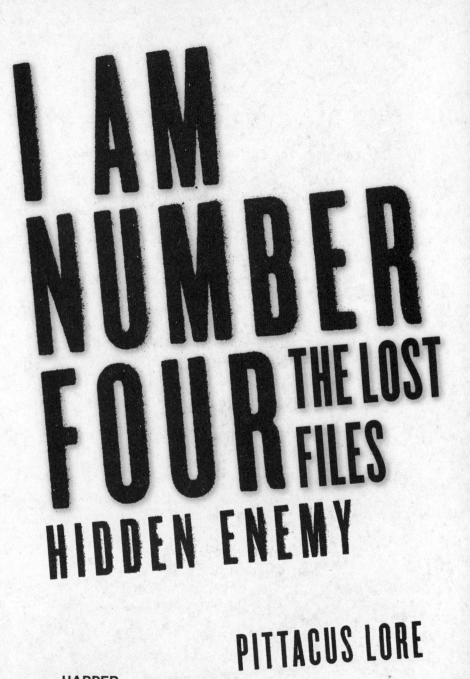

I AM NUMBER FOUR

THE LOST FILES

HIDDEN ENEMY

PITTACUS LORE

HARPER
An Imprint of HarperCollinsPublishers

I Am Number Four: The Lost Files: Hidden Enemy

I Am Number Four: The Lost Files: Five's Legacy © 2014 by
Pittacus Lore

I Am Number Four: The Lost Files: Return to Paradise
© 2014 by Pittacus Lore

I Am Number Four: The Lost Files: Five's Betrayal © 2014
by Pittacus Lore

www.epicreads.com

ISBN 978-0-06-228768-7

Typography by Ray Shappell

16 17 18 CG/RRDC 10 9 8 7 6 5 4
❖
First Edition

CONTENTS

I AM NUMBER FOUR
THE LOST FILES
FIVE'S LEGACY

CHAPTER ONE

"THE MOGS ARE HERE!"

My eyes shoot open as I jerk upright, hoping that sentence was just something from a bad dream.

But it's not.

"They're here," Rey whispers again as he crosses over the floor of our little shack to where I'm sleeping on top of a pallet of blankets.

I'm off the floor in seconds. Rey's solar-powered lantern swings in front of my face, and it blinds me. I flinch away and then he turns it off, leaving me in complete darkness. As he pushes me towards the back of our home, all I can make out is a sliver of silver light peeking through the window.

"Out the back." His voice is full of urgency and fear. "I'll hold them off. Go, go, go."

I start grabbing at the air where he'd stood moments before but find nothing. I can't see anything: My eyes still burn from the lantern.

"Rey—"

"No." He cuts me off from somewhere in the dark. "If you don't go now, we're *both* dead."

There's a clattering near the front of the shack, followed by the sound of something—or someone— slamming against the front door. Rey lets out a pained cry but the inside of the shack is still nothing but an abyss of black in my eyes. I know there's a metal bar over the door that's not going to hold up against much more than a little force. It's for show more than anything else. If someone *really* wanted into our shack, they could just blow through the flimsy wooden walls. And if it's the Mogs . . .

There's no time to think, only to react. It's *me* they're after. I've got to get to safety.

I rip away the piece of cloth that serves as a makeshift curtain and throw myself through the little window. I land with a plop in a three-inch puddle of mud, slop, and things I don't even want to imagine— I'm in the hog pen.

A single thought runs through my mind. *I'm going to die a thirteen-year-old boy covered in pig shit on an island in the middle of nowhere.*

Life is so unfair.

The hogs squeal—I've disturbed their sleep—and it snaps me back into the moment. Old training regimens and lectures from years before take over my brain and I'm moving again, checking my flanks to make sure there are no Mogs that have already made their way to the back of the hut. I start to think about what their plan of action might be. If the Mogs actually *knew* I was on the island, I'd be surrounded already. No, it must be a single scout that stumbled upon us by accident. Maybe he had time to report us to the others, maybe not. Whatever the case, I have to get out of the line of fire. Rey will take out the scout. He'll be fine. At least that's what I tell myself, choosing to ignore how frail Rey's looked lately.

He *has* to be okay. He always is.

I head for the jungle behind our shack. My bare feet sink into the sand, as if the island itself is trying to slow me down. I'm dressed only in dark athletic shorts, and branches and shrubs around me scratch at my bare chest and stomach as I enter the cover of the trees. I've done this sort of thing before, once, in Canada. Then, coats and a few bags weighed me down. But we'd had a little more warning. Now, in the sticky-hot night of the Caribbean, I'm weighed down only by my lack of stamina.

As I hurl myself through the dense vegetation, I think of all the mornings I was supposed to spend jogging along the beach or hiking through the forest that I *actually* spent playing solitaire or simply lazing around. Doing what I really wanted to do, like drawing little cartoons in the sand. Coming up with short stories told by stick figures. Rey always said I shouldn't actually write anything down—that any journal or notes I wrote could be found and used as proof of who I am. But writing and drawing in the sand was temporary. When the tide came in, my stories were gone. Even just doing that caused me to work up a sweat in this damned climate, and I'd return to Rey, pretending to be exhausted. He'd comment on the timing of my imaginary run and then treat me to a rich lunch as a reward. Rey is a taskmaster when it comes to doling out things to do, but his lungs are bad and he always trusted that I was doing the training he told me to do. He had no reason not to—no reason to think I wouldn't take our situation seriously.

It wasn't just the avoidance of having to work my ass off in the heat that kept me from training. It was the monotony of it all that I hated. Run, lift, stretch, aim, repeat—day in and day out. Plus, we're living out in the middle of nowhere. Our island isn't even on any maps. I never thought the Mogs would ever find us.

Now, I'm afraid that's coming back to haunt me. I wheeze as I run. I'm totally unprepared for this attack. Those mornings lazing around the beach are going to get me killed.

It doesn't take long before there's a stitch in my side

so sore that I think it's possible I've burst some kind of internal organ. I'm out of breath, and the humid air feels like it's trying to smother me. My hands grasp onto low-hanging branches as I half-pull my way through thick green foliage, the bottoms of my feet scraping against fallen limbs and razor-sharp shells. Within a few minutes the canopy above me is so dense that only pinpricks of the moonlight shine through. The jungle has given way to a full-blown rain forest.

I'm alone in the dark in a rain forest with alien monsters chasing after me.

I pause, panting and holding my side. Our island is small, but I'm only maybe a fifth of the way across it. On the other side of the island a small, hidden kayak is waiting for me, along with a pack of rations and first aid gear. The last-chance escape vessel, something that'll let me slip into the dark of the night and disappear on the ocean. But that seems so far away now, with my lungs screaming at me and my bare feet bleeding. I lean against a tree, trying to catch my breath. Something skitters across the forest floor a few feet away from me and I jump, but it's only one of the little green lizards that overrun the island. Still, my heart pounds. My head is dizzy.

The Mogadorians are here. I'm going to die.

I can't imagine what Rey is doing back at the shack. How many Mogs are here? How many can he take on?

I hope I'm right, and it's just a single scout. I realize I haven't heard any gunshots. Is that a good sign, or does it mean the bastards got to him before he was able to fire off a single round?

Keep going, I tell myself, and then start out again. My calves are burning and my lungs feel like they're about to split open every time I inhale. I stumble, hitting the ground hard and knocking what little breath I had out of me.

Somewhere behind me, I can hear movement in the trees.

I glance around. Without a clear view of the sky, I can't even tell which direction I'm going anymore. I'm totally screwed. I have to do something.

I abandon the plan to cross the island. I'm in no shape to do so. For a moment I think of burrowing down into the brush—maybe finding something to hide in until I can slip through the forest—but then I think of all the fist-sized spiders and ants and snakes that could be waiting there for me, and imagine a Mogadorian scout stepping on me by accident.

So I head up instead. Gathering every ounce of strength I have, I use a few sturdy vines to pull myself hand over hand up to a low branch on a nearby tree. All I can think of are the many different types of beasts Rey's told me the Mogs can command, any one of which would like nothing more than to tear me apart.

Why don't *we* have giant hell-beasts to fight for us?

My arms are shaking by the time I squat on the limb, the wood creaking under my weight as I stare into the blackness, hoping over and over again that nothing will emerge from it. That I can just wait this out.

That it will all just go *away*.

There's no telling how much time passes. If I'd been more put together or hadn't been so taken by surprise, I might have remembered to grab my watch on the way out the window. It's weird—time always seemed like it didn't mean anything on the island, and now it means everything. How many minutes before more of them arrive? How many seconds before they find me? I try to keep from trembling, and my stomach from turning over—between the running, my fear, and the damp smell of pig that clings to me in a thick coat of sludge, I'm teetering on the edge of vomiting. Maybe the stinking layer of crap will help keep me camouflaged, at least.

It's not a very reassuring silver lining.

Finally, a silhouette starts to take shape in the darkness. I draw in closer to the tree. The figure is human sized. Maybe even a little hunched over, leaning on a cane as he steps into the dim moonlight. He's wearing a blue linen shirt, khaki cargo pants, and sneakers that might have been white at some point. His beard is white, streaked with black, his wild hair almost silver.

I recognize him immediately, of course. Rey.

He's got something held against him, wrapped in a piece of cloth. I start to call down to him, but he's already staring holes into me, his lips quivering, as if he's fighting every urge to yell. He simply stands there, the silence hanging in the thick air between us. Finally, I break it.

"Well? Did you get him?"

Rey doesn't respond immediately, just looks away, staring down at the ground.

"What'd you forget?" His voice has a slight rattle to it.

"What?" I ask, my breath short.

He throws his parcel down on the ground. Part of the cloth falls back, and I can make out a familiar corner.

"The Chest?" I ask. My *Loric* Chest. The most sacred thing I own. The treasure I'm not actually allowed to look into. The container that supposedly holds my inheritance and the tools to rebuild my home planet, and I can't even peek inside until Rey thinks I'm ready to—whatever *that* means.

"The Chest." Rey nods.

I scramble down the tree, half falling to the earth.

"We should get going, right?" I ask. My words are spilling out now, my tongue stumbling over the letters as I try to say a million things at once. "You don't have any weapons? Or our food? Where are we going now? Shouldn't we be—"

"Your Chest is the second most important thing you have to protect after your own life. It was stupid to leave it. Next time, it's your priority to keep it safe."

"What are you—"

"You made it half a mile into the forest," he says, ignoring me. His voice is getting louder now, filled with barely restrained anger. "I didn't want to believe it, but I guess this is proof. You haven't been doing your training. You've been lying to me about it. Every day."

"Rey . . ."

"I already knew that, though." He sounds sad now. "I could tell just by looking at you."

My mind is racing, trying to figure out why we're still standing here. Why he's worried about my training when there could be a whole fleet of Mogs on their way after us. Unless . . .

"There aren't any Mogs here," I say quietly.

Rey just shakes his head and stares at the ground.

This was a test. No, worse than that: This was Rey's way of trapping me and catching me in a lie. And even though, yes, I technically have been less than honest about my training regimen, I can't believe Rey would scare me like this.

"Are you kidding me?" Unlike Rey, I don't have the power to keep my anger from clouding my voice. "I was running for my life. I thought I was going to *die*."

"Death is the least of your worries for now," he says, pointing at my ankle. Underneath the layer of mud and crap is an ugly red mark that appeared a few days ago. A mark that's starting to scab over, and will soon turn into a scar. The mark that—thanks to some other-worldly charm—shows me that another one of my fellow Garde has been murdered. Two is dead. Three and Four are all that stand between death and me.

I am Number Five.

I suddenly feel stupid for thinking I was about to be killed. Of course I wasn't. Numbers Three and Four have to die before I can. I *should* have been worried about being captured and tortured for information. Not that Rey ever tells me anything.

And I realize what this is about. Ever since the scar appeared, it's like something within Rey snapped. He's been getting sicker the last few years, and I'm not anywhere as strong as he thinks I should be. I haven't developed any of the magic powers I'm supposed to have. Neither of us can put up a good fight. That's why we're here on this stupid island, hiding.

Rey's eyes have been on the ground, but he finally raises them to mine, looking at me for a long moment. Then he nods at the Chest.

"Carry it back," he says. Then he's shuffling off into the darkness, leaving me in the sparse moonlight, staring at the duffel bag that contains my Chest.

We weren't under attack. It was only a test.

I'm not going to die on the island. At least, not tonight.

I pick up my Chest, hugging it close to me, letting the corners dig into my stomach.

I stare into the blackness that Rey has disappeared into, and in that moment there's only one emotion filling me. Not fear or relief or even shame for being found out. It's the feeling that the only person I have in this world has betrayed me.

CHAPTER
TWO

THE SUN RISES AS I WASH OFF IN THE OCEAN
and think of Canada, the first place I remember living
here on Earth.

I really liked Canada.

In Canada we ate butter tarts and French fries covered in gravy and rubbery globs of cheese, all served
out of carts on the sides of the roads. Even when it was
summer there it wasn't all that hot. I learned a little
bit of French. Rey didn't like the cold, but I did. He
was Albert in Canada, a name he'd picked after seeing Alberta on a map, thinking it would make him
sound like more of a local. "Old Al" he called himself
sometimes when talking to servers or cashiers. I always
thought it was funny when he dumbed his personal-
ity down and pretended to be my grandfather at times
like that, using words like "whippersnapper" that he'd
picked up from the TV. No one questioned the kindly

old man and his grandson.

I was Cody then. I liked being Cody. I was a person, not just Five. At night, Rey would tell me about Lorien and the Mogadorians and the other Garde—my kindred spirits scattered across the world—and how one day we'd bring about the glorious return of our home planet. Back then, everything seemed like a fairy tale. All the aliens and powers and other worlds were nothing but stories to get me to do my chores. Didn't clean up after yourself? Lorien didn't stand a chance. Forget to brush your teeth? The Mogs would get you for sure.

Then they actually came.

We'd been living up near Montreal for six months— maybe a whole year—when Rey found out they were coming for us. I'm still not sure how. All I know is that suddenly I was running through the woods behind our little cottage while a few Mogadorians tracked me. I was six years old, scared out of my mind. Eventually I'd hidden in a tree. I thought I was a goner until Rey appeared, taking out the Mogs with a broken-off shovel and a shotgun he'd bought on the black market. He's always been good with tools.

"Albert . . ." I'd said from the tree. We always called each other by our false names, never knowing who was listening. "Are they gone?"

"Albert's dead," Rey had said. I knew what he meant, even though I was so young. I'd felt it in my gut. It meant we weren't safe. It meant we couldn't stay there, in that place I liked so much.

So we went on the move, and we didn't stop for a long time.

Rey was Aaron after that, followed by Andy, Jeffrey, and then James. I was Zach, Carson, and then Bolt, which was the last name I got to pick before Rey started choosing them. Maybe I'm forgetting a few in there—it all seems so long ago. I know that I was Carson when Rey's cough first appeared, along with the dark hollows under his eyes. We were camping in the Appalachians. He thought it was the cold that was making him sick, so we started moving south, making our way through the United States and towards a warmer climate. Eventually—after a few sketchy boat rides Rey arranged for us—we set up camp in Martinique, where we stayed for a while. But Rey's cough just got worse. He kept telling me he was feeling better, but at some point I stopped believing him.

I was always the better liar.

As a kid, I thought of lies as little stories or games. Sometimes people we came across would ask questions—Where were my parents? Where was I born?—and I'd just start talking, making up these elaborate histories for Rey and me. Having secrets means you do a lot of lying. Not because you're evil or a bad person or anything like that, but out of necessity.

Really, Rey *trained* me to lie about all those morning runs and hikes. I make a mental note to tell him this later.

Sometimes I wonder if Rey is crazy. Like, what if he's just a really messed-up old guy who stole me from a loving, normal home and all of this alien stuff is simply made up? Maybe he gave me drugs or brainwashed me into having fake memories of some place that couldn't possibly exist. All my life I've heard about Lorien, but the only proof I have that any of it is true is a few weird-looking guys who came after me in Canada.

Well, that plus two scars that appeared like magic on my ankle and a Chest that's supposed to house all kinds of treasures. A Chest that doesn't open no matter how much you prod at it—I know, because I've tried about a million times to find out what's inside over the years.

The treasure of Lorien. Sure. A lot of good it's doing out here in the middle of nowhere.

I don't mind the beach, really. I mean, I get why people go there on vacation. When we first got to the Caribbean, we stuck to the bigger, more populated resorts, just living on the fringes. We'd watch the tourists roll in every year, their brand-new beach clothes a parade of bright colors as they sipped drinks out of giant coconuts and pineapples that weren't even native to the islands (not that they'd have known). But when

One died—when that first scar formed on my ankle—
Rey flipped out. I was nine years old and it was like
the final string keeping him in check snapped, and he
went into full-on survival mode. No more people. We'd
have to live life completely off the grid. And so he'd
cashed in whatever possessions we had, bought a few
supplies and a small sailboat, and headed out to find
the most deserted, godforsaken place he could. Gone
were the restaurants and air-conditioning. No more
TV, video games, or hot showers. Just a beach and a
shack. I don't know what kind of deal Rey must have
struck to find this island, but I'll give him one thing—it
must be hidden away pretty well. A few times a year
people mistakenly wash ashore here, but Rey always
gets rid of them fast.

And that's where I am now. Washing up in the ocean.
A dark cloud forms around my body as I scrub the pig
shit off in the clear water at the shoreline. That's what
the future holds for the great Number Five, one of the
seven most important people left on the planet.

It's not fair.

I remember watching old kung fu movies on cable
right before we came out here. The main characters
were always going to the tops of mountains to train
with ancient masters who taught them to throw ninja
stars and kill people with chopsticks and stuff. When
One died and Rey moved us to the island, he told me

he was no longer the grandfather he'd pretended to be, but my teacher. I'd be his disciple. And I was excited about this at the time. I thought I was going to live out one of those old movies or something. And at first, I *did* do the training—Rey could still walk and move well, then, so we practiced rudimentary martial arts moves. But soon he was sleeping most of the day and trusting that I was doing everything he told me to do. Life on the island turned out to be nothing like those old movies. In those, it'd only take a five-minute montage for the student to become the master. On the island, the training was brutal, unending, and above all, monotonous.

I used to dream of being taken away. That the Garde would all show up one day and tell me they'd been looking for me, and that they were going to take me to their space clubhouse or something. But for all I know, the other Garde don't care about me at all.

"Five!" Rey calls from the shore. Here, where there's no one, there's no point in pretending to be who we're not.

"What?" I yell back, still mad about this morning.

"Come here," he says.

I glance up to see him waving me toward the shack. Instead of listening to him, I fall backwards, letting myself float in the warm water as the sun creeps higher over the horizon.

"Five, get—" but his shout is interrupted by a fit of coughing.

For some reason, this just adds to my annoyance. I'm one of the nine Garde—Lorien's last hope—and *this* is who they sent to protect me? Out of all their magic and powers, *he* was the best they could do to keep me safe? A magic numbering system and a sick Cêpan to look after me. Thanks a lot.

A terrible thought rises in my mind, and even though I try to ignore it, it's there, taunting me, making me hate myself not only for having it, but for thinking that it might be true: The Rey that was supposed to protect me died a long time ago. Before he got sick. When we were still in Canada, with the cold air and hot food. When I was just a little kid.

I hate this feeling—the bitterness that sometimes bubbles up to the surface when I'm upset with Rey. It's not his fault he's sick. I know that. But he's the only person I have to be mad at.

The coughing continues. I crack, and I'm headed up the shore, toes digging into the sand. I shake my brown hair to try and dry it. It's been a long time since I had a proper haircut, and my hair is long and matted against my neck. I pick up a coconut that's fallen from a palm tree as I pass by it. We can break it open and have the sweet meat with breakfast. If I'm even getting breakfast. Rey's no doubt about to chew my ass out and probably send me into the forest to live on my own for a few days to teach me a lesson about lying.

He's breathing normally again by the time I reach him.

"You shouldn't be out here," I say. "You should be resting."

He ignores me and holds a hatchet out. Behind him, I can hear the hogs freaking out about something. They sound spooked.

This is the give-and-take of our relationship: neither of us doing the things the other one says we should be.

"What's this for?" I ask, hesitating to take it. He's probably going to force me to chop wood or something to start making up for this morning. I'm sure he *also* would like an apology, but I'll wait until I'm not mad about the whole "tell Five that aliens are here to murder him" thing.

"To protect us," Rey says, pushing the hatchet closer towards me. "I've coddled you for too long, and now I'm afraid it's too late."

My face scrunches as I shove the coconut under my arm and take the tool. The hogs are still going crazy in their pen.

"What's going on?" I ask slowly. I'm suddenly afraid he's going to have me butcher one of the pigs. I mean, I'm totally on board with eating them; I just don't want to have to kill them myself.

Rey nods towards the pen. The pigs are running around, snorting like mad. If they could scream, I'm guessing that's what they'd be doing.

And then I see why. They're telling us that something has infiltrated their home. That danger has come for them. On the other side of the pen is a coiled-up length of scales and muscles. A viper. A lance head. Nasty little bastards with a habit of making their homes a little too close to humans. Once, in Martinique, I saw a boy who was thirteen or so—about my age, now—who was being carried on a backboard to the hospital. He was suffering from a lance-head bite. Well, suffering might not actually be the right word. He was unconscious, and the bottom half of his left leg from the knee to the foot was a mess of black and green, like he'd been bitten by a zombie or something. It was the only lesson I ever needed in keeping an eye out for slithering when walking through the forest.

It's not the first one I've seen on the island. Usually Rey takes care of any that wander too close to us.

"Kill it," Rey says.

I stare at the coiled snake. The last thing I want to do is get close to it. It's not that I'm a coward. I just don't want to end up losing a limb. And there's something else: I've never killed anything before. Nothing bigger than a spider or one of the giant mosquitoes that plague us here.

"Why?"

"You have to," Rey says. "If you don't, it'll kill one of the hogs. Or us. Either way, we'll be in for more trouble than is necessary."

"I . . . I can't. I mean . . ." But I don't have any real argument to make. My fingers uncurl from around the hatchet I'm holding and it falls to the sandy beach. The coconut falls beside it, and I realize I'm shaking. "You do it."

Rey mutters something under his breath.

"You're supposed to keep me out of danger," I argue, trying to save some face. "I mean, that's what your *job* is, right?"

"My *job* is to help you get prepared for what's to come," Rey says, snatching the tool from the ground with a chastising quickness. "If you can't kill a simple snake, what are you going to do if the Mogs discover you and you find yourself up against an actual enemy, huh? One that can think and understand you. One that's been *trained* to take you out? What are you going to do when it's *just* you and no one—" His rant is interrupted by another fit of coughing, and Rey buries his face in the tattered sleeve of his blue linen shirt. When he finally stops, he spits blood on the ground.

Blood.

He talks softly, more to himself than to me. "Maybe I should've spent more time teaching you to fight instead of hiding. I thought I could hide you away until you were stronger. But I failed to make sure you developed like I should have. I was too weak. The other Garde . . . they'll probably have already gotten their first Legacies by now. Probably masters of all kinds of weapons and combat."

"Hide well enough, and you'll never have to fight," I say, parroting one of his favorite lessons. I'm trying to make him happy now, but I just keep thinking about the fact that he's coughing up blood. That's bad. That's what always happens in the movies a few scenes before a character dies.

I ignore it and keep talking.

"We can start doing more fight training again. I'll do it, I promise. I'll get good at it."

Rey doesn't respond, just nods a little bit and turns away. The hogs squeal louder. The viper's up and ready to strike now, warning off the animals and humans around it, its body swaying slightly in the air like a constricted *S*.

"I'm afraid I've failed you as a Cêpan," Rey says. He holds a hand out and grips my shoulder, squeezing it once. He smiles, but it's a sad, far-off sort of expression. When did he start looking so old?

Rey turns and throws the hatchet with a flick of his arm. It sails through the air, spinning horizontally. The blade hits the snake a few inches below its head, and then embeds itself into the side of our little shack. The pigs scramble to the far side of the pen as the serpent's body wriggles frantically on the ground, its nerves working out the last of their power.

Rey just keeps walking, hunched over, with a shuffle in his steps.

I don't respond to Rey's comment. I don't think he expected me to. Instead, I replay what he said earlier about how the other Garde would probably be so much more advanced than me. So much more prepared for the future.

I feel like a disappointment.

But then, part of that is his fault, too, right? It's not just me. It's not my fault.

The last place I want to be is inside the hut with him now—or anywhere near the dead viper in our backyard—so I grab the coconut and get an old parasol that's leaning against the shack and head farther down the beach, to where the trees give way to nothing but sand and crystal-blue water. I sit near the tide's edge and plant the giant umbrella in the sand beside me, unfurling it. I burn easily, even after a few years of living in the tropics. I'm not meant for this sort of environment. *I should be somewhere else.*

Rey seems to have decided that if we're out of sight and hidden, we'll never have to fight. Which is a good thing, since I don't think either of us could stand a chance against the Mogs.

Which also means we can't leave. I'm stuck here, with Rey. And the hogs. And a forest full of deadly snakes and spiders and God knows what else.

I dig little ditches in the beach with my heels and sink my toes into the soft earth, cooling them down, and stare at the two scars on my ankle. I know Rey's right. If the Mogs showed up I'd be defenseless. I'd have to rely on him to fight for me. I'm a failed Garde with a frail Cêpan. Again, I can't help but think that Lorien has cheated me in all this. Surely this wasn't how the Elders had meant everything to be.

In the pocket of my shorts, I find a little red rubber ball I've had for ages—the kind you get for a quarter in convenience store toy machines. I let it roll over the back of my hand, across my knuckles, then between my fingers, over and over again. A little sleight-of-hand craftiness.

I shouldn't be here. The thought floats through my head again. I glance over at the little sailboat that's tied to a post up the beach. It would be so easy to just get in, cast off, and float to the nearest civilization. Martinique isn't far away, if I remember correctly. They have restaurants and hot showers and carnivals there. Street fairs packed with games and every type of food you could ever want. Not that far away.

It would be so easy.

I stare at the coconut as I grow more and more frustrated with the state of my life. My right hand curls into a fist at my side, shaking.

A jolt of energy rushes through me—something I've never felt before. The hairs on the back of my neck stand on end.

The coconut explodes.

For a second I'm stunned, then I just stare at my hands.

Did I just do that?

CHAPTER
THREE

THERE'S A NAME FOR THE POWER I HAVE: TELE-
kinesis. It's the first of my Legacies—my special gifts.
I know this because Rey has told me for years that this
day would come. I'd almost stopped believing him, but
they're here now. I can feel the energy coursing through
my veins.

I can feel the *power*. It feels good.

With just one exploded piece of fruit I suddenly have
a newfound outlook on life. I see a future that doesn't
include this island. If I can move things with my mind,
I can wipe out enemies—knock down entire armies.
People will look up to me. Maybe even fear me. And
Rey—he'll never look at me like I've disappointed him
again. He'll know he hasn't failed me as a Cêpan.

I don't tell him about the coconut, or my newfound
ability. I keep it a secret, practicing with it in my free
time. I'm going to get good at it, and then show him

how capable I am by pulling a tree out of the ground and batting away our little shack. Or something. Something big to prove to him that we no longer need to be on the island. That I'm ready to get out of here and back into the real world, because *I'll* be able to fight the Mogs if they show up now. I'm so tired of this damned sun and humidity. This island. I'll show him. He'll take us somewhere else.

I start out with coconuts. They're light and easy to crack, and I rip them apart with my power. I let the small green ones float above my mouth and drink the sweet-tasting water from inside. Then I slingshot them into the ocean, where they fly through the air and blend in with the sky before splashing down into the salty water on the horizon.

The only problem is that Rey is being better at making sure I actually *am* running all the miles I'm supposed to. He's started popping up at random places around the island, stopwatch in hand, making sure I'm jogging—or at least walking really quickly. Fortunately that seems to take a lot of energy out of him, because he spends the rest of the day napping.

Perfect time for me to hone my badass new superpower.

I move on from coconuts to rocks and fallen logs. On the end of the island opposite our shack, I haul in a huge piece of driftwood against the tide with nothing more than force of will. The larger, heavier objects are a little harder to maneuver at first, but I'm getting better at it. Building my telekinetic muscles. This is the best I've felt in months.

On the day I've decided to tell Rey about my powers, thick black clouds start to roll in from the sea. I recognize what this means: The wet season is approaching, and it's going to be nothing but rain for the next few months. I stop halfway through my morning jog and practice my power just a little more. I find a log on the ground and toss coconuts into the air, trying to bat them into the sea like some giant's version of baseball. I don't know how long I stand there trying before I actually make contact with one of the coconuts. It's not the home run I've been imagining—both the coconut and the dead branch shatter, sending bits of wood and coconut milk raining down on me—but the destruction is incredibly satisfying.

It's only then that I realize the sun is higher in the sky than I expected, and I wonder how long I've been standing there. My face is sunburned—I can feel it stinging as I head back to the hut. My stomach rumbles. I hope Rey's made lunch already.

I see his white hair first. It's practically shimmering in the sunlight. He's facedown in the sand, just around the next curve in the shore.

My heart stops.

I yell his name as I run to him, over and over until my throat burns. *No,* I think as I run. And *shit.* Those two words repeat in my head as I get closer, trying to figure out how he got there and if he's moving at all.

I practically slide into him in the sand, kicking up a little cloud around us. I roll him over. Grit and sand stick to one side of his face.

"Rey! Rey, wake up. Rey, can you hear me?"

His chest is rising up and down, but just barely. I stop talking long enough to hear his breath, which is wet and shallow. I wonder how long he's been out here—why he's so far away from the shack to begin with—but it's obvious. He was out making sure I was training. Or trying to figure out what was taking me so long. Looking for me.

It's my fault he's like this.

He's too heavy to lift with my body, but I can lift him with my Legacy. I jog beside him as his body flies through the air, lifted by my telekinesis.

He'd be so proud if he could see everything I was doing right now. If he'd just wake up.

I've spent the last few days honing my power and thinking of how I could survive anything now that my first Legacy has surfaced, but if Rey dies I don't know what I'll do. Every time I've ever thought of abandoning him or running away from the island on my own, I've always known in the back of my mind that there's no way I could do that. Even sick and frail, Rey is the only one I have in the world, on this planet that's not even technically my home.

By the time we reach the shack, I'm frantic. Inside there's nothing much. We sleep on mats surrounded by netting, but his mat is elevated like an actual bed. I set him down, then scramble around, trying to figure out what I can do to help. There are a few barrels of water. I fill a cup and bring it to him, but of course he's not awake to drink. I splash some of it on his face, but am too afraid it's going to go up his nose and into his lungs to pour the whole cup on him. He doesn't move at all. So I pull up a chair and wait. Staring at him. Willing him to open his eyes and reprimand me for taking too long on my run. Then we'll cook lunch and I'll show him how I can lift tree trunks and juggle coconuts just by thinking about it. And he'll be happy.

An eternity passes before he speaks my name. It's a rasp, so soft that had I not been sitting in a chair beside him with my eyes glued on his face, I might have missed it.

"Five," Rey says again, then coughs into one of the blankets.

"Hold on," I say, springing up. I find the lantern and flip it on, then refill the cup of water and bring it over to him. He waves it away.

"I was looking for you," he says. His voice is weak

and he only seems half coherent, like he's talking to someone far away.

"I know."

"I want you to listen to me," he says, and I shake my head. He just needs to drink some water and rest and I'll listen to him lecture me later.

"I have all the time in the world to listen when you're better. I have nothing to do here except listen to you."

His eyes look at me but also through me, as if he's struggling to focus on my face.

"The Garde are still hidden," he says softly, ignoring what I tell him. "If you go searching for them, you'll expose yourself to the Mogs. You'll be safer here. On your own. Until you're stronger."

"Rey. It's okay. It's going to be okay. Look, I have to show you what I can do now."

He shakes his head once, and even with how weak he is, it causes me to stop moving and listen. His expression is so solemn, what can I do but hear what he has to say?

"My job was to protect you," he continues. "I know I haven't taught you everything I should have, but . . . I tried. I tried to do my best, but my body didn't agree with this world."

"No," I whisper.

It finally seeps in that this might be the end of us.

There is something so unnatural about thinking

that I might wake up in the morning and Rey would be gone. Not just out on the boat or across the island, but nowhere. Forever. I could probably count the times I didn't know exactly where he was on one hand. His absence is inconceivable. It doesn't compute. Suddenly I think of all the times I wished for another Cêpan or to run away from the island and hate myself.

I start to cry, tears falling in salty drops to the floor.

Rey starts gasping, and I stand, my chair falling backwards, feeling so helpless as I stare at him.

"Just tell me, what do I do to help you?"

The gasping turns into a fit of coughing that seems like it will never end. Blood trickles from his mouth.

"What do I do?" I repeat. "What do I do?"

Finally, he speaks, this time in such a low whisper that I have to kneel beside him to hear.

"Stay alive," he says.

His eyes look more lucid now as his hand reaches out and grips my forearm.

"Five, don't follow the Loric into this war until you're ready. Trust your instincts." He inhales again, deeply and unevenly. "When the time comes, trust yourself. You're the future. Do whatever it takes to survive."

His breath rattles again and then it stops.

And then there's nothing. His chest doesn't rise up. His eyes don't open. Everything is quiet and still.

The silence is the worst thing I've ever heard.

"Rey?" I ask softly, then louder when he doesn't respond, hoping that he just hasn't heard me.

Nothing.

He's gone.

My brain floods. All I can think about are the times I've disobeyed him, or cursed him—even if it was only in my head. I'm filled with regret.

I'm alone.

I run outside. It's the only thing I can do. I'm barely aware that rain is pelting me, signaling the beginning of the wet season. My body shivers, even though the rain is warm. This tiny island suddenly feels huge and full of danger. Random thoughts keep shooting through my brain: *You'll have to do something with his body. He never knew how powerful your telekinesis had become. All the chores he'd done on this island are now yours—* as I sink down to my knees. There's distant thunder and the hogs squeal.

It's all too much.

Alone, except for a bunch of pigs.

It takes me a while to catch my breath as I sit on my knees, bent over the wet sand. My eyes fall on the reddened scar on my ankle. Two's symbol.

I almost laugh.

There were nine of us and now there are seven, and we're the ones who are supposed to defeat the Mogadorians. An entire army of aliens. And so they sent us to Earth with fragile protectors and scattered us across the globe. Hoping what? That at least one of us would survive?

The rain beats down on me. I feel like my head's going to explode—like something's got to burst out of me. I shout from somewhere deep inside. The two palm trees nearest to me splinter in half under the power of my Legacy.

CHAPTER FOUR

I BURY REY IN THE FOREST.

I wanted to send him out to sea—to put him in the sailboat and just push him out. I remember seeing that in some movie about Vikings once, and Rey taught me the basics of sailing. But I was too afraid the currents would push him back to the beach. That I'd wake up one morning and find his body washed up on the shore, eyes pecked out by seabirds and body shriveled up like jerky. I couldn't see that.

Burial seemed like the only solution. I couldn't just leave him out in the elements as something for the little green lizards to pick at. So I find a place where there's enough open land—once I've cleared away a few bushes—and start in with the shovel. Digging his grave is the hardest work I've done in a long time. Under different circumstances I'd joke that this was Rey's last laugh—finally getting me to do some hard labor. But I miss him too much to do that.

The rain doesn't let up. For every shovel of mud I scoop out, twice as much floods back in rivers of brown. Before I even realize I'm doing it, I'm punching into the earth with my newfound power, mud coating my body and face. I use my telekinesis to burrow out the rest of the hole and keep the mud back.

And then, once he's in the bottom, I let all the mud and sand and earth and water fall in over him. His body is covered almost instantly.

He's gone.

I carry on, alone on my island, through the wet season. Rey has taught me well—how to survive off the land— even if I didn't realize he was doing it at the time. I know which plants to eat, and how to keep our shack dry on the inside as the sky continues to dump rain on me day after day. I continue running, and training— more so than I ever did when Rey was alive.

I keep thinking that someone will show up. If the Garde's deaths are burned into my leg, is it the same for the Cêpans? Will Rey's mark show up on the Loric guardian who's looking after Three? Or Four? Will one of them come and find me and tell me what I should be doing next?

But no one does.

And after weeks—maybe even months—of waiting

for something to happen, I know what I have to do. Rey told me to stay on the island until I was stronger, but he didn't know about my power. I *am* stronger now. Besides, he also told me to survive, and if I'm going to do that, I'm going to have to leave. If I stay, I'll go crazy.

Technically I can do whatever I want. I'm free. There's no one looking after me. I'm alone.

I can go anywhere I want.

Martinique. It was the last island we were on. I didn't mind it there. And it's close. Or at least, it *seemed* close when we sailed from there.

On a day when the rain finally starts to die down, I act.

I empty out Rey's pack and stuff it with some rations. It goes in the sailboat, alongside all the coconuts I can find and several canteens of water. Once I'm on the big island . . . well, I'll have plenty of time at sea to figure out what to do next. Maybe I'll try to track down the Garde. Maybe I'll just find a way to get back to Canada and that home I so liked when I was a kid.

I toss my duffel into the boat, along with my Loric Chest. I take Rey's big, broad straw hat to keep the sun off me. There's no lower deck to the boat, so I'll be exposed the whole time I'm at sea.

My last act is to break down the hog fence. I do it with a single burst of telekinetic power.

They'll be fine, I tell myself as they reluctantly

cross over the broken wooden slats and onto the beach. *They'll get a taste for all those lizards running around.*

It takes me a few tries to get the two sails up on the little boat, and even longer to try to read the sea map I find on board. There are no markings in the place where I think our little island is, but I'm sure that Rey always said we were just east of Martinique. There's a compass and a telescope in the drawer as well—all the things an amateur sailor could need.

I want to leave immediately, but I have to wait for high tide, and that means I have to sit around rethinking my decision until dusk. Finally, the ocean rolls in under the boat, and I use my power to push off into the water. Then I work on adjusting the sails to the direction I need to be going. By the time I get the course set it's almost completely dark, the moon and stars obscured behind thin clouds. I can barely see our island as I turn back for one last look at it. I wave, even though I know there's no one there to see it.

"Good-bye, Rey."

The boat and I sail into the black night.

I wake up confused, unsure of where I am at first.

I'd meant to stay awake the whole night—by my guess, it shouldn't have taken all that long to get to Martinique—but after working the sails and using my power so much, I must have passed out leaning against the wooden dock.

The morning sun shines down on me. Soon it will be mercilessly frying my skin. The boat bobs. I rush to my knees, expecting to see land. . . .

But there's nothing. Just a world of ocean. Blue as far as the eye can see.

I try to remain calm, but panic is causing my heart to pound against my ribs.

In no time the map is out in front of me, spread on the deck. I'm sailing east, into the rising sun, which means that I'm still going in the right direction. I just haven't hit Martinique yet. I'm not moving as fast as I thought I would.

Or I passed the island in the night. I realize that it's possible I was wrong all along, and our little island wasn't where I thought it was. I could be anywhere. There could be nothing ahead of me until Africa.

Africa.

I panic. There's no way I'm making it all the way to Africa.

I can't believe that Rey didn't have some kind of GPS.

Or maybe there was one that I just didn't know about. One that's still at home. In the shack on the beach. A place that sounds much more appealing than it did last night.

I stare at the map for a long time as I gnaw on some

of the jerky-like meat I brought with me. In the end, I take out the compass and set myself sailing north-northwest. At least that way I'm bound to hit some islands.

Right?

After searching in vain for a glimpse of land with the telescope, I lean back against the deck and take the red rubber ball out of the pocket of my shorts. Running it over the backs of my knuckles, I find a pack of cards in my bag.

Everything's going to be all right, I tell myself as I shuffle the cards and begin to lay them out. *Just keep yourself busy, or you'll go nuts out here before you get to land.*

What is all this useless shit?

It's my fourth day in the boat before I discover I can unlock my Loric Chest. Rey always said it was something that we had to open together, and it hadn't dawned on me to try now that he's gone.

A bounty of shiny, useless-looking items gleam in the sunlight. I had hoped that there'd be a water filtration system magically waiting for me, but it looks like I'm out of luck. Which is worrisome, because I've already made my way through all the coconuts, and the rest of my rations are starting to look dangerously meager. It looks like the Chest is just filled with trinkets from a dollar store. My fingers pass over a little black flutelike instrument. I dig through a few more things and pull out a long glove. I slide it on, tugging it all the way up my forearm. When I flex my wrist, a blade shoots out. It comes within an inch of stabbing me in the eye, the entire silver blade almost a foot in length.

I'm too tired to even flinch.

Great. If I don't want to die of dehydration, at least I've got this.

I shudder at the thought.

All of it's useless. Or at least, none of the stuff has come with an instruction manual. I pack everything back inside except for the knife-glove. I can practice with that. Just in case.

The Chest goes back into my duffel, and I guzzle the last of a container of water. Then I use my telekinesis to push the boat farther, faster along the water, hoping with everything I have that I'm going in the right direction.

I bet the other Garde have better stuff in their Chests. Or that their Cêpans are there to explain what they're supposed to do with them.

I've wondered plenty of times what the other Garde are like. What they're doing. If their Cêpans keep them hidden away from the world in the farthest corners of the globe. But for the first time I wonder if I'm the only one missing out. Is it possible that the other Garde are all together somewhere, fighting and training with one another, wondering where I am? Would they even *care*?

Did Rey keep me hidden away because he was afraid they'd rush me into fighting? To make sure I stayed alive?

All I have are questions, and the only answer I get is the sun beating down on me.

My tongue feels swollen and rough in my mouth. I haven't peed in a long time, which I think is probably a really bad sign. I'm not even sweating anymore. It's nighttime, but I should still be sweating.

So much for making it out in the world on my own.

My seventh night at sea is the night I'm going to die. So long, Five. It only took a week for you to fuck up completely by disobeying all of Rey's last wishes.

Is it even possible for me to die? Rey told me the special charm meant I'd be safe from death as long as one of the Garde before me was alive—that being *captured* was the real thing to fear—but does that mean it works against starvation and dehydration and exposure to the elements as well? Because I don't want to be some kind of half-living, dried-up mummy washing up on the shores of Cuba a month from now.

My lips are chapped and peeling but my tongue has no moisture to wet them.

I can barely move—I feel so tired—but I pull my duffel bag closer, hugging it, looping my arms through its straps. I can feel the Loric Chest inside. My whole body hurts and I can barely keep my eyes open.

There's a strange tickle in my chest, and I wonder if it's some kind of death rattle—if this is what Rey felt right before he died. It grows, until my entire body feels alive, on fire.

So this is what it's like to die. So much for the charm.

I close my eyes and hug the bag tighter. I wonder if my symbol will end up burned onto the other Garde's legs even though I'm dying out of order.

I'm dying out of order. I refuse to have that be my last thought.

I crack my eyes open and my breath catches in my throat.

I'm not in the boat. The boat is still there, but it's several yards beneath me. I'm floating towards the cloudless night sky, still holding my bag to my chest. I wonder for a moment if all the Garde get shot back into space when they die. Maybe this is part of the stupid plan that forced me to live out in the middle of nowhere. With my sick Cêpan.

My parched lips curl down into a frown as I speak my final words.

"Fuck Lorien."

And then I'm shooting forward, the wind beating against my face. Flying.

CHAPTER FIVE

I DON'T KNOW HOW I'M DOING IT—OR WHERE I'M finding the energy—but I soar through the air. It feels different from my telekinesis, like it's coming from somewhere else within me. I feel like I'm in some kind of trance as I shoot through clouds, focused only on looking for somewhere to crash that isn't water. It doesn't feel like too long before I see land. I picture myself on it, and like magic I'm lowering, until I'm bouncing on a beach, forming a little trench of sand.

I'm too exhausted to properly react to the fact that I was just *flying* through the air. All I can wonder is where I am and hope that no one saw me.

No such luck.

A female jogger is by my side before I can climb out of the little ditch my body's made in the sand.

"Holy crap, what happ—"

I must look terrible, because when she gets a good

look at me she stops in the middle of her sentence.

"Water," I croak out, my throat feeling like it's full of dust.

She pulls a bottle from her workout belt and hands it to me. I squeeze the cool liquid into my mouth, hardly stopping to savor it. My eyes are dry and stinging, but the water keeps coming, so I just keep swallowing.

"Careful, careful," the woman says. "There's plenty more."

I look around warily. I'm on a beach, but not one that I recognize. It's dawn, or just before—there's hardly any light out at all. My mind spins.

"Where am I?" This doesn't look like any place I remember in Martinique.

"Lummus Park," the woman says. She's looking less worried about me now and more confused. Her eyes keep looking out to the sea in the direction I came from.

"No, what island is this?"

Her face wrinkles.

"This is South Beach. Miami."

Miami?

"Where do you live?" she asks me. "Was there an accident? Do we need to call for help? How did you— I mean, it looked like you were *flying*."

I'm quick to shake my head.

"No accident," I say between gulps. "No help. Don't call anyone."

A few people gather around us. People start asking if everything's okay. After downing the last of the water, I start to get to my feet, but my legs are wobbly.

"No, no, no," the woman says. "Stay right there. You need more water."

She looks up at the handful of people gathered around us and someone offers her a bottle full of bright green liquid.

"Perfect," she says, handing it to me. "Drink this. It'll be good for you and help out with your electrolytes."

I hesitate for only a second before I'm chugging the sweet liquid. My heart starts to pound, as if it's been paused for the last few moments.

Something sparks in my mind and I look around. I'm still wearing the glove with the sheathed blade but I don't see anything else on the beach.

"My bag . . ." I say, starting to get frantic. The Chest may not have had anything I thought I could use in it, but Rey talked about it as if it was Lorien's last hope— other than me and the rest of the Garde, that is. There's no way I can lose it.

It's the only thing I have left.

A few yards away, I see a guy picking up my duffel bag. He tosses back the canvas flap and starts to pull out the Loric Chest.

"Hey!" I shout in the loudest voice I can muster.

Before I can think about what I'm doing I reach out

my hand and feel a spark of telekinetic energy. The bag and Chest fly from the man's hands and into mine. He's stunned, but it looks to everyone else like he's just tossed it over to me. I clutch it against my torso.

Someone snaps a picture of me on their phone.

"Hey." The woman beside me stands up, sounding annoyed. "What are you trying to do, man? This kid's obviously been through something and you want to take pictures of him?"

"I thought we'd need pictures to run if it's a story," the photographer says. "If this 'something' is big, we need to document it."

They start to argue. I get up and start to run.

"Hey!" someone is shouting behind me—the woman, probably—but I don't look back. I just put my head down and make a beeline toward the closest bushes and trees. Anything that will give me cover. My legs feel like jelly and my head pounds, but I keep going until I can't hear anyone yelling behind me anymore.

It's been so long since I've been in real civilization that I've almost forgotten how to function. Clinging to my bag, I do everything wrong. I almost knock down a few people as I run with my eyes looking over my shoulder. I catch bits and pieces of curses as I pass.

"Watch it, you little piece of . . ."

". . . damned punk. I should . . ."

". . . the hell do you think you're doing . . ."

But I ignore all of them. Running, suddenly desperate to get away from the people and the rest of the world.

I come across another park, all lush lawns and palm trees, with a few rows of big shrubs. That's where I head. The sun is rising, and people are already starting to fill the beach a hundred yards away, but I nestle down into the bushes until I'm as far out of sight as I can be. My body aches. My chapped lips burn. But at least I've gotten a little water.

Rey's voice rings in my head, like some kind of taunting ghost. I know exactly what he'd say.

This is what you wanted, isn't it? You're off your little island. You got what you asked for. Welcome back to the real world.

I groan. It's all I have the strength to do. Then I close my eyes and slip into darkness.

When I wake up, the sun is starting to go down. I've slept through the entire day, but I'm better for it. I'm still weak getting to my feet, but I don't feel like I'm immediately going to collapse.

What I do feel is hunger. So much hunger that my stomach cramps at just the thought of food.

I have to find something to eat.

I take a quick stock of everything I own—dirty linen shirt, cargo shorts, sandals that are about to fall apart, and a duffel bag that holds an alien Chest. It's not a lot to work with, but I've also got telekinetic powers.

And flight.

I wonder briefly if the flying has to do with my telekinesis or if it's something different altogether. I'm anxious to try it out again, but my stomach twists and I know I'm not doing anything unless I get some food in me. I find a water fountain in the park and drink until I feel like I'm going to burst, but it doesn't really help that much with the hunger pangs.

In the near distance are buildings and lights, and I head in that direction. If there are lights, there are probably people. And if there are people, there's probably food.

It doesn't take long before a sweet smell invades my nose. It smells like food I remember eating at a carnival in the Caribbean before we went off the grid. I follow it through a few streets as the buildings get bigger and the lights get brighter, keeping to the shadows as best I can. People pass me by, but they don't pay me any mind. In fact, it looks like they're purposefully avoiding the sight of me—probably because I look like a homeless person, and the last thing they want ruining their night is to have to talk to some destitute kid.

Perfect.

And then I find it: a street fair or carnival or whatever it is they call it here in Miami. The road is blocked off and swarming with people, but more importantly, it's packed with food trucks and little stalls selling what look like crepes and burritos and tacos.

It feels like all the blood in my body is rushing to my head. People. Everywhere. After so long on the little isolated island, it's intimidating to see such crowds.

Calm down, I tell myself. *Just take this one step at a time.*

I grab a seat on steps leading up to yet another little park—it's as if they can't get enough of them in this city—and start to stake out my options. I could use my powers to float a taco over to myself, but the stands are small and the food is being watched. Besides, Rey was always our cook, so I don't even know what half the things I'm seeing are.

I realize how terribly unprepared I am to be back in the real world. I should have planned better. I thought I'd show up in Martinique with a boat—something to *trade.* I don't have any money. Not even a penny. Just my Chest.

And my Legacies.

My stomach twists again with hunger and I realize what I'm going to have to do: steal. Use my telekinesis to lift some cash off someone down here. Somewhere in the back of my head an alarm is going off—this is an abuse of your Legacy!—but I ignore it. I'm *starving.* I'll worry about paying the people back later.

My eyes scan the crowd. There's a group of people standing nearby. They're well dressed in suits and dresses and polished shoes. They definitely look like they could afford to lose a few bucks. It takes me several tries—the first few times I tug at someone's wallet, they reach to their back pocket to make sure it's still there—but eventually a leather billfold slips out, and I quickly shoot it into the bushes.

I don't move yet, but count backwards from one hundred, watching to see if the guy notices his wallet's missing or not.

As if on cue, my stomach makes a terrible gurgling noise when I get to "one."

I stroll casually over to the bushes and retrieve the man's wallet. It's packed with cash. I grin, shove the bills into my pocket, and then head for the food stalls.

I stop at the first one I see. It's some kind of Cuban food, and I end up with a greasy sandwich of pork and cheese that drips all over my hands when I bite into it. It's the best thing I've ever tasted. When it's gone, I move on to tacos, then ice cream. My stomach is filled up quickly, but I push through and keep eating.

I'm halfway through my ice cream when I realize someone's watching me.

A policeman.

I casually walk away, and he less-than-casually follows me from a distance. I glance over my shoulder just long enough to see him tap something into his cell phone, his eyes never leaving me. It's possible he just thinks I'm trouble based on how destitute I look, but it's equally possible that after I ran away from the beach this morning, whoever it was that snapped a picture of me reported me to the police.

I can't take that chance.

I make a beeline for a side street. Once I'm around the corner, I start running. The last thing I need is for an officer to start questioning me, or report me, or worse, try to take me into custody. Then I'd have to make a scene and use my powers and probably alert half the Mogadorian army to my presence. No, I just have to get away.

I immediately regret eating so much food.

It sits inside my stomach like a pile of bricks, and I feel like I'm going to vomit after just a few blocks of jogging. Over my shoulder, I see that the officer is keeping up with me. When I duck into an alleyway, I hear his footsteps turn into a run somewhere behind me.

Go, go, go, I shout at myself in my head. And I'm running as best I can through the alleys and across a side street and behind a huge building and past some fences, and then . . .

The alleyway dead-ends, and I'm screwed.

Or at least, I *will* be screwed if I don't figure out this new flying thing. It's not like I know how to make it happen. I stare up at the roof ten stories above me. I have to get up there. And so I clench all my muscles and envision myself floating up, and suddenly I'm not just floating, but *shooting* up into the air. I go way past the top of the building as my heart pounds, and for a moment I can see out over the ocean for what looks like forever. Then I try to calm down and *gently* float back to the top of the roof. I land with a bit of a thud, but it's not bad for my second conscious attempt at getting out of the sky. Certainly better than crash-landing onto the beach.

I'm basically an alien superhero.

I peek over the edge of the building. The cop is standing in the alleyway, looking puzzled. Two more people soon join him there, though only one of them is in uniform. The other's just wearing a suit, from what I can tell. They're too far away to make out any specifics. After looking around for a while, they disappear.

I sink down and lean against the waist-high bricks at the edge of the roof. I can sleep here tonight. The air is cool, and I doubt anyone will bother me.

I pull the leftover money from my pocket and count it. It's not much, but it'll get me through the next few days while I figure out what to do next. Then I'm weirdly relieved to find the old red rubber ball in my pocket as well. I stare at the stars while I roll it over the backs of my knuckles.

It's kind of strange that they're the same stars as the ones I used to see from the island. When I look at the sky, it's almost like I never left. For the millionth time in my life, I wonder if any of the stars I'm seeing are Lorien's sun.

When we were on the run, moving through Canada after that Mog found us outside of Montreal, we always slept in shifts. That's what we called them, at least. In actuality Rey would stay most of the night watching over me. My shift would just be the few minutes in the morning while Rey showered or went to get us food or something. Even in our shack, I think sometimes he'd stay up half the night by the door if he had a feeling or hunch that something would happen. I'd always kind of laughed it off as paranoia, but now, alone on the rooftop of a building in a town I've never been in, I wish more than anything that I had someone to look out for me.

CHAPTER SIX

I MAKE A HOME FOR MYSELF IN SOUTH BEACH.

I don't have a roof over my head or anything, but I get familiar enough with the little area that it starts to feel like I *know* it, at least. Clubs, restaurants, and hotels line the beaches, and from the sidewalks I can see inside, into other worlds that seem so detached from what I grew up with that they're completely alien to me. There are flashing lights and bands and dancers that spill out into the street. In Martinique I'd seen carnivals and festivals that had dancers but never anything quite like this—Rey had always made sure I was kept inside after dark. But now, alone, I'm free to wander.

I think about heading up towards Canada, but I'm still weak from the voyage. Besides, I need to practice the hell out of flying before I even begin to think of flying all the way there, which seems like the easiest way to avoid any issues with border patrol or police.

At first it's hard for me to fly—without a rush of adrenaline or a near-death experience, I can't seem to figure out where the power comes from. But over the course of a week or two I get better. Levitating just a few inches off the ground at first, then rising into the air as high as I can before I get freaked out and come falling back to the ground. Sometimes when it's extra dark, I fly over the ocean, low enough that no one will see me, darting between buoys. I'm getting good at it.

The rooftops serve as my bed at night. They feel safer than sleeping on the beach or in alleys. During the daytime, I get really good at picking pockets with my telekinesis. I stop feeling bad about it after the second or third time. I'm *surviving*. If I'm going to make it to Canada—or anywhere else—I'm going to need plenty of cash and supplies. And there are countless targets walking in droves in and out of expensive-looking shops all over the island. I buy a new set of clothes—jeans to cover the scars of One and Two on my ankle—and keep a few other fresh shirts in my bag. In my clean T-shirt and with a wad of cash in my pocket, I'm just another kid in Miami whose parents have given him too much allowance.

I stay careful when it comes to my powers. They could easily give me away. That and my bulky, heavy Chest, which I carry with me everywhere I go.

I think about the Garde quite a bit at first. About

maybe seeking them out and trying to find them. But how would I even go about doing that? Post "Missing" ads or something? For all I know they could be in shacks in Africa or Indonesia or Antarctica. And if they're not—if they're banding together . . . well, no one ever came to find *me*.

So I think of them less and less. Every time I discover something new about the city, part of me curses Rey. We could have been doing this all the time instead of being stuck in the middle of nowhere. I spend my days exploring or playing in arcades or reading books on the beach—doing all the things I didn't get a chance to do on *our* island where there were no bookstores or electrical outlets. I feel like I could probably play video games or watch movies forever. I eat up all the stories. I wish I could create them myself.

I make up for lost time.

I know what Rey would say. He'd call me lazy. He'd trot out parables about ants and grasshoppers. But I refuse to feel bad about actually living my life for once instead of cowering in fear.

It's almost *too* easy here. I get comfortable.

Maybe even careless.

And that's how she finds me.

Normally any wallets I lift go straight into my duffel bag, and I go through them later when it's dark and I'm not in a crowded area. But I'm hungry and low on cash and end up leaning against a palm tree on a nice, quiet section of beach. I'm rifling through my haul when she speaks from behind me.

"You're just *looking* to get busted, aren't you?"

I flinch and twist around, pulling my bag closer to me as I get a good look at the person this high, slightly raspy voice has come from. She looks like she's a few years older than me, with deeply tanned skin and shiny black hair that's pulled back in a ponytail. She's wearing a lot of dark eye makeup and a gray tank top over cutoff jean shorts.

I stammer the beginnings of a few words and scramble to my feet. She laughs a little.

"Don't worry," she says with a shrug. "I've got enough reasons of my own to avoid the cops."

She stares at me with dark brown eyes, waiting for me to say something, but I don't know what to do. I've been avoiding people the whole time I've been here— old habits—and no one's really gone out of their way to talk to me. But this girl seems . . . nice.

"Okay, so do you not talk or something?" she asks. "What's your name?"

I open my mouth, and then stop. It's a simple question, but of course I have no answer. At least not one I can give her truthfully. So I think back to a person I liked being.

"Cody," I finally say. The name I used in Canada.

"Cody," she repeats. "It's nice to meet you finally. I'm Emma."

Shit. What does she mean by "finally"? I stare at her face, analyzing it, looking for signs that she might be a Mog—ready to fight or fly at a moment's notice if it comes to that.

"Oh, please. I've seen you lurking around. It's impossible not to. I'm surprised the police haven't picked you up yet. You look totally sketch when you're on the prowl. It's crazy that you even get close enough to people to lift off them."

Oh. Well, the good news is, she doesn't seem to notice that I'm able to pick pockets because of my Legacy. The bad news is, apparently I'm not nearly as stealthy as I thought I was.

"No offense," she continues, squinting at me a little. "You don't talk much, do you?"

"I guess not," I say. I've never really thought about it. "I used to talk a lot when I was younger and then it was just me and . . ." I don't know how to finish the sentence—realize that I've said too much already.

Luckily, Emma simply nods her head.

"You working for anyone?" she asks.

"No, it's only me," I say. Then I'm confused about what she's even asking. "Wait, what do you mean?"

Stupid. I don't know why, but I'm slipping up. I haven't told her anything important—haven't even scratched the fucked-up surface that is my past—but there's no reason I should be telling her *anything*.

She just smiles and nods at my bag.

"Buy me an arepa and maybe I'll tell you."

If Rey were here, we'd be fleeing. Gone. I wouldn't have even been given the chance to talk to Emma. But as much as I imagine Rey's voice shouting at me to excuse myself and blend in with the crowd and make a break for the nearest sparsely inhabited island, he's not *actually* here.

Besides, I haven't talked to anyone in a long time. Not really. Maybe I'll learn something useful. And if anything goes wrong and she leads me into a trap or something, I've got telekinetic powers and the ability to fly away. I'm practically untouchable.

"Okay," I say, forcing a little smile. "What's an arepa?"

She takes me to a little food stand up the beach and I order two arepas. When the cart owner tells me it'll be six dollars, Emma says something in Spanish and the owner scowls.

"Three dollars," he says, handing over two golden disks that shine in the sunlight. I pay and we walk away. The beach is on one side of us, a row of luxury hotels on the other.

"What was that about?" I ask. I bite into my arepa, which turns out to be one of the most delicious things

I've ever eaten—savory-sweet corn cakes sandwiching melted white cheese. I'm in heaven.

"Just keeping that guy from taking advantage of you," Emma says. "He thought you were a tourist."

"What'd you tell him?"

"Just that I knew he was overcharging you." She pauses for a beat. "*Maybe* I mentioned my brother's name. He's kind of a big deal around here."

"What do you mean?" I ask.

"Let's just say if you *were* lifting those wallets for someone, it'd probably be him."

"What, is he like . . . a gangster?" Even as the words come out I realize how dumb they sound, but my mind immediately went to a mob movie I caught the day before when I'd spent half the waking hours in a theater. Cheese strings from my mouth to the golden half moon in my hand.

"Something like that." Emma looks at me and smirks. I feel stupid, like some kind of naïve kid.

"So do you work for him?" I can't picture her as one of the femme fatales from the movies. She's too young, obviously, but also too friendly. "Is this the part where a black car drives up and I get shoved in and held for ransom or something?"

"I'd probably choose someone who wasn't picking pockets if I was going to try to get some kind of ransom money," she says with a little smirk. "No, I don't work

for my brother. I'm nothing like him. Don't even talk
to him, really. Besides, the last thing I want is someone telling me what I can or can't do. *Especially* if that
someone is as stupid as my brother."

I smile, genuinely. I can kind of get where she's coming from.

"Besides," she adds. "He thinks I'm too young and
that he doesn't want me involved." She lets out a long
sigh between bites of her snack. Her mouth is half full
when she speaks again. "So where are you from?"

"Why are you talking to me?" I ask, ignoring her
question. She looks a little confused. "I mean, why did
you come talk to me on the beach?"

"I wanted an arepa."

"Sure."

"Okay. I saw you around and knew what you were
doing. I figured you could use a few pointers. I thought
maybe you'd be my new beach buddy. I'm tired of working alone."

"Working?" I ask. "What do you mean?"

She stops in the middle of the sidewalk, grins and
then pulls a black leather billfold from her pocket. The
first wallet I stole—the one I carry my cash around in
now. My hand reaches to my back pocket and confirms
what I already know. Somehow she's managed to snag
my wallet. I never felt a thing.

"Not everyone's as easy a mark as you," she says with

a mischievous glint in her eyes. "I could use a hand if you're up to it."

"You want me to steal wallets for you?"

"*With* me."

I hesitate. Walking around and talking to Emma is one thing, but I can practically hear Rey yelling at me and telling me not to get close or make friends with anyone but him. But she's obviously not a Mog.

"Come on," she says, sensing my reluctance. "Look, I don't know where you're from but it's obvious you're not as familiar with this place as you should be if you were about to shell out six bucks for some street food, even if it was delicious. Let's meet up again and get into some trouble. I'm so bored this summer. *That's* why I came and found you."

Her last words stand out to me. She sought me out, came and found me on the beach. The least I can do is consider hanging out with her a little more.

"Sure," I say.

Her face lights up a little.

"Great." She pulls out her cell phone and grimaces at the screen. "Shit, I gotta go. What's your number?"

"I don't have one," I say, a little sheepish.

"What do you mean you—" she starts. Then her face falls a little. "Well, meet me on the beach tomorrow. Same place I found you today. I'll be down in the afternoon."

I nod. "Yeah. Okay."

She flashes one more smile and tosses my wallet to me. I fumble with it, uncoordinated. By the time I have it back in my pocket, she's halfway to the street, disappearing into the throng of tourists.

Holy shit, I think. *Did I just make a friend?*

The realization that I'm not sure because I've never had a friend in my life other than Rey is crushing. How am I supposed to save a planet overrun with a warmongering species if I can't even figure out how to interact with other people?

My thoughts flash to the other Garde. What if I don't get along with them?

CHAPTER SEVEN

INSTEAD OF WAITING FOR EMMA IN THE SPOT where she snuck up on me yesterday, I stay half a beach away, loitering between some bathrooms and a thick line of plants. That way I'll be able to see if she shows up with a Mog brigade or something—though I don't *really* think she's going to. I'm just trying to be cautious.

And I don't want her to catch me by surprise again.

Emma appears early in the afternoon. She looks around for me before shrugging and sitting underneath the palm tree where she found me. She waits for a while—twenty minutes maybe—as I try to talk myself into walking over.

It's weird how nervous I feel. This is just so foreign to me, meeting up with someone. Talking to someone new at all. I feel awkward.

When she stands up and looks like she's going to

leave, I grit my teeth and head her way.

"Hey!" she says with a grin when she catches sight of me. "I thought you were going to stand me up."

"Sorry," I say, shoving my hands into my pockets. "I, uh, lost track of time."

"No problem. It's nice out today. Let's hang out here for a while."

And so we sit and chat. Or, mostly she talks, and I respond to questions as vaguely as I can—or with out-right lies. Where am I from? Around. Where do I live? Not far from the beach. What about my parents or family? They're here and there. They travel a lot. I'm left to my own devices. I pick a pocket or two on occasion because I think it's fun.

Emma doesn't press me about anything, which almost makes me feel bad for all the lies I tell her—that I've got a home to go to at night and a loving family somewhere. She's easy to talk to in a way that Rey never was. Mostly because she talks a lot about herself, and everything she says is new to me. Sometimes she slips into Spanish and it sounds so pretty that I don't even point out to her that I can't understand her.

Emma isn't at all the person she made herself out to be when we first met, so self-assured and street smart. As she talks I can see the cracks begin to show. Her brother might be some kind of criminal guy—that much I think is true—but she's just a rebellious girl who has gotten good at sneaking things from other people, looking for some adventure during the summer. Emma really *does* have a loving family and a home to go back to every night. But from what I can tell she's hungry to be a part of something, to get a taste of danger.

It's funny: I never imagined people would actually go out looking for trouble or danger. I guess when you spend your life hiding from everything to keep something bad from happening, stuff like that loses its thrill. Still, when she suggests we go out and lift a few wallets or purses, I go along. I think of it as a game, or training. Lying. Hiding. Stealth. These are all things that Rey would *technically* approve of since they're skills that'll help keep me hidden away from the Mogs.

Right?

I find out pretty quickly that I'm not the best thief when I'm not using my powers. I only have to be chased through the streets of South Beach once to figure that out. Emma can't see how I've made it so far without getting caught, but I just shrug. My role becomes that of the distraction. I'm the person who stops and asks for directions, or falls down in front of a mark while she picks their pocket.

That I'm not terrible at: I'm basically just lying and telling stories.

And before I know it we have a system that works and are making a lot of money. At least, enough that

I'm never hungry or wanting for much, with a little left over to put in my Canada fund. We get good at what we do. We make a code—a sort of Robin Hood pact. We steal only from those who look like they can afford to lose a few bucks. They're easy to spot, coming in and out of designer stores or hotels. We target tourists, not people who look like locals.

We see each other most days. About a week after first meeting Emma, I ask her why she's into breaking the law and stealing from people. I've deduced by this point that she probably comes from a good enough home that she could just ask her parents for money or something.

"Respect," she tells me as she tosses some woman's now-empty wallet into a trash bin on the beach. "That's what I want. That's what *we* need. When people respect you, you can do anything. That's how you get real power in a city like this. Your name has to mean something to people."

I want badly to tell her that my name *does* mean something. To a lot of people. I'm a savior. And a target. But the more time I spend with Emma, the less pressing these things seem, and the farther away Canada lies. With her I'm just a kid eating ice cream and street food every day, spending the afternoons sneaking into movie theaters and lazing around the beach at dusk.

Over the course of a few weeks Emma and I *do* get a reputation around the beaches—at least enough of one that Emma's brother hears about us and tells her to lay off before she gets into trouble. I can tell that the locals have changed the way they think about me just from how they look at us when we pass them by. Some with respect. Some with a hint of fear. All of them with knowledge of who we are and what we can do.

It feels good to be acknowledged.

I carry my Chest with me wherever I go, too scared to leave it hidden somewhere. It's all I have left of the island, and of Rey, which both seem so far away now. At night, I sleep with it pulled close to me. It's in the moments between sleeping and waking that I find my thoughts drifting to my destiny and the rest of the Garde, to the war and fighting that surely waits in my future. I dream that I never have to be Five again. That I can do whatever I want, no longer bound by the destiny forced upon me by the Elders of Lorien.

But I know that's something I can't escape. Not entirely. Either I'll fight alongside the Garde—seven super-powered soldiers who've never met one another, trying to take down an entire army—or the Mogs will kill all of us and take Earth as well.

I wish there was another way: a third option I'm not

thinking of. But for the life of me I can't think of one.

I might as well enjoy my time on this planet while I can.

␥

One night, I spot the perfect target.

Emma and I are hanging out behind one of the fancy hotels that back up to the beach, divvying up what we've taken throughout the day. It's nighttime, and the only people to bother us are a few late-night joggers who just nod to us as they pass us by.

The mark is in his midthirties or so and well dressed in a crisp black button-down shirt, gray pants and shiny black shoes that are impractical for a walk on the beach—even if he is keeping to the sidewalk. His dark hair is swept back and accentuates his pale skin, meaning he's almost certainly not from Miami. And, most importantly, he's alone.

Perfect. He's practically begging us to lift his wallet.

I glance at Emma, who gives me a mischivious grin, one I recognize easily by now.

"What's the story?" she asks.

"We lost our cat," I say. "It's black as night and we've been looking for hours."

She smiles and nods, backing away from me. This is what we do. I provide the story and she does the "heavy lifting."

As the man approaches, his eyes drift between the

two of us but he doesn't pay much attention. When he's passed Emma, I step into his path. Emma positions herself behind him.

"Hey, mister. Have you seen a black cat running around here? We've been trying to—"

The man moves fast—faster than I would have thought—and in the blink of an eye he's got Emma out beside him, her arm twisted in his grip. A red leather wallet falls from her fingers and bounces on the sidewalk. The man tightens his fingers around her, and Emma falls to the sand with a small cry. She lets out a string of curses in Spanish.

Shit.

I move forward, but he raises a hand to me, and there's a command about his presence that causes me to stop. I don't know what to do. He speaks to Emma in Spanish, saying something that makes her eyes go wide. She mutters back to him, and he responds. His voice is low and smooth. There's some kind of dawning recognition that sweeps over Emma's face. Clearly she's puting things together that I don't understand, and I start to feel like I'm completely in the dark about what's actually happening in front of me.

All I know is that I have one friend in the world right now, and she's on the ground in front of a man who she's obviously afraid of. So when he reaches for her, I can't help but react.

I send him stumbling backwards with a telekinetic blast.

The attack isn't much—more of a flinch of my Legacy than anything—but it serves to put some distance between all of us. The man looks surprised for a moment, and then narrows his eyes at me. I puff out my chest and clench my fists.

"Cody, what are you . . ." Emma looks confused. "Listen, I know who this guy is. Sort of."

The man bends down slowly, hands out in front of him, and picks his wallet up off the ground. He flicks two cards out from it. They land on the sidewalk.

"If you're ever looking for work, call this number," he says. Then, as if it's an afterthought, he tosses a fifty-dollar bill onto the ground as well.

Then he walks right past us. Away. Like he doesn't have a care in the world. There's something about him that permeates the air and makes him seem untouchable.

When he's out of earshot, I turn to Emma.

"Are you okay?" I ask, concerned.

"You have no idea who that is, do you?" Emma asks, her eyes never leaving the man's back.

"No. Who?"

Emma picks up the two cards and holds one out to me. It's white, with nothing but a black phone number printed in the center of it.

"His name is Ethan," she says. "I've heard my brother

talking about him lately. He's some big important guy who is shaking things up around the city now. Do you know what this means?" She stares at me, but I just shake my head. She grins. "He's our ticket to the next level."

CHAPTER
EIGHT

EMMA CALLS.

She doesn't talk to Ethan, but the person on the line seems to know who both she and I are. It makes me nervous, but it's only a fake name that they know.

Ethan is apparently in dire need of couriers—people to run packages and documents across the city for him. It's not exactly what Emma had in mind when she called, but she agrees on behalf of both of us.

"I thought you didn't want someone telling you what to do," I say when she's off the phone.

"I *don't*." She frowns a little bit. "But I'm getting bored lifting off of randos every day. Aren't you?"

Not really, I think, but I just shrug.

"So, what, you're going to work your way up to master cat burglar or something?" I ask with a smirk.

She punches me in the arm and laughs.

We call in for our assignments. Usually they include

picking up envelopes at specific stores or locations and delivering them to stores on the other side of town. Emma hates it, but I don't mind. I get to see parts of the city I never knew existed. Voodoo shops in Little Haiti and chandeliers hanging in store windows in the Design District. Sometimes we have to split up to get the work done. Mostly we're running around the city together.

One day on a solo assignment, I meet Ethan again.

He sits in a big corner booth at the back of a restaurant. I have a package for him. The place is fancy, or at least fancier than the fast food and street vendor food that I usually eat. He grins widely when he sees me, flashing perfect white teeth.

"There's my best worker," he says, motioning to the other side of the booth. "Please, have a seat."

"Thanks, uh . . ." I realize I don't know what to call him.

"Please, call me Ethan."

"Ethan." I nod.

I plop down in the booth, setting my duffel down at my feet. Before I can say anything else, food starts arriving: plates upon plates of seviche and roasted chicken and pasta swimming in sauce. Ethan encourages me to eat as much as I want, and I practically shovel food into my mouth.

Ethan talks while we eat. "I don't normally get my

hands dirty with small-time crooks or gangs in this city," he says, cutting into a shrimp on his plate. "But reports get back to me. From people on the streets. From cops. When someone of interest pops up, I know about it. And you and your friend are definitely people of interest. You had a solid partnership before you came across me. Tell me, what brought you to pickpocketing? Why do you do it?"

"To survive."

Ethan smiles. He gestures to me with his fork.

"You're young. About fourteen I'd say, right?"

I nod. He continues.

"I lived on the streets when I was your age. It made me a damned good thief and forced me to grow up fast. But it's not an easy life. And it's dangerous. My brother didn't make it." His voice goes quieter. I freeze. It feels inappropriate to keep eating while he's telling me about his dead brother, so I sit there with a huge chunk of cheese squirreled away in one of my cheeks as he keeps talking. "I had to look for him for days before I finally found him. Another gang had . . . Well, it's not important. I don't want to scare you. More importantly, I see a lot of him in you. It's uncanny, really. I think he would have survived if he had your talents."

I tense up. As far as Ethan knows, my talents include delivering mail and taking wallets. I think back to when we met on the beach and I stupidly pushed him with my telekinesis. Has he figured out what that was?

No, I tell myself. *He probably thinks it was the wind. How could he know?*

"Uh, yeah," I say. "I'm sorry to hear about your brother."

"It's all in the past," Ethan says. "But you—you're the future."

Ethan's lips curl up in a smile.

"Tell me more about yourself," he says.

And so I start talking. Nothing about Lorien or the island, but about the things I like. Arepas, movies, books, arcades. And Ethan looks fascinated. It turns out he's a movie buff. He's waxing on about a long list of films I should have seen when I suddenly start to wonder how I managed to end up in a fancy Miami restaurant talking movies with some high-ranking criminal mastermind.

What would Rey say? I wish he were here. I wish he could see how well I was doing on my own. How important I'm becoming.

⌐

Emma is always hungry for more, wanting bigger and better assignments.

Eventually, we get one.

Ethan wants a series of warehouses bugged to keep tabs on competitors or something like that. As usual, we don't ask questions. Emma and I are supposed to sneak in at night when the buildings are empty and plant a few tiny devices Ethan has supplied us with. It's an extremely simple task.

So of course everything goes wrong.

Emma and I split up to get the work done, and I'm halfway through planting the bugs in a small warehouse filled with row upon row of boxes and shelves when a dozen guys show up. If I lived in a superhero movie, they'd be stereotypical henchmen.

"Uh," I say as they form a half circle around me. "Hi. I was just looking for a place to sleep tonight. I'll move along and—"

"Ethan sent you, didn't he?" one of the men asks.

"Ethan?" I ask. "Who's that?"

The man answers by throwing a punch at me.

At first the rudimentary training Rey had given me during hand-to-hand fighting comes in handy, but I'm rusty and was never really that good at it to begin with. And there are just so many of them. I dodge a few punches and then a fist lands in my gut and I crumple. Then I'm on the ground, kicks coming from every direction, my vision sparking as someone's heel meets the back of my head.

They can't kill me—there are still two Garde standing between me and death—but they can break me. Incapacitate me. Send me to the emergency room or abduct me.

I only have one chance of getting out of this.

Telekinetic energy erupts from my body, sending all the attackers sprawling backwards. I don't give anyone a chance to recover. I use my Legacy to send them flying into walls and one another, lifting them into the air and then slamming them down onto the concrete. I lash out and use my powers in ways I never imagined. It's strange how naturally it comes to me, this destruction. It feels so good—like I'm stretching a muscle I haven't used in a while. I realize that I miss using my telekinesis so often, like I had on my little island or when I was first picking pockets. Bodies fly all around the room, crashing into shelves and lights, until someone calls my name and I freeze.

Emma.

I turn to see her standing in one of the open loading bay doors, half silhouetted by the moonlight. She makes no move to come forward. There's a look on Emma's face I've never seen before. Her eyes are wide, the whites standing out in the near darkness. Her hands are shaking.

She's terrified.

Around me, all the attackers fall from the air, hitting the ground with thuds.

"Emma," I say, stepping towards her.

She takes a step back.

"What are you? How did you—" she says.

Her eyes fall on someone lying a few yards away from me.

"Marcus?" she asks. And then she's running towards him. He doesn't respond when she shakes him, and tears start to fill her eyes.

It takes a moment for me to figure out why I know the name Marcus, and then it clicks. I hadn't immediately recognized the name because she usually just calls him her brother.

Marcus appears to be alive but his leg is twisted in a way that I know means it's broken. He's probably cracked a few ribs from the drop in the air too.

What have I done?

"I'm sorry, I—" I start, but I'm cut off by Emma's glare, one of pure hatred.

"You monster," she says. "You fucking freak. Are you possessed? How did you do this?"

I take a step forward but she's on her feet, a pipe from one of the shelves I knocked down in her hands.

"Emma . . ."

"Don't you take another step closer."

"It's okay," I say. "It's me. Cody."

She shakes her head. Or maybe it's just trembling—it's hard to say. At her feet, her brother gurgles something unintelligible.

I take another step forward.

"Let me help you—"

And then she swings. The pipe connects with the side of my head and everything goes black.

When I wake up I'm in a car. A really *nice* car, all gray leather and touch screens. A man in a suit drives. I sit in the back passenger seat. Ethan sits beside me.

"Welcome back to the world of the living," he says.

My head pounds. I raise my fingers to find a throbbing knot on the side of my skull.

"Emma . . ." I murmur.

"It was quite the swing. You've probably got a concussion. I can have one of my doctors look at you if you feel dizzy or off."

"Where is she?"

"She stayed behind. Apparently one of the men was her brother. She called for help. I came in as soon as I heard there was trouble and took you. Didn't want you getting hurt more or arrested or anything like that."

I nod my head a little, but that just makes it hurt more. The pain makes it difficult to piece together everything that's just happened. A hundred different places on my body hurt. My white T-shirt is stained with drops of blood. My Loric Chest . . . there's a thump in my heart when I think of it. I look around the car. My dirty duffel bag sits at my feet on the floorboard.

I reach for it, frantically ripping back the cover. The Chest is still there. I exhale.

Ethan continues. "So, you have a few tricks up your sleeve you hadn't bothered to tell me about. No wonder the two of you were so good at the jobs I gave you."

"She didn't know," I say.

I regret the words immediately. They're an accidental admission of truth—that I do have powers. That I'm different.

But he knows that already. He saw what I did just as clearly as Emma did.

"Ah, that explains her reaction."

A monster, she called me. I thought she was my friend.

I stare out the window, unsure of where we're going. Maybe I should just roll down the window and fly out into the night. Find some other place to go. Start over again.

Maybe it's time I finally do go back to Canada.

A question forms in my sore head: Is this what my life is going to be like now? Moving from place to place, with no idea of what I'm supposed to be doing? No way to find the other Garde. No way the Garde are going to find me. If they're even looking for me. I could cause a scene or show off my powers, but the Mogs would probably have me killed before the Garde ever came out of hiding.

I wish there was another way.

"What were you to her? Partners? Friends? More than that?"

I roll this question around in my head for a moment, trying to see what he's getting at.

"Friends," I say. "I mean, I think we were."

"A friend wouldn't have reacted as she did, Cody," he says, leaning back into his seat. "A friend wouldn't have turned her back on you. I hate to say this, but I think it's possible that Emma has been riding on your coattails, trying to get anything out of you that she could. Using you."

I start to protest, but he raises a hand, stopping me from speaking.

"Do you know what you are to me?"

I shake my head slowly. "An employee?" I ask.

"Potential," Ethan says. "Raw power. I am not a fool. I know talent when I see it, and I respect it. I've been all around the world. I've seen some pretty crazy, unexplainable stuff in my day. Stuff you wouldn't believe even if I swore an oath on everything I hold dear and holy. I've seen men in Indonesia who can tell you your darkest secrets. Women in the Caribbean who can resurrect animals. Nothing surprises me. You don't have to tell me about yourself or your history. But you don't have to hide anything either. I'll never look at you like you're a freak. Whatever power or gifts you have, it means you're stronger than most people, right? It means you're someone who is going to endure. To survive. And that's why you're here now." He gestures back and forth between us. "We have a lot to offer each other. If we worked together, we'd be unstoppable."

"What about Emma?" I murmur.

"Emma has a family. Her foolish brother, yes, but parents and a home as well. You, on the other hand, are alone, aren't you?"

"What makes you think that?"

"Cody, I run a very tight ship when it comes to my business. I do thorough background checks on everyone I work with. You, my boy, have been something of an anomaly."

It occurs to me that he hasn't seemed shocked at all by anything that's happened. My powers, or Emma's leaving.

"You've been following me."

"You need to work on your stealth." Ethan pushes his dark hair back behind his ears. "That's something I can teach you. And from the looks of it, you could use quite a bit of hand-to-hand combat training as well. But most important is that ability you seem to have. You can move things around just by waving your hands."

"Telekinesis," I say.

What am I doing? I should go, should jump out of the car and disappear into the darkness.

But Ethan already knows. And I suddenly realize he's the only friend I have now. The way Emma looked at me—I know there's no going back to her now. I'd be surprised if she ever talked to me again. Besides, all this talk of training—maybe this is actually a really good thing. Ethan is obviously a powerful man. If he can train me to be like him, I can use that later. I mean, I can always leave, right?

"People like you and me are different, Cody," Ethan says. "You're special. I knew it the moment I met you on the beach. I could tell that you were the talented one of your little duo. You're powerful, but I can help you become someone that people truly admire and respect. Would you like that?"

"Yes," I say. I don't even really have to think about it.

"Good," he says with a smile. "We have a bright future ahead of us."

The driver turns towards a towering wrought-iron gate. It parts, exposing a long driveway leading up to a house that looks like something out of a movie about Hollywood millionaires.

"What is this place?" I ask.

"Your new home."

CHAPTER NINE

IT'S KIND OF STRANGE HOW QUICKLY TIME GOES by after Ethan takes me under his wing. I tell myself I'll stay a day or two, and then weeks pass like nothing. I keep thinking, "I'll leave tomorrow." But it's always tomorrow and never today, and I stay.

There are no more courier assignments or picked pockets. I live in luxury.

With a place like Ethan's it's difficult to imagine going back to sleeping on rooftops or in a shack. His house has everything you could ever want. A library, game room, beachfront view—there's even a little movie theater in the basement, which is where I spend a lot of my free time. Everything's locked and unlocked with a little key card I carry around in the expensive wallet Ethan bought me. There's a staff that cleans up after me. And there's a cook. A *cook*. He's probably my favorite person in the house. Aside from Ethan, who watches movies with me almost every night.

I like to remind myself that Rey would have wanted me safe. What could be safer than a place like Ethan's? A *compound*. Ethan sets me up in a room bigger than our entire shack on the island. I practically have the whole second floor to myself. Everything I could possibly want. Things I didn't even know I *needed*. We never had floss on the island, much less computers. I use the internet to try to find anything I can about the Garde— any news article or blog posts I can find that might lead me to them—but every time I think I'm getting close, the internet turns into a brick wall. I get an error message in the browser telling me the link is broken or the website is having difficulties. I figure the other Cêpans are doing this, trying to cover their tracks. If Rey were alive and we had the internet, I'm sure he'd be going around deleting things I posted too, or hacking into news sites.

That, or the other Garde are just too scared to come forward or do anything other than sit around waiting for something to happen for them to react to.

Not like Ethan. Ethan's like a dream Cêpan. Anything I want, he gives me. And anything he wants, he just takes.

"Everything out there can be yours," he says at least once a day, and when he does it sounds like he means it. It makes sense. What better display of strength and power is there than being able to do whatever you want when you want to. Ethan forgoes the running and weight training and instead focuses on my Legacies. I tell him I don't know where they came from, and he says it doesn't matter—all that matters is that we have them to use now. And he trains me, some days on the precision of my telekinesis, and other days on its strength. Flying comes easier and easier, until I can lift off with hardly a thought. His staff is well paid and wouldn't dare speak of anything they see. And he assures me he's *definitely* not telling anyone about what I can do. I'm his secret weapon. He has incredible things for my future. When I'm ready.

It's a future I'm excited to discover.

Ethan believes in power. I think he's obsessed with it. It's not hard to see how happy he gets when he takes us to a fancy restaurant or some incredibly expensive boutique and the servers and employees treat him like a god who's come down to Earth to order a filet mignon. I get it. I feel that way, too, when I'm with him. The thrill of being looked up to, of being *envied* even.

It's like an addiction.

But envy and money aren't the only aspects of power that Ethan values. His trade requires intimidation.

It's not something I'm good at.

A few months after the incident at the warehouse, one day after lunch, we walk through some trendy part of downtown Miami that's all billboards and lights. Ethan wears his normal dark suit and I've got on a T-shirt and jeans that cost enough money to probably buy the entire island I lived on with Rey. Gone is my long, matted brown hair. I've got a buzz cut now. I wonder how I survived in the tropics so long with so much hair on my head.

As usual, I keep an eye out for Emma. I don't know if I really want to see her again, but I don't want to just run into her on the street by surprise.

The last thing I need is another concussion.

We pass by a handful of kids a little older than me sitting outside a coffee shop—two guys and two girls. I don't notice the dog at their feet until it barks at me, and I jump back, startled, half knocking Ethan into the street.

The table erupts in laughter. One of the girls apologizes and pulls the dog back on its leash.

"Pansy-ass douche bag," one of the guys mutters to his friend.

"What was that?" Ethan asks, stepping up to the table.

I can see all of them begin to look uncomfortable.

"Nothing," the guy says.

"Did you hear what he called you?" Ethan asks me. I recognize the tone in his voice. He's turned on teacher mode, ready to impart some important lesson.

"Yeah . . ." I say.

"And are you a douche bag?"

"Hey, man," the girl says. "We're sorry. He didn't mean anything. He's just a jerk."

Ethan ignores her. Instead, he talks to me.

"That boy disrespected you."

"I guess." I shrug.

Ethan looks around for a moment. We're off to the side of the shop. There are not many people on the street. No one near us, at least.

"Then *show* him he should respect you."

The guy at the table stands up. He's twice my height, and at least two heads taller than Ethan.

"Leave it," the guy says.

I look over at Ethan hesitantly.

"You have to start at the bottom of the food chain and work your way up," Ethan says quietly. He turns to meet my eyes. "If you don't teach them that you're more powerful than they are, they'll never fear you. It's time for you to take action."

I nod to him.

"Look," the guy says, "I said—"

I raise my hand out in front of me and suddenly the boy flies three feet backwards, crashing into the wall of the coffee shop. He starts cursing and frantically trying to move, but I've got him a foot off the ground. He has no leverage. I'm in control.

The others at the table gasp and start to freak out.

"The girl's got a phone out," Ethan says calmly.

With my other hand I use my Legacy to rip it from her fingers and throw it to the ground. The screen shatters.

"The boy is going to run for it."

One of the other guys at the table is heading towards the side entrance. I take his legs out from under him with a flick of my wrist.

"There's someone behind you."

I swing around, both palms out, ready to fight.

But there's no one there.

I turn to Ethan. He's smiling.

"Perfection," he says. Then he glances around quickly. "We should go."

I let the boy drop to the ground. He's shaking and gasping for air as we walk away as if nothing has happened. His friends gather around him. My heart is thumping in my chest. I feel dizzy and light and weirdly satisfied.

I can't help but grin.

"You look pleased with yourself," Ethan says. "How did that feel?"

"Wonderful," I say.

It felt wonderful.

A year after being at Ethan's—almost down to the day— I'm pulled out of sleep in the middle of the night. My calf is on fire. I yelp, howling at the pain as I knock half the things off the nightstand trying to find the light. Even before it's switched on, I know what the burning means.

Death.

Another one is gone.

A swirling, reddish symbol has appeared on my leg above two similar ones. Three is dead. This red mark is likely the only kind of tombstone he or she will get. Another Garde sacrificed for the Lorien cause. Only one person rests between me and death now, if what Rey always told me was true about the order in which we had to be killed.

Number Four.

I stagger out of bed, wincing a bit every time I put weight down on my ankle. And it's more weight than usual. After a year of meals served up in Ethan's house any time of day I might be hungry, I look nothing like the sunburned, skinny kid from the island. I'm built like a tank now. Solid. Maybe a little on the chubby side. Definitely a lot pastier than I was a year ago. I've been focusing much more on my Legacies than keeping my body in shape.

The death of Three takes me completely by surprise.

I haven't necessarily *forgotten* about Lorien and the Garde, but without Rey constantly badgering me about them, all that has kind of lived in the back of my mind. I've spent so much time lately living things up with Ethan that the Garde have once again become stories. I've forgotten that they're actual people. I've tried to ignore the fact that I may end up the next target on death's numerical list.

One more way I tell lies, I guess. Only these are told to myself.

My mind is finally catching up with my body's wakefulness, and I start to think of all the implications this new development might have. Maybe Four's death isn't that far away. There's always the chance that Three and Four were together. I *do* always imagine the other Garde working together without me.

I walk around the room holding my breath, waiting for a new searing burn to take over my leg. But after a few minutes nothing comes. Still, if another scar does appear, it means I'm next. I'm the new big target.

Me, and anyone else I'm around.

I stop pacing.

I could leave right now. Ethan would never be any wiser to what's actually going on. I could fly away to a different city. A different *country*. Finally up to Canada—just a while later than I'd planned.

But I don't want to be on my own again. Maybe Ethan

would want to go with me. For someone who doesn't like big groups of people, the thought of not having *one* person to rely on scares me.

Even then, though, the Mogs might track me back to him. We haven't necessarily been subtle with the use of my powers. I feel so stupid all of the sudden. As good as it felt displaying my superiority over people like that asshat at the coffee shop, I never should have let Ethan talk me into it.

I have to tell him about what's happening. It's the least I can do for how good he's been to me.

As I slip out of my room, I can almost hear Rey's voice in the back of my head. *Tell no one who you are. Tell no one what you know. Secrecy is your greatest weapon.* But Rey's not actually here now, and the world hasn't exactly been the labyrinth of fear and persecution that he always said it would be. I've been in Miami for over a year and I haven't even heard so much as a whisper of the word "Lorien." If Rey *were* still alive, we'd probably be fishing sea snails out of their shells with bamboo shoots while we sweated and half-starved on some tropic island.

No, I have to tell Ethan. Maybe he can help somehow. He's smart and rich—maybe there's some titanium-plated safe house he can take me to. Or weapons. Maybe he knows someone in the military who can nuke Mogadore.

Or something.

I slink through the dark house. Ethan's bedroom door is cracked, but he's not inside. No lights are on in the bathroom or closet. He's not there.

Gone.

My heart skips a beat.

They've already come. They've taken him. It's too late, and I'm fucked.

Then I notice Ethan's bed. It's still made. He hasn't gone to sleep yet.

Maybe he's still awake.

I make my way downstairs cautiously, looking for lights in the kitchen and den, but there are none. I'm about to go outside when I hear the faintest strains of music floating through the air from somewhere farther inside the house. One swelling measure, and then it's gone.

Tiptoeing through the halls, I figure out where it's coming from. The door to Ethan's private study— the room that shall not be entered—is cracked open. There's a sliver of light shining through.

No way.

I've been over every inch of this house for the past year and this is the only room my key card won't open. I even tried to jimmy the lock with my telekinesis one day when Ethan was out, with no luck. It's always been an impenetrable fortress.

Until now, I guess.

I push the door open just a little more and am surprised by how heavy it is. The thing must be made of metal or something. I peer in.

There's a wall of bookshelves on one side, but most of the rest of the room is covered in charts and graphs. A big circular desk in the center of the floor has a map spread across it covered in pins and little flags. Ethan sits at his workstation. There are three—no, make that *four*—computer monitors hooked up to a couple of PC towers, and a laptop opened off to the side. Music pours out of speakers hidden around the room, the volume just above a whisper. Beethoven, I think, but I only know that because Ethan dragged me to a symphony once thinking I might take a liking to a bunch of violins or something.

Ethan's back is to me, but I can hear him. He's talking to someone. It looks like a video call. I can almost make out the person on the screen.

My body freezes. "Person" might be the wrong word.

The figure on the screen has black hair, slicked back, with some other black marks—birthmarks? Tattoos?— peeking out at the sides. His eyes are dark orbs. On the sides of his nose are shining little slivers of flesh, like monstrous gills standing out against his ashen skin.

I've seen faces like that before. Only once. In Canada.

A Mogadorian.

Before I can wrap my head around anything that's going on, Ethan speaks.

"What about Four? Have you got a lock on him?"

My head pounds.

What's going on?

"We have a few leads." The Mog grins, exposing rows of gray teeth. "It shouldn't be long now. It's only a matter of waiting for him to slip up now that Number Three has been taken off the board. We'd had leads connecting him to Florida, but it seems like those were probably all pointing to your charge."

No, no, no, none of this is right.

"More than likely." Ethan nods. "None of our eyes in Miami have reported anything, at least."

His charge. The Mog is talking about *me*. My heart leaps into my throat. They know where I am.

Is Ethan working for them? Is he *one* of them?

Nothing's making sense. My thoughts race. The red mark on my calf burns.

"And Number Five?" the Mog bastard asks. "I trust his training continues as planned."

My hands tremble.

"He remains well," Ethan says. He cocks his head to the side just a bit. "In fact, he's here right now."

A little cry escapes through my lips.

"I'll have to call you back," Ethan says, tapping on the keyboard. The Mog disappears.

So do I.

I have to get out of this house. Whatever is happening, my cover's been blown, and I can't afford to stick around and try to figure things out.

I dart for the front door, but it's locked. My key card is upstairs, but I have a sneaking suspicion that it wouldn't do any good.

I head to the back door—the sliding one that opens up to the patio, the one that's never locked—but it won't budge. I pick up a nearby chair and slam it into the glass. It should be more than enough force to shatter it. Instead, the chair just bounces off.

This house suddenly seems like one big prison.

"Bulletproof," Ethan says from behind me.

I whirl around, holding up my fists, ready to punch him or use my telekinesis against him. He just stands there unarmed with his hands out in front of him, the sleeves of his white dress shirt rolled up to his elbows.

"Explain yourself!" I shout with a fury I didn't even know I had in me. I'm running on pure adrenaline now.

"Look, there's no reason for us to fight. I don't want to, and we both know there's no way I could even attempt to match you if—" He takes a step forward and I blast him back, sending him toppling over a gray couch in the living room, crashing through a glass coffee table.

When he looks up, he seems oddly pleased.

"I deserved that."

"Explain yourself," I say again. Not as loud, but more earnestly.

What has he done? What have I done?

Ethan gets up slowly and sits on the edge of the couch. He pulls a piece of glass out of his palm, wincing slightly.

"All right," he says. "Let's be honest with each other for once."

I nod. He takes a deep breath and then starts to talk.

"I am not a thief or playboy criminal or anything like that. Not originally, at least. That was just a persona that was created for me. We have so many ties to the people that run this city—both the criminals and the politicians—that it was easy to plant me here."

"How did you even *find* me?" is all I can manage to sputter.

"You flew to shore last year. That sort of thing gets noticed. Maybe not by the media or the police, but people talk. And we were listening."

"Who are you? You don't look like a Mog."

"Do you know about the Greeters?"

That word brings up memories of Rey talking. An image of us in Canada flashes in my mind, me tucked into bed and my Cêpan telling me about our escape from Lorien. Ethan just keeps on talking.

"The Greeters were humans who met the Cêpans when you first arrived on Earth. They helped the Garde transition into life here. That sort of thing."

Garde. Cêpan. It's so strange to hear these words coming out of Ethan's mouth—words I've kept hidden for so long.

"Right," I say. "So what does that have to do with you?"

"I was supposed to be one of them."

"You're a Greeter?"

"I was a part of this message board that a man named Malcolm . . . You know what, that part doesn't matter. What matters is that I predicted the future. I know power—know *potential*—when I see it. That part of me is true. And I could see that there was no way that Lorien's squad of children could ever hope to stand up to the Mogadorians. So when the Mogs came to Earth looking for you, I struck a deal with them. In exchange for my service, I will be spared. Earth's future belongs to the Mogadorians, and when they take over they'll remember that I was the one who helped them." He slumps a little, and when he talks again it's more to himself than to me. "I chose correctly too. The Greeters haven't necessarily had a great life since then."

"You sold me out so you could live," I say quietly, backing up against the door. My eyes dart outside. Suddenly I realize what this means. "They're here to kill me already, aren't they?"

"Whoa, whoa," Ethan says, raising his hands again, one of them bloody from the glass. "You misunderstand. I'm not helping them by handing you over to them so they can kill you. They don't want to hurt you at all. I'm helping them by training you. You're going to rule here, Cody. The Mogadorians want you to reign alongside them."

My mouth drops open.

"What?" I ask again dumbly, but it's the only word I can summon right now.

"The Garde are done for," Ethan says. "You've got another scar, right? That leaves six of you. The Mogadorians have an entire army—hell, entire *worlds* at their disposal. Do you really think Lorien poses any threat? That *Earth* could stop them?"

I don't answer, just stand there trying to make sense of everything that's happening.

"Why me?"

"They have others. Number Nine is in their custody *right now*, but he's not leadership material. I know, because I've met him. You're the one that's got what it takes. The power and the hunger. All this—this house, the staff, me teaching you—everything was put together for you. To make you stronger."

"You have Nine?" My mind races. For so long the other Garde have just been stories and scars—it's almost shocking to hear that Ethan's actually met one of them.

"Oh yes," Ethan says. "You wouldn't like him. He's arrogant and cocky. A pretty boy. And do you know where he and his Cêpan were while you were picking pockets on the beach to stay alive? In a giant apartment in Chicago. Living a life of luxury. The life you *should* have been leading—and *have* been leading since you've been in my care."

The last year of my life has been a lie. No wonder I haven't felt like I've been hunted while in Miami—I've been in their care the whole time.

"But . . ." I struggle for words. "Rey . . . my destiny . . ."

"Your destiny is whatever you make of it," Ethan says. He pats at something in his pants pocket and I can hear a metallic click in the door behind me. "You're free to go if you want. But think about what that would mean. Three have fallen. The rest will fall in time. You can die with them, for some fight that you inherited, a fight that was forced upon you, or you can live like a king. The Mogs will give you Earth. They'll give you anything you want. You were raised to think of them as the enemy, but that's just because it's all you knew. It's a weird form of brainwashing. Try to put things in perspective. The Mogs are not your enemy. They're your only chance for survival."

No.

Before Ethan can say anything else I've used my telekinesis to push open the back door and am soaring through the sky. I worry for a moment that something might shoot me down—that there are guns or lasers hidden in the trees around Ethan's compound—but nothing stops me from going.

I fly out over the water, low enough that no one should be able to see me. The Garde. Ethan. The Mogs. My mind is a mess and I can't think straight. It doesn't help that I'm surrounded by nothing but ocean now, bringing back memories of Rey's little sailboat and being lost out at sea, near death.

How is it possible that everything I've done has been so wrong?

I fly back to the mainland—miles and miles away from Ethan's home—to try to calm down and think rationally. I land on the top of the tallest building in downtown Miami, perch on the edge of the roof. And there I sit, trying to make sense of it all.

Everything about my life after I crash-landed on the beach might have been arranged by the Mogs. Well, not everything. It would have taken a while for word to spread about me. Everything after meeting Ethan on the beach has probably been staged, but things before that might not have been.

Like Emma. Did she know about me? Was she just a

plant to get me into Ethan's sights? Part of the plan all along? For some reason, the answers to these questions nag at my brain. When she called me a monster, was it because she really thought I was one or because she was told to do so?

I take the little rubber ball from my pocket and roll it over the backs of my knuckles. It's the only little piece of my past I have left. That and . . .

Shit.

My Loric Chest is back in my room at Ethan's. Of course I forgot it. I'm such an idiot. Rey would be furious if he were alive to know I'd left it like I did during his fake Mog attack back on the island.

But Rey's not here. It wasn't even a Mogadorian that killed him. It was this planet. Or his own body.

Rey's not here. No one is. It's just me.

I'm alone again.

My thoughts flash to the other Garde. The Mogs have Nine. That means there are only five of us alive and free. Five of us against the world. Against *several* worlds.

I wonder if Ethan might be right. Maybe Lorien's last-chance plan of enchanting a bunch of little kids and sending them to another planet never had any hope of success. We never even got to question whether that was what we wanted to do or not. No one asked us if we wanted to be the chosen ones.

I'm suddenly reminded of a movie Emma and I saw together before everything went to hell—some horror flick we'd laughed our way through. There was an island inhabited by a cult and a man was stranded on it. He and the rest of the audience knew that the people in the cult were crazy, but they didn't. They'd been a part of the cult their whole lives and just couldn't see that they were the bad guys.

Was that my story too?

I wish Rey were here to make sense of things. Already he's fading from my memory. And the things I do remember vividly are his rules, or his disappointment, or his failed training.

And his last words. *Do whatever it takes to survive.*

I stay on the roof all night. By morning, I still don't know what my next move should be. And even though I know I shouldn't—that it's probably being watched—I go to the beach where I first met Emma.

I find the arepa stand where I bought us snacks.

It takes the owner a few moments to recognize me with a few extra pounds and close-cropped hair. When he finally does, he looks spooked.

"Have you seen Emma around?" I ask him.

He shakes his head a little.

"She's gone."

"What do you mean, she's gone?" I ask. My heart

races. If the Mogs killed her . . .

"Her family moved a few months ago. Her brother had been in the hospital for a while, but when he finally got out, they wanted to start over somewhere new. They hightailed it out of here."

His face is going pale. At first I think the Mogs have shown up behind me or something, but then I realize it's me. Emma must have told him, or the other locals, what she'd seen. About what a freak I was.

The man crosses his hand over his head and chest. He keeps talking, but I walk away.

I wander aimlessly, frustration growing inside me. Four other Garde are free, but hidden away. Probably living in high-rises or penthouses like Nine was. And here I am alone again. Forgotten. Having to start over.

Something hot boils up inside me. I slam my fist against the brick wall of a store beside me. And then, something strange starts to happen.

My body changes.

I can feel it stiffening and growing heavy. My skin grows dry and looks brittle.

I take a few steps away from the wall and back into a stop sign on the street. I wrap my fingers around it for balance—my head is spinning—and squeeze. The metal crumples under my touch.

Then my skin changes again. It takes on a silvery sheen. I stumble forward, pulse quickening. I lean against a storefront window. Again I change. I raise my hand. I can see through it.

Glass. I've turned into glass.

At first I think I'm dying—maybe I've been poisoned somehow. But with every step I take and every different material my fingers graze, it becomes more apparent what's happening.

I'm turning into the things I touch.

My hands shake. My eyes grow wide and dry. It's everything I can do just to keep breathing at a normal pace.

It's early in the morning, and there aren't many people around, but that will change. Soon, there'll be crowds everywhere. Whatever is happening to me, I can't stay out in the open.

I have to get to safety. To shelter.

I don't want to be alone.

There's only one person I know who can help me. Only one person I know, period.

I somehow manage to turn into a normal, fleshy human again, and then I'm in the air, flying faster than I ever have before, throwing caution to the wind as I soar high over the city. When I crash onto the beach at the back of Ethan's property, one of the maids sees me and runs inside.

I try to stand on the beach, but suddenly I'm sinking—no, not sinking, I'm falling apart as my legs disintegrate, breaking up and turning into tiny pieces of earth. I'm becoming one with the beach. I scream as I start to collapse in on myself.

What's happening? I wonder frantically. And then another, more pressing thought appears. *I'm going to die a pile of beach.*

"Cody!" someone shouts. It's Ethan. The maid must have found him.

My torso's falling apart now. I try to shout to Ethan but the only thing that escapes my throat is a dry wheeze. I reach forward, but my arm is already starting to break down.

He runs straight for me, grabbing my hand as best as he can, but half of it slips through his fingers. Part of me touches his watch and I start to solidify again, this time taking on a gold, metallic sheen. The rest of my body follows suit.

I hyperventilate. My heart thumps in my chest, and I swear for a moment it sounds like metal, clanging against my rib cage. That makes me freak out even more, and I can't catch my breath.

"Calm down," Ethan says. "This is . . ." He struggles to find the right word. "I guess you're developing new powers or something."

Calm down? Is he joking?

"Breathe, Cody," he says.

I almost shout, "You know that's *not* my name," but stop myself.

The maid reappears. She hands a little black bag to Ethan. He says something back to her that I don't hear while I continue to have the panic attack to end all panic attacks.

He pulls out a little vial of something from the bag. He snaps it in two and holds it up to my face.

"What—" I start.

"Just something to help you relax," he says.

Some kind of white smoke drifts out of the vial and I start to feel light and dizzy.

"There you go," Ethan says.

He grabs my hand to help me to my feet, and I don't know if it's the weird smoke or touching real human flesh, but suddenly I'm me again—flesh and bone and not looking like some kind of gold robot.

Before I know it I find it hard to think of anything—to even *feel* anything—and all I see is black.

When I wake up, I expect to be restrained or locked up somehow, but I'm still just lying on top of the covers. The window is even open. My duffel bag is on the bed beside me, my Loric Chest still inside.

Ethan sits in a chair at the foot of the bed.

"Good afternoon," he says. There's hesitancy in his

voice, like he's unsure how to act. Or how *I'll* act.

I glance around, looping my arm through the straps of my bag.

"What did you give me?" I ask, thinking back to the strange white smoke.

"Nothing harmful," Ethan says. "Just a little tranquilizer. I was afraid you were going to hurt yourself if you didn't stop changing."

My heart starts beating furiously as I remember the feeling of breaking apart on the beach.

"No," Ethan says in his most authoritative voice. "Calm down. Breathe deeply. You don't want to start morphing again."

I nod, trying to focus on taking long, slow breaths. There's a residual numbness from whatever the drug was. I feel alert and focused, but relaxed.

Ethan's eyebrows knit together. Either he's genuinely worried about me or he's a really great actor. I'm not sure which is the case at this point. He throws his hands out to his sides.

"I'm sure you have a lot of questions," he says. "It's just you and me."

"Like I'm supposed to believe you."

"It's important to them that you come of your own free will. That only makes sense. The Mogadorians don't want someone they've forced to rule. They want someone who *wants* to be a part of their cause."

"Free will?" I mutter. "That's what you call all the lies you've told me?"

Ethan frowns.

I grip the handles of the duffel bag. I can be out the window in an instant if I need to be. But a huge part of me really wants to talk to Ethan, to find out why he's done these things. To answer all the questions welling up inside me.

"Was Emma in on this?"

"Emma," Ethan says with a frown. "No, she didn't know anything that was going on. The men who attacked you at the warehouse *were* staged, but I honestly had no idea her brother would be one of them. They were just lackeys. I believe her family has moved to Tampa since you've been here. We keep tabs on them. I could have her brought here if you wanted."

"No," I say. All that means is that her hatred of me—her calling me a freak—was real. She was not really my friend. I wonder if that's how all humans react to Legacies and superpowers like mine.

"You found Emma yourself. All I did was nudge you. Hell, all I did was show up on the beach and give you an opportunity. You came to us. You just didn't know who we were." He leans in a little. "Think about it. The Loric never gave you the choice we're giving you. They put a spell on you and sent you away. They told you who you had to be. All I'm offering you is another way. A *better* way."

"What about the other Garde?"

He shrugs.

"Maybe they'll learn to see reason too."

"And if I leave?"

"I'm not going to stop you," Ethan says, looking very serious. "The last thing I want is for you to be hurt. But once you leave I can't protect you any longer. If you turn down this offer, you're the enemy. You won't even be safe here. You've probably guessed it by now, but this isn't *my* house. The Mogadorians arranged for it."

"If I leave, you've failed your mission, haven't you?" I ask.

Ethan nods. I know what this means. I've heard enough stories about the ruthlessness of the Mogs to know that they don't tolerate failures. If I leave, Ethan is probably as good as dead.

I stare at him. Everything has happened so fast. Everything's *changed* so quickly.

"I know you, Five," Ethan says. "How good it makes you feel to be in control and respected. You can feel like that forever when you're ruling with the Mogs. I've seen their power. It's amazing. And they want you to be a part of it. They want you to be on their side, be *one* of them."

"Everything out there can be yours," I say, quoting Ethan's favorite motto.

"Everything," he says.

I close my eyes. It's all too much to take in. But what Ethan says makes sense. At least, mostly.

The Elders left me with a dying old man to protect me. The Mogs built me up and gave me anything I wanted. *Groomed* me. *They're* the ones who have shown me the most respect in my lifetime.

They're the ones who can keep me alive.

I think of the other Garde. What easy lives they've probably had. Competent Cêpans. Homes in cities. One day in the future they will likely look at me and tell me that I've betrayed them. But who knows? Maybe they'll see reason. If I can just talk to them, maybe they'll start to see things differently. Why should we be hunted down like animals when we could be rulers? The humans don't have powers like ours. They think we're freaks. Monsters. We could show them what we truly are together.

"Okay," I say slowly. "What do we do now?"

Relief washes over Ethan's face, and his smile erupts again, the one I know so well by now.

"I'll let them know," he says. "Get your things together. They'll want to talk with you as soon as possible."

I nod, and head to the stairs.

"Hey." Ethan turns back to me before leaving. "I'm proud of you. You're doing the right thing. You're doing the *smart* thing. That's the biggest test of all."

I move as if in a daze. My body functions, but it's as if someone else is controlling it. I wonder briefly if I'm in shock. That's what they always say on TV when someone's been through something crazy like this.

"We're heading up north," Ethan yells from the stairs. "Grab a coat."

I pull some cold-weather clothes out of the back of my closet—stuff Ethan bought me a while ago that I've never had reason to wear. Then I head for the door.

I pause and then turn back. I pick up my duffel bag and take my Loric Chest out, placing it on the bed. All the useless stuff is still there. I run my fingers over the items before picking up the hidden blade.

It might be smart to keep this handy, just in case we run into trouble.

I slip the bracer on over my hand and wrist, and then put a glove on over it.

Just in case we run into trouble.

There's a chopping noise coming from outside my window. I look out and see a black helicopter landing on the sprawling yard of the house.

CHAPTER
TEN

WE'RE IN THE HELICOPTER FOR WHAT SEEMS like a long time. It's small, but fast. I don't know who the pilot is and I don't ask. All I know is that we have to wear these big noise-canceling headphones with radios built into them, and that's the only way the three of us—me, Ethan, and the pilot—can talk to one another. None of us does, which is all right with me. I'm too busy trying to remain calm, focusing on the grass and roads flying by beneath me. Pretending the cars and trucks are toys.

Ethan keeps grinning, like he's just won the lottery. I imagine the Mogs will reward him somehow for helping to recruit me. I start to pick apart everything he's said and done in the past year, but I have to stop. Every time I start doing that, I begin to second-guess myself. So instead I just stare at the clouds and cities and pastures sweeping by beneath us, trying to steel myself for whatever's coming next. I take deep breaths and keep my hands clasped together, trying not to freak out about the fact that I'm heading to Mog central.

For some reason I think they're going to take me to some kind of alien ship or even an old Gothic mansion, but we land at a big, sterile-looking building. It's still dark outside, but from what I can tell the place looks like a big office—not at all the HQ I would have expected the Mogs to be using.

Men in black suits meet us at the front doors. They look human enough, and nod—almost bow—to me in reverence when we approach. I try to keep my body from shaking, which takes a lot of effort. Everything is new and different and terrifying, and for a few passing moments all I want is to be sitting on the beach on my little island, even though by this point I probably couldn't even find it if I tried.

"Welcome, sir," they both say.

Inside, we're escorted past a front desk and around security. I notice a placard on a wall as we pass: Federal Bureau of Investigation.

"Is this, like, a *government* facility?" I whisper to Ethan.

"I told you," he says. "They've got eyes all over the place. They've got resources everywhere."

He winks at me, though this fact is both impressive and unsettling. I'm beginning to see just how useless all the hiding and moving was.

We continue to silently wind through a few halls, down a set of stairs, and into what must be an underground level. Finally, we come to two doors next to each other.

"You're in here," one of the men says, motioning from me to the first door. Then he turns to Ethan. "You're in the other one."

"Wait," I say, stepping forward. They can't separate us. I don't want to be alone in here. Panic starts to rise up in me. I can feel my skin start to change, taking on the properties of my duffel bag handles, all leathery and smooth. "Why can't we—"

"It's fine," Ethan says in the most soothing voice he can. It works, because I start to calm down. "They just want to talk to you. It's probably classified info or something like that. It's okay. You're their VIP. Don't worry."

I nod reluctantly. Ethan disappears into his appointed room. I stand in the hallway for a few seconds before one of the men clears his throat. I shoot him an annoyed look and then go inside.

It's the kind of room I recognize from watching too many crime shows on cable over the last year. It's empty except for a swinging light, a few chairs, and a big metal desk in the center of the room that looks like it could double as an operating table. An interrogation room. I swallow hard.

"Please, have a seat," someone says.

I turn to see the Mogadorian Ethan was videoconferencing with last night standing in the corner. His gleaming black hair reflects the swinging light, black eyes twinkling. His lips spread across his gray teeth. He has to be seven feet tall, at least.

"We've been expecting you, Five," he continues, his voice rich and low as he waves towards one of the chairs. I hesitate, and then take a seat. The Mog sits across from me.

I'm sitting across from a Mogadorian.

Suddenly, all I can remember are stories Rey told me growing up. About how the Mogs invaded, and about all the terrors they brought with them to our planet. You'd think that they were monsters—and though this guy is definitely creepy and intimidating, he doesn't look all that different from me, all things considered.

Still, it's hard for me to keep my fingers from drumming on the table. I pull my hands back, crossing my arms. That's when I feel the Loric glove and its hidden blade.

Rey always told me that if I was caught I'd be tortured. If that's what this is really about—all one setup to try to torture me—will I be fast enough to use the blade to escape? Either by destroying the Mogs or myself?

"We're very pleased with your decision to join us, young Lorien," the Mog says.

"I don't have much of a choice if I want to live," I say.

"An intelligent boy. I always knew we were correct in placing our bets on you. If only more of your kind were able to see the true extent of our might and the inevitability of the Mogadorian rule, we might have saved many casualties."

"You've been in contact with the others?" I ask.

"In some ways."

"What's your plan? Are you going after Four next?"

"Based on the charm that protects all of you, that *would* make sense," the Mog says, grinning widely, exposing those hideous teeth once again. "Of course, it's possible that charm has its limits. How many times do you think it will work before it finally fails? We have so many soldiers and scouts willing to test out the spell's longevity, happy to die in the name of securing our future."

He's going to try to kill me, I think. In an instant, I've got one glove off and a hand on the table. It's as if by instinct. I haven't trained with my newest power, but I take a chance. Sure enough, my skin goes silver as I absorb the properties of the metal. If nothing else it should buy me some time if he attacks me.

The Mog laughs a little.

"Oh, don't worry. We have *others* we could test that

out on. Isn't it obvious by now that we have a much brighter future prepared for you?"

"You have other Garde *here*?" I remember Ethan mentioning Nine being held captive. The idea of meeting another of my kind makes my pulse pound.

I don't want to do it. Not now, at least. I couldn't face one of them as someone who turned on them. Not until I'm stronger, until I've got my head on right and can really talk some sense into them.

"In due time, you'll learn about all the ways that we've ensured our success in the extermination of the Garde. But we can't just go around telling you all our secrets, now, can we? Not if you were planning on double-crossing us or were to report back to the Garde. You must prove your loyalty to us before we can continue."

I hesitate, and focus on my breathing. On calming down. My body changes back to normal, and I place my palms on the table before me.

"A useful power," the Mog says. "Ethan had not mentioned it in his reports."

"It's new," I say. "Very new."

He just nods.

"We can help you with that. With all your skills. By the time we're through training you, you'll be one of the most powerful players in our ranks. There is not a place on this planet that will be *worthy* of your rule."

Something sparks in me. The memory of a place. A destination I never made it to.

"Canada," I say.

"I'm sorry?"

"Canada. I would want to rule over Canada."

The Mog looks confused for a moment, and then smirks.

"How about all of North America. To start with."

I nod. I don't know how else to respond to being offered a continent.

"But, first, your loyalty," he continues. "This is the sort of deal that is usually inked in blood."

Blood?

"What do you want me to do?"

The Mog turns his head, nodding toward Ethan's room.

"He has served us well."

"What?" I ask. *Ethan?* My stomach turns. Surely he can't mean what I think he means—that he wants me to kill the only person I have in the world. "But you made a deal with Ethan." My voice threatens to shake.

I start to go on, almost pleading, but the Mog just lets out what might be a laugh, but sounds more like choking.

"No, no, dear boy. We aren't asking you to hurt Ethan. That human has served us very well. And we honor our deals. I simply point out that Ethan went through some of the same trials you will have to go through in the future to prove his intentions to us. Your loyalty to him is commendable, but we're going to have to harden your resolve."

I exhale long and hard.

The Mog places a folder on the table.

"There *will* be a sacrifice to us. Not immediately, but once you're ready. When we've trained you, and helped you unlock your full potential. There's a picture of your target in here." He slides the folder across the table. "Would you like to see who it is?"

I don't touch the document.

"We are offering you the world, Five. Prove yourself, and we will make you a god on this planet. If you are serious about joining us, this is the way it must be. Not only as proof of your loyalty, but proof that you have what it takes to rule in the name of Mogadore. There is much to come. We have no room for the squeamish."

And if I *don't* do it, he'll have me thrown into a cell and probably tortured. Ethan too. This he doesn't say, but I know it must be true.

For a moment this scenario seems strangely familiar. My mind flashes back to our little shack on the island. The hogs snorting wildly, practically screaming in their pen. The scared snake, raised halfway off the ground like a clenched spring, ready to strike. Rey telling me to kill it before it harmed one of us. It was the snake or us. It just had to be that way.

The memory seems so far away. So long ago.

I'd simply stood there, not wanting to have to do anything. Hoping that everything would work out somehow—that the danger would go away on its own.

But that's not how the world works. It's no use just sitting around waiting for danger to come to me. At least with the Mogs, I'll know the danger. I'll *be* the danger.

Do whatever it takes to stay alive.

Rey's last words to me.

"All right," I say. My voice wavers a little, and I try to even it out as I continue. "If that's what it takes to show my allegiance."

The Mog grins.

I stare at the folder. I don't have to open it, but I realize that this—like so many other things in my life—is a test. To see if I have the stomach for what's to come. I'm going to have to get used to this sort of thing. Harden myself. The Mogs won't coddle me—of this I have no doubt. They're ruthless and powerful. That's what I'll have to become.

I take a deep breath and open the folder.

I AM NUMBER FOUR

THE LOST FILES

FILES

RETURN TO PARADISE

CHAPTER
ONE

I HAVE TO KEEP REMINDING MYSELF WHO I AM the first week at the new school. Not, like, I lost my memory or something. I *know* who I am in a literal sense. But I have to keep forcing myself to remember what being me means. So all week I keep a single thought repeating through my head:

You are Mark James.

It's what I think on Monday when some douche bag trips me while I try to find an empty seat among a precalc classroom full of strangers.

You are Mark James, the guy everyone at your old school looked up to. These idiots will learn.

And Wednesday when someone loots my locker during weight training and forces me to walk around in sweaty gym clothes for the last two periods.

You are Mark James, all-conference quarterback. They're just jealous.

And at lunch on Thursday when I sit on the tailgate of my truck and someone in a loud old Camaro zips past, hurling an oversize Styrofoam cup of orange soda at me while yelling what I think is "ass pirate."

You are Mark James, and you are the best fucking athlete the Paradise High Pirates ever saw.

If someone had asked me a year ago what my future held, I'd probably have said something like "Mark James, Ohio State star quarterback." Maybe if I'd had a beer or two I'd go so far as to say, "Mark James, first-round NFL draft pick."

What I wouldn't have said—what I couldn't have even imagined thinking—was anything remotely close to "Mark James, survivor of an alien attack."

For my entire life, the future seemed set for me. As soon as I threw my first pass, I knew what I wanted to do. Paradise High QB, college football star, NFL hopeful. But now the future is this stupid, dark thing I can't predict, and I feel like my whole life has been heading towards something that doesn't even matter. Might not even exist if we end up conquered by a bunch of superpowered aliens. I mean, my all-conference trophy was used to *murder* an alien. A Mogadorian. A bunch of pale, janky-looking assholes from another planet came to Earth hunting for a very human-looking alien named John Smith—*ha*—and his invisible friend. Then they destroyed my school. My kingdom. Almost killing me in the process.

Some people did die. I guess I should count myself lucky, but I don't *feel* lucky. I feel like someone who's just found out that vampires exist or that reality is actually an elaborate video game. Everyone else keeps going on as usual, but the world has changed for me.

There are only a few people who know what really happened at Paradise High. Everyone thinks the school's in shambles because weirdo-drifter/new student John Smith went crazy and jumped through the principal's window one day, then came back that night and caused massive amounts of damage that took out half the building. Then he fled town. Word is that he's some kind of teenage terrorist or member of a sleeper cell or a psychopath—it depends on who is telling the story.

But one exploding school can't stand in the way of education, so now everyone from Paradise is being shipped to the next town over where there's an actual building for us to go to. It just so happens that the next school over is Helena High, our biggest rival, who I beat in the best football game of my life, capping off an undefeated season by completely annihilating their defense. So, yeah, I guess I can see why I'm not the most loved guy in school. I just never thought I'd spend my last semester of high school washing orange soda out of my hair. Maybe if I was still the same old Mark James I'd think it was kind of fun even. I'd be dreaming up ways to get back at the other students, ways for me and my football buddies to prank them and get the last laugh. But filling someone's locker full of manure isn't as high on my list of priorities now that I know beings from another world are walking among us and that a complete alien invasion is possible at any time. I *wish* manure were still higher on my to-do list.

A bunch of my teammates have told me I've gotten quiet and seem different since it happened, but I can't help it. It's kind of pointless to talk about cars and partying when I was literally almost squashed by some kind of extraterrestrial monster. How am I supposed to go back to being fun-loving, beer-chugging Mark James after all that? Now I'm "Paranoid That Aliens Are Going to Hunt Me Down" Mark James.

I can deal with the new school. Hell, I probably deserve it for the shit I put people like John through back in Paradise. It's only a semester, and then I'll have graduated. Maybe they'll even be able to fix up the school auditorium in time for me to walk the stage in Paradise. What sucks is that I can't tell everyone what's going on. They'd throw me in a mental institution. Or worse, those bad aliens—the Mogs—would be after me to try and shut me up.

At least I have Sarah to talk to. She was there. She fought with me, almost died beside me. As long I have Sarah, I don't feel like I'm going to go crazy.

CHAPTER
TWO

THERE ARE BIG SCHOOL BUSES SHUTTLING KIDS back and forth between Helena and Paradise, but I was able to talk the principal into letting me drive myself. I told him I wanted to stay late and work out—that I didn't want what happened in Paradise to keep me from being an unstoppable college football machine. He said that was fine: I'm guessing partly because he hopes anything I do in the future will make Paradise High look good, and partly because everyone in town still feels kind of bad for me because I threw a party and some kids accidentally burned down my house.

I don't *think* that had anything to do with aliens. At least, I've made sure to tell everyone who insinuates that John blew up my house that it was really a couple of stoners down in the basement who were lighting stuff on fire for fun. That usually shuts people up—especially adults who like to pretend that stuff like that never happens in good old Paradise. Besides, John saved Sarah and both of my dogs. There's a YouTube video to prove it. No one should be giving him shit for that night. He gets a free pass on that one.

I meet Sarah in the parking lot after the last bell on the Friday of our first week in Helena. She waits for me at my truck. It's kind of gray outside, and she's got on a plaid sweater that makes her eyes look like they're practically glowing blue. She looks gorgeous.

She always does.

Sarah Hart was—*is*—the love of my life. Even after she dropped cheerleading and came back to school as some kind of emo hipster who suddenly didn't want to be dating the star QB. Even after she dumped me and started sorta dating an alien.

I smile at her as I approach, all teeth. It's a reflex. I can't help it. She smiles too but not as wide as I'd like.

Even with the "You are Mark James" mantra in my head all day, sometimes I don't feel like me at all. Instead of being the cool, put-together guy I've always been, I start worrying about intergalactic war and if Mogs are watching me have breakfast. But even when I start to wonder if I should be building a bomb shelter out in the middle of the woods or something, part of me wants to stay planted in the world I knew before there was definite proof of aliens on Earth, where I'm just a dude who's trying to win back his ex-girlfriend.

If this whole ordeal has had any bright side, it's that I see a lot more of Sarah than I did before. I like to think that me saving John's life impressed her, maybe even showed her that there's more to me than she thought. Someday when this is all said and done, Sarah is going to come to her senses and realize that even if John is a good alien, he's still freaking E.T. And I'll be waiting, even if it means fighting off space invaders to keep her safe and show her I'm better than he is.

The waiting totally blows.

"You're begging to get jumped, aren't you?" she says as I get closer.

At first I'm confused, but then I realize she's nodding at my chest, where my name is embroidered in gold over the heart on my Paradise High varsity letter jacket.

"What, this?" I ask, flexing a little and puffing out my chest. "I'm just repping our school. Trying to bring a little bit of Paradise to hell. That way we all feel like we're at home."

She rolls her eyes.

"You're provoking them."

"They're the least of my problems these days."

"Whatever," she says. "Your truck still smells like orange soda."

Once we're in my truck, Sarah leans her head against the passenger window and exhales a long breath, as if she's been holding it in all day. She looks tired. Beautiful but tired.

"I got a new name in bio today," she says, her eyes closed.

"Oh yeah?"

"'Sarah Bleeding Heart.' I was trying to explain that John wasn't a terrorist who was going to try to blow up the White House. Like, literally, someone said that they heard he was going to blow up the White House."

"Now who's the one asking for it?"

She opens her eyes just enough to glare at me.

"I feel like all I do now is defend him, but everyone else refuses to listen. And every time I try to say something about how they don't know the whole story, I lose a friend. Did you know that Emily thinks he kidnapped Sam? And I can't even tell her that it's not true. All I can say is that John wouldn't do that, and then she looks at me like I'm part of some big plot to destroy America or something. Or worse, some lovesick loser who's in denial."

"Well, you've still got me," I say reassuringly. "And I try to defend John whenever I can. Though I don't think I've been very good at it. All the guys on the team think he was able to kick our asses after the hayride because he was trained as a special agent from Russia or something."

"Thanks, Mark," Sarah says. "I know I can count on you. It's just . . ."

She opens her eyes and looks out the window as we speed past a few empty fields, never finishing her sentence.

"Just what?" I ask, even though I know what's coming. I can feel the blood in my veins start to pump a little faster.

"Nothing."

"*What*, Sarah?" I ask.

"I just wish John was here." She gives me a sad smile. "To defend himself."

Of course, what she really means is that she wishes John was here because she misses him. That it's killing her not to know where he is or what he's doing. For a moment, I feel like my old self again as my hands tighten around the steering wheel. I want to find John Smith and punch him square in the jaw, then keep hitting him until my knuckles bleed. I want to go straight into a rant about how if he really loved her, he wouldn't have left her here to get picked on and laughed at. He would have manned up. Even if he did leave to find other aliens like him to save our planet. If I were in his shoes, I'd have figured out a way to keep Sarah *and* the world safe. And happy.

I can't believe these are the types of conversations I have with myself on a daily basis now.

Being super pissed at John just makes me sound like the Mark that Sarah broke up with. So instead of talking shit about him, I swallow my anger and change the subject.

"I've been thinking a lot about what's happened lately. How the FBI and stuff have been handling it. My dad says that it's kind of weird how they're keeping the local law enforcement in the dark. I mean, he's the sheriff and they aren't telling him anything about what's going on."

"Yeah, but isn't that so they can keep a lid on the investigation?" Sarah asks. "That's the FBI's *job*, right?"

"My dad doesn't think so. He should at least be kept in the loop, even if he can't tell the rest of his officers about what's happening. Plus, I know they found some bodies at the school and there was a lot of damage, but John got moved straight to the FBI's most-wanted list. That seems a little extreme, right? Especially considering there's no *actual* evidence that John was the one behind all this."

"So, what? Do you think this is some kind of government conspiracy?" She sits up straighter in the passenger seat, leaning towards me.

"I just think maybe they know more about what's going on with John's people than they let on. I'm *guessing* some of the people in black suits are smart enough to realize that it wasn't just some angry teenager who dug gigantic claw marks in the football field."

"Jesus, Mark, you're starting to sound like Sam," she

says. Then she shrugs a little. "But I guess he was right about some of that stuff we all thought was crazy. That would make sense. I mean, if stuff like this is happening across the country, *someone* is keeping track of it all, right? The FBI swooped in here really fast. Maybe they're working with John's . . . species?"

I can't believe Sarah has fallen for someone who could be classified as another species.

"Or else they're working with the monsters with all the glowing swords," I say. "Which would mean we've just allowed the opposing team to set up shop in town."

Sarah lets her head fall against the window again.

"Where are you, John?" she whispers, her breath fogging up the glass in front of her. "Where are you?"

We're quiet for the rest of the drive home.

All I can think of is the promise I made to John when everything was going down at the school—that I would keep Sarah safe. Of course I'll do that. I'd be doing it even if he hadn't asked me to. But it makes my insides twist up to know that he's the one she's thinking of while *I'm* the one whose actually looking out for her.

CHAPTER
THREE

AFTER I DROP SARAH OFF AT HER HOUSE, I switch into detective mode.

It's only been a little while since the whole "aliens are real and attacking your school" thing, but since then I've been trying to get as much information about what's going on as possible. I'd like to say that it's so that if Earth has to fight, I can take on the bad guys, but I think it's mostly just because I need something to do. And because I like to be a person in the know. Preferably the one calling the shots. Maybe that's what made me such a good quarterback. It's surprisingly tough to go from being the guy who knows everything that's going on in school to some dumb jock who didn't even realize there was a war going on around him.

I can fix that. I just have to gather info.

Plus, it gives me something to talk to Sarah about other than whether or not I think John—and the others, but mostly just John—is okay or not. Even if it does make me sound a little like nutso Sam.

I take the long way home and drive past the high school. Not that I can get anywhere close to it—the authorities have the whole area around it pretty locked down. It isn't the police who are running the show now. If so, I could probably camp out on the school lawn if I wanted to since my dad is the sheriff. No, there are people *much* higher up running the investigation. The FBI, and I'm guessing some other three-letter government groups that we civilians aren't even supposed to know about. There are a lot of people in black suits walking around Paradise these days, which I guess makes sense since this is some grade-A Area 51 shit. Once I'd tried to sneak over to the school through the woods that border it, but they've got all the surrounding areas lit up with giant floodlights at night. I couldn't get within a few yards of the edge of the trees or else someone might have seen me.

It would have been a nice time to have that alien girl—Six—and her invisibility powers around.

Today I recognize the cop who's posted to make sure that no one turns down the street that leads to the school. Todd is only three or four years older than me. He was a big town football star back in the day and always likes to corner me and talk stats and plays when I'm at the station. I hesitate for a second and then decide to try my luck. I want to know what's going on at the school. Maybe if I can get close enough to see what kind of detective work they're doing, I can get an idea of how much they do or don't know. Maybe I can even talk one of them into spilling a few secrets if I don't see any pale dudes walking around.

I make a loop and come back to the school. As I'm doing so, I take off my letter jacket and toss it into the backseat, shoving my backpack on top of it.

"Hey, man," I say, pulling up beside Todd. A couple of traffic barrels sit in front of my bumper. "How's it going?"

"Just freezing my ass off to protect this sacred ground," he says, shoving his hands into his pockets and nodding his head towards the school. I can't tell if he's joking about the sacred ground or not because he's definitely the kind of guy who will be talking about his high school glory days until his dying breath.

"Yeah," I say, trying my best to sound casual. "What are they doing over there, anyway? I mean, I heard the place is a mess, but Dad says they aren't telling you much about whether they're finding anything useful or not."

"It's all classified intel," Todd says, raising his eyebrows just a little bit to make it sound really important.

"You know. Homeland-security-type stuff. Apparently the government doesn't like it too much if you try to destroy a school."

"I bet, man." I nod. "Hey, so I actually left my letter jacket in the locker room back before all this shit went down and—I know this is stupid, but I feel kind of naked without it. Do you think I could just run in really fast and grab it? I mean, you probably felt the same way about yours when you were racking up touchdowns, right? It's like a second skin."

Something weird happens to Todd's face. He's quiet, and it looks like he just got a big whiff of something foul. Finally, he just shakes his head.

"No can do, buddy," he says slowly. "The place is off-limits. I'm not even supposed to go all the way to campus."

"Yeah, but—"

"No," he says again. This time there's no room for argument.

I squint my eyes and try to see as far down the street that dead-ends into campus as I can, but all I can make out is a handful of big black SUVs and a couple of moving figures dressed in dark clothes.

Todd clears his throat, and I snap back to the present.

"It's cool," I say. "I just thought I'd ask." I force a grin. "But if something happens to my jacket, I'm going to haunt you for the rest of your life."

Todd gives a little smile as I back up and head away from the school.

They won't even let him all the way up to campus? I think. *What the hell are they doing there?*

CHAPTER FOUR

MY GRANDMOTHER'S HOUSE IS AN OLDER HOME IN the country, two stories tall and filled with so much wood paneling that it feels kind of like a cabin on the inside. It's where my parents and I are staying for the time being since our house is basically a pile of ash. My parents were going to start looking at building something new when everything in town went crazy, so now we're camping out with Nana—my dad's mom—indefinitely.

I'm hardly out of my truck before Abby, our golden retriever, is on her hind legs and trying to lick my face. Dozer, our bulldog, stands up on the porch and looks for a moment like he's going to come greet me too before he just falls back down and starts to snore.

Inside, the house smells delicious—like pot roast and mashed potatoes. It's my dad's favorite, which means he's probably in a bad mood today and Nana is trying to snap him out of it. My guess is justified, because when my grandmother peeks around the corner from the kitchen, she tells me Mom's staying in Cleveland for another few weeks visiting her family, which, knowing my mom, is code for "I'm going crazy in this house with my mother-in-law." She's been acting kind of weird and distant since the whole house fire thing, but I keep telling myself things will be fine and she'll come back to Paradise once everything's blown over.

Dad gets home not much later than I do. I guess that's one of the perks of being cut out of a big investigation— you get to have dinner on time every night. He tosses his dark sheriff's hat on a table near the front door and heads to the guest room he's staying in upstairs. Soon he's back down in a sweatshirt and jeans, and the three of us sit down for dinner at Nana's ancient round dining-room table that must weigh two tons.

Nana says grace and asks us about our days. I give a vague answer about school going well—as far as my family knows, there's no difference in who I was at Paradise and who I am at Helena. My dad asks a few questions about whether or not the administration has decided if Paradise will have a baseball team this spring or if we'll get merged with our new school, which would be worse than having no baseball at all. I shrug and dig into my dinner.

Eventually, I get to prodding about the investigation.

"I saw Todd today," I say between bites of meat. "He told me they're not even letting him up to the campus, even though he's supposed to be protecting the site."

"Officer Charleston," Dad says, chewing through Todd's last name, "is not supposed to be gossiping about police affairs. And certainly not about any ongoing investigations."

"It was my fault. I stopped by when I saw he was manning the roadblock. Forced him into talking to me. Don't worry; he wouldn't let me step so much as a foot past him."

Dad doesn't say anything, just keeps on chewing with his eyes on his plate. I clear my throat a little and keep talking.

"So, uh. Have you been over to the school? What have they got going on over there? Any ideas about who or what was behind everything?"

"The Smith kid and his father were behind it," Dad says, parroting the same thing everyone else has been saying.

I want to correct him and tell him that Henri wasn't actually John's father. That he was some kind of guardian who protected me and Sarah and the others—who *died* doing so. And that I watched his body burn in a ceremony behind a slummy motel close by.

But as far as Dad knows, John Smith was just a quiet

guy in some of my classes, and I was nowhere near Paradise High the night everything went down. So instead I just ask: "How can they be sure it was him, though?"

"They're sure." Dad's voice is gruff, meaning he's done talking about the subject.

"Who wants more rolls?" Nana asks.

"Yeah, but what *proof* do they have?" I ask, feeling a little bad for ignoring my grandmother. "They must have something on him if they keep telling everyone he did it."

Dad drops his fork down on his plate and looks across the table at me.

"Do you know who the 'they' is you keep mentioning, Mark?"

"Uh, sort of. The FBI, for one."

"And you've probably seen enough movies to know how the FBI works. And what happens to people who ask questions about top-secret investigations, right?"

"Sure," I say. "Black bags over your head and stuff."

"I don't know about that, but the last thing I want is for my son to end up in trouble because he was poking around in things he should've let be. It's bad enough that Sarah was involved with this boy. The last thing I want is for you to get wrapped up in it too."

"Of course," I say.

He picks up his fork and keeps eating, but my head spins. *Sarah was involved with this boy.* It's not the fact that this is true that makes my stomach drop, it's that my dad knows. I rack my brain, trying to think of a moment I might have mentioned that Sarah and John were dating before, or even after everything happened, but I can't think of one. Talking about a guy who kicked my ass and stole my girl is not exactly the type of thing I would bring up with my family. If Dad knows Sarah was "involved" with John, it's from the investigation. Meaning the FBI and whoever else is in Paradise right now must know too.

"You got another letter from Ohio State today," Nana says as she tries to force a second round of mashed potatoes on me.

The nice thing about living in a small town is that if your house burns down, the mailman can probably still find you.

"I'll look at it later."

"Just like the letters from other colleges you said you'd take care of, right?" Dad asks. "The ones that have piled up on your desk? I went and looked at them earlier, and half of them haven't even been opened yet."

"It's just—," I start, but he won't have it.

"Jesus, Mark. Do you have any idea how lucky you are? Do you have any idea how many other kids would kill to have schools clawing at each other to have you attend. To have even *half* of the scholarship money some of these places are offering you just to do what you love? To play football? How ungrateful . . ."

He keeps going, but I zone out a little bit. When I think back on how hard and boring I thought the application process was for colleges, I feel like an idiot. But it was the most important thing in my life at the time, trying to remember whether or not I'd sent off all the right transcripts and letters of recommendation. Now I realize there are much, much bigger things to worry about.

Dad keeps lecturing me. He's normally a really nice guy. Good to us. Always there when I need him. The one thing he doesn't like, though, is when he feels useless. When things get taken out of his hands or jurisdiction and he gets cut out of the loop. Then he gets cranky and starts to become a real dick at home.

I guess that's something I must have inherited from him.

CHAPTER
FIVE

ALEX DAVIS TEXTS ME AFTER DINNER. HE'S A wide receiver a year younger than me who was part of my close circle at Paradise High. Apparently his parents are out of town for the weekend, and he's managed to score a whole keg. Everyone we know is going over there. "No open flames lol," he says. I text Sarah to ask if she wants to go, but she says no, as I expected. Inviting her is just a gesture. Neither of us is really in the mood to party lately. Pick any Friday night in the years before Mogs invaded Paradise, and I would have been out with friends—maybe out with Sarah—partying at someone's house or in a clearing in the woods that we'd circled our cars around. But now, I just don't see the point. There's *an alien war* that could break out here at any moment. When that happens, I don't want to be trying to recover from my third keg stand.

My friends—my teammates—bothered me about

my newfound lack of social life a lot at first. Then I told Sarah's friend Emily that I was weirded out about parties ever since my house burned down. That's not actually true, but Emily's kind of a gossip, and pretty soon no one was giving me shit about staying home so much. Or at least, most people weren't.

I text Alex and say I'll pass and he calls me a little bitch and for half a minute I think that maybe I'll go over there to kick his ass and remind him which one of us was MVP, but then I just click my phone to silent and head upstairs.

My room at the house used to be my granddad's office before he died. At least, everyone called it his "office." Really it was just the spare room where my grandmother stored all his old history books and navy trunk and stuff like that. But there's a desk and a fold-out couch in there, which is all I really need.

The first thing I do when I sit at the desk is log on to this blog I've started following called "Aliens Anonymous." I stumbled on it by chance, back in the first few days after the battle at the high school, and despite its dumb name, it's turned out to be pretty interesting. One of the guys running it—a dude who goes by the name GUARD—posted a story from the local paper and wrote a bunch of stuff about how the whole destruction at the high school might be a cover-up for alien activity. At first I thought GUARD might have been from around here, but the Paradise incident was actually just one of many accidents or events he'd pegged as being somehow linked to aliens. In this case, at least, he'd guessed correctly. He'd even made the connection that the "John Smith" that everyone kept pinning stuff on was probably not exactly of this world.

Searching through the blog's archives, I'd come across a few stories that sounded like they might have had to do with the Loric or Mogs. The site is mostly a lot of posts that look like they belong in one of those "Elvis Still Lives!" magazines at the grocery store, but some of them sound true—or at least like they could be true, given what I've seen. I knew I could help the blog by telling them some of what I know, and by doing that I could get them to help me search for clues as to where John and Sam and Invisible Girl might be now.

So after browsing the blog for a while, I'd contacted GUARD and told him I was from Paradise and that I thought he might be right. There were a couple of weird emails from him full of instructions that had made me wonder if I was dealing with some kind of messed-up lunatic wearing a tinfoil hat—a guide on how to hide my IP address, passwords to access restricted sections of the blog, rules on when and how I could contact him—but after a while we started to get to know one another. I guess I started to trust him, because before long I'd told him about what happened at the school that night.

GUARD doesn't know *everything*, though. I've seen enough specials on the news to realize that I should question the identity of anyone I meet on the internet, especially now that I know the Mogs would do anything to find John and the others. I didn't tell him my name or anything. Just that I saw things that made me a true believer. On the blog I go by the name JOLLYROGER182, which I stole from the skull-and-crossbones flags flown at the Paradise Pirates football games and some of my granddad's old navy stuff that's framed in the upstairs room. He was part of the Fighting 182nd in the navy. I wonder what he'd say if I told him I was gearing up to maybe have to one day fight for Earth.

There are a couple of other people who are regulars on the blog, or "editors" as we call ourselves. Usually it takes a long time to earn that title, but I must have really convinced GUARD that I was legit, because he gave me full access to the blog pretty fast. The others are fine and all, but GUARD is the de facto ringleader, and the dude who's the most serious about everything that's going on.

I'm happy to see he's online. We start chatting immediately.

JOLLYROGER182: wassup man
JOLLYROGER182: anything new 2night?

GUARD: Hey, JR. Still trying to make sense of that thing in TN.

GUARD is convinced that a freak storm in Tennessee was caused by one of the Loric's powers, but we haven't been able to track down any evidence. The story came from a police officer who had too much whiskey one night and started yelling to everyone at a bar about how some magic kids with the power to control thunderstorms were tearing across the state, and somehow that made it into the local paper. I called to see if I could talk to the officer, pretending I was someone from the Paradise police department, but they told me the guy had been transferred to a different county and they couldn't put me in touch with him. I have a sneaking suspicion that's the FBI's version of sending a dog to a nice farm upstate, which probably provides more evidence that it was John and the others than anything else.

JOLLYROGER182: want me 2 look into it some more? i can try to call around again
GUARD: No. Take a look at this. Sound familiar?

He sends me a link to a post on an online journal. It belongs to some girl named Meredith down in Miami. It starts out really sad—her parents think she's on drugs and have had her in and out of institutions—and I can't figure out why GUARD is interested in it. Then, after a few paragraphs, I get to what he's talking about: the reason her parents think she's on drugs is because she says she watched some random dude on the streets of Miami use what she describes as "mind powers" to shove her boyfriend up against the wall of a coffee shop, keeping him pinned there a few feet off the ground.

My chat window dings while I'm reading.

> GUARD: What do you think? Telekinesis?
> GUARD: Could this be your friend? The time stamp on the journal entry is yesterday, but she doesn't say when the coffee shop event happened.
> GUARD: Emailed to find out more info but she hasn't gotten back to me.
> JOLLYROGER182: hold on

Luckily, this girl's listed the facility her parents had checked her into *and* her full name. Not exactly smart stuff to put on the internet, but great for me. I look up the hospital and call the front desk.

"Hi," I say when a woman picks up. "I'm trying to get in contact with Meredith Harris."

"Just one minute," the woman says. I can hear the clacking of keys in the background for a few moments before her voice comes back again. "Oh, I'm sorry, sir, but Ms. Harris was checked out a few days ago."

"Oh, um . . . ," I say, trying to come up with my next question. I realize that I probably should have thought this through more before I called, but thinking before I act isn't really my style. I go off instinct.

"Um, that can't be right," I continue. On my computer screen, I see the date of the journal post, and something clicks in my head: *It'll be easier to figure out if it was John in Miami if I know when this chick first got sent to the hospital.* "Maybe I have the wrong number. When was your Meredith Harris checked in?"

"Well . . . ," the woman says. I can tell she's hesitant to give me any more info.

"Please, ma'am, this is my sister. I'm just trying to make sure I know where she's at."

I must have come up with the right amount of sob story, because she gives me a date—one that puts Meredith Harris going into the hospital at the same time I was trying to kick John's ass on the hayride.

I thank the woman on the other end of the line and hang up, then turn back to GUARD.

**JOLLYROGER182: no dice. i called the hospital.
the girl was admitted while John Smith was
here**
GUARD: Maybe the actual incident occurred

before he came to Paradise?
JOLLYROGER182: i don't think his powers came
until he was here

At least, that's what John told Sarah. In all our conversations about the Loric and the Mogs, I've gotten to know basically everything he ever told her about himself.

GUARD: Ah. Okay. Maybe it's another Loric then.
JOLLYROGER182: must be a dumb one begging
to become Mog food.
GUARD: So much stuff happening these days. A
lot of weird activity.
GUARD: I get the feeling everything must be
coming to a head sometime soon. Don't you?

I hate that I agree with him.

I poke around online a little more before calling it a night, my eyes strained too much and a headache coming on. I lie in bed and think of the same scene that's been replayed in my head a million times since everything went crazy. It's not even one of the weirder moments, like when a damned lizard monster attacked us or John's dog turned into some kind of dragon. Or when alien bad guys turned into *ash* after being stabbed. It was when I was at John's house.

It was when I'd found out that aliens existed.

I'd gone over to John's house to ask about the video. That *stupid* video someone had shot on their phone of John flying like Superman out of my burning house, Sarah and the dogs with him. I'd ended up in the middle of a fight between him and the guy I'd thought was his father, Henri. And then weird stuff started happening. Henri stopped moving, like he was frozen in place, which I now realize meant that John was using his telekinesis. They were talking about Sarah being in trouble, and then John was just gone. Running, I guess, all the way to the school.

After he'd left, Henri was able to move again. I'd been furious that no one was answering my questions, but I couldn't help but feel bad for the guy. He looked like he was about to break in every way possible. I'd kept asking questions, but he kept ignoring me. He ran into another room. When he came back out, he was carrying a shotgun and this locked box with all kinds of weird symbols carved into it. I could tell he was on some kind of mission as he headed to his truck. I was fast, though, and got there before him, planting myself in the passenger seat. I needed to know what was going on. Especially if Sarah was involved.

"I don't have time to deal with you," Henri had said as he jumped into the truck. "Out!"

What was I supposed to do? How was I supposed to react to that?

"If Sarah's in danger, you take me to her," I said. "No matter what." And I meant it. Suddenly that was the only thing that mattered.

Henri had looked at me long and hard before starting his truck. As we peeled out of his driveway, he shoved the locked chest into my lap.

"What's this?" I asked.

Henri just shook his head.

"Boy, you've got a lot to learn in the next five minutes."

Then everything went to hell.

Lying on my pullout bed at Nana's, I think about this interaction, wondering why I got in the truck in the first place. I don't know, really. Looking back on it, I should have called my dad. Or let Henri go alone. Or any number of options that wouldn't have put me at Mog ground zero. But something had told me to go with him. I'm glad I did. I mean, I saved John that night, and probably Sarah too.

But a little part of me wishes that I'd never gotten into that truck. That Henri hadn't told me about the war we were driving towards—a battle on Earth between two alien races.

Part of me wishes I'd just walked away. Life would have been a lot less complicated that way.

CHAPTER
SIX

THE NEXT MORNING I REALIZE I NEED TO TELL Sarah that the FBI and the police know about her and John. We'd assumed they had, but every concrete piece of information we can find helps us build a clearer picture of what's going on. Plus, I want to tell her about the stuff I've been researching with GUARD. I've only ever talked about "Aliens Anonymous" in an abstract way, mentioning articles I've found online but not explaining that I'm now a part of a super-nerdy alien conspiracy blog. Maybe today's the day to tell her.

She agrees to meet me for lunch, and by the time I get to the pizza place on the downtown square, she's already there.

"Hey," I say as I slide into a booth opposite her. She looks at me with concern, her eyes darting around nervously. I'm confused. "If you don't want pizza, we can go someplace else."

"No," she says, forcing a smile. "I'm just having kind of a weird day."

"How so?"

"Is there a woman with red hair in a black suit behind me?" Sarah whispers.

I scrunch my eyebrows together in confusion and then look over her shoulder. Sure enough, there's a red-haired woman in dark clothes drinking a coffee alone and reading from an electronic tablet a few tables behind us.

"Yeah, why?"

Sarah exhales a long, steady breath, shaking her head.

"We went out for dinner last night, and she was there. This morning I went on a run, and she drove by me four times. Now she's here."

"Shit," I murmur. "Well, there goes what I had to tell you."

"What do you mean?" She sits up straighter, concerned.

"Just that my dad mentioned the FBI knew you were connected to John in some way. I didn't figure they'd have you *followed*."

"Crap," she says.

We sit without saying anything for a few moments, trying to figure out what to do next. The silence is finally broken when the waitress comes by to take our order.

"Hey, Mark," she says sweetly. I've eaten enough pizza here in my lifetime to receive hall of fame status. She knows me well. "What can I get you?"

"Hey. Uh, we'll take a medium half meaty, half veggie." Mine and Sarah's old standby order. "I'll have a soda."

The waitress smiles at me and then turns to Sarah. She sneers in a way that makes it obvious she wants Sarah to notice.

"You want anything?" she asks, an edge to her voice.

This is Sarah's life now—the mad bomber's girlfriend. I want to cause a scene but swallow down the urge because apparently we're already getting enough attention as it is. Sarah turns her head and locks eyes with the waitress, giving her a look that I recognize. I've been on the receiving end of it too many times— the kind of glare that makes you think your face is going to melt off.

"Diet soda, ma'am," she says, emphasizing the last word.

The waitress rolls her eyes and walks away. Sarah just sighs.

"Jeez, some people," I say.

"It's not *some* people. It's *all* people. I mean, half the town thinks I'm some kind of terrorist floozy. Even if they don't say it, you should see the looks I get. And that's not counting the people who are following me."

"Okay, so what do we do now? Run away and try to find John and the others? I'll go with you if you do. Hell, I'll drive."

I have no desire to go on a blind search for the Loric, but if Sarah wants to go, I'm not letting her go alone. And I have to admit, the idea of a road trip with Sarah is appealing—even if it *is* to track down her alien boyfriend.

"How would we even find them?" she asks.

"Actually," I say, lowering my voice, "I've kind of been doing some research on the whole . . . Well, you know. Everything. There are other people out there who know about this stuff. People like Sam, who the rest of us thought were just kind of crazy. I've been talking to some of them, and we think we might have figured out a little more about what's going on."

"What do you mean?" Sarah says, perking up. "What kind of stuff?"

"Well, now that I've seen John and Six in action, I kind of get what you'd need to look for. There was a girl in Miami who saw her boyfriend get picked up using telekinesis. It wasn't John, but it might have been one of the others like him. Maybe someone who's in contact with John. And one of the other bloggers has been keeping track of this guy in India who some of the locals have been worshipping as a god."

"Yeah, but how do you know these bloggers or the people they're writing about aren't just a bunch of crazy people?"

"Well, a day or two after John and the others left Paradise, a police officer in Tennessee had pulled over some teenagers driving a suspicious car, but before he could arrest them, some kind of supernatural winds basically blew him out of the way." Sarah raises her eyebrows, a glint of hope in her eyes. "Sound familiar?"

"Six."

"That's what I think."

She grins, but it only lasts for a few seconds before the reality of the situation sets in.

"They could be anywhere by now," she says.

"Yeah."

"So there's nowhere for us to even start our search."

We pause as the waitress comes back and sets down my drink in front of me, then half slams Sarah's onto the table, sending little drops of diet soda lapping over the rim of the glass. She leaves without saying a word.

"We could go anyway," I suggest, trying not to sound enraptured by the idea of all that alone time with Sarah. "Skip this small town and let everything blow over."

She gives me a little smile and shakes her head.

"My family . . . ," she says, but I can tell I've over-stepped my bounds in her mind and am sounding too much like an ex-boyfriend who's trying to drop the "ex" part. "Plus, if John came back looking for me, he'd be heartbroken if I wasn't here."

"He'd be an *idiot* if he came back to Paradise," I mut-ter. The words come out before I can stop them, so I try to explain. "I mean, with all the suits running around here."

As if she overheard this as her cue, the red-haired woman gets up and walks over. She slides into the booth beside Sarah. Before I can react, there's another dark-suited person sliding in beside me—a man who looks like he's in his late twenties, with olive skin and close-cropped black hair.

We're trapped in the booth.

"What the—," I start.

"You're Mark James," the red-haired woman says. "The sheriff's son. And you're Sarah Hart."

"What do you—," Sarah says.

"My name is Agent Walker, with the Federal Bureau of Investigation, and this is my associate, Agent Noto. I hope you don't mind if we join you."

"We do," I say, narrowing my eyes.

Agent Walker smiles. Noto hasn't said a word or done anything but stare back and forth between Sarah and me. I wonder how close he was to us. Did he hear me talking about the blog earlier? Does he know what we've been talking about?

"We're just trying to get an idea of what happened with John Smith here in town. As you probably know, he's a person of high interest. There are several incredibly generous rewards that are being offered for any information on his whereabouts." She turns her attention to me. "I was sorry to hear about what happened to your home, by the way. But I'm sure the reward money could go far in rebuilding."

Is this woman *really* trying to bribe me into telling her about John?

"After all, I'm told the blaze started at a party you were throwing," she continues. "I'm sure you've been wondering how you can make things up to your parents after something like that."

My mouth drops open a little, and I feel like I've been punched in the gut.

"You've been watching me," Sarah says, changing the subject. "I've *seen* you."

"Of course you've seen me," the woman says. "We wanted you to know that we're here, keeping the town safe."

"You're following me," Sarah says, gritting her teeth a little.

"I'm simply doing my job by ensuring that we follow up on every lead."

"And you think Sarah is a lead?" I ask.

"We think you know more about John Smith than you might even realize." Walker never takes her eyes off Sarah. "You were dating him. You must have some information that would be relevant to our investigation. Something that might help us to decipher exactly what happened at your school."

"I hardly knew him," Sarah says, staring down at the table. "We weren't dating."

"We saw a video that looked like he was flying out of your burning house," the woman says to me. She turns back to Sarah. "He was carrying you."

Sarah smiles.

"It's crazy what you can do with cameras and a few hours on the computer, isn't it?" she asks.

"Sam was always good at stuff like that when we had presentations at school," I add. "He probably did it."

Sarah kicks me under the table. I can't figure out why until the agent turns to me and smiles.

"Samuel Goode. His mother, Patricia Goode, is a nurse. Father is Malcolm Goode, a . . ." She pauses for a moment before smiling a bit. "Current whereabouts unknown. Sam hasn't been home since that night either. His mother is worried sick about him. It would be nice if she had any assurance that her son was alive."

"Sam is . . . ," Sarah starts, but then stalls. I recognize the look on her face. She's trying to connect all the dots and carefully plotting out what she's going to say.

Speaking carefully has never been my strong suit.

"Sam Goode is a conspiracy theory nut job," I say, lounging back in my booth a little. "That little twerp wears the same NASA T-shirt every day of the week. You should hear the kinds of things he talks about. Aliens. The Illuminati. Personally, I think it's his way of trying to get people to notice him when all the attention goes to me and my buddies on the team. He probably finally had enough of it and ran away, using the school thing as an excuse. He's smart, but he's also a total wuss. Trust me when I say he can't handle himself in a fight. Not exactly terrorist material. If you ask me, he's probably hunting for Sasquatches in the woods somewhere. That's where I'd try to find him, at least."

I take a big swig of my soda and glance over at Sarah, who's looking at me with a mixture of disgust and confusion. I give her a little kick under the table, and she manages a smirk.

I take a chance and lean forward, grabbing Sarah's hands in mine. They're soft and tremble slightly. I have to hold them still against her initial urge to pull away.

"Isn't that right, babe?" I ask, flashing the toothiest grin I can muster her way.

"That's probably true," she mutters.

"Well, that's very *enlightening*, Mr. James," Agent Walker says.

"I think I'm ready to go now," Sarah says, scooting towards Walker.

The agent doesn't move.

"But you haven't even eaten yet," she says. Agent Noto still hasn't so much as breathed as far as I can tell.

"I'm not hungry," Sarah says.

"Why don't we talk a little more?"

"Oh, are you charging us with something?" I ask.

"What would we have to charge you with?" Walker says with a smile that's just a little too forced.

"Nothing." I shrug. "I just know you can't keep us here unless you are actually going to arrest us or something. That's how my father's always said the law works."

Walker gives a few short laughs, which seem to say, "How very cute that you think that's how things work around here." Still, she slides out of the booth. Agent Noto follows her.

"If you happen to remember anything," Walker says, pulling a business card from her suit pocket and holding it out to Sarah, "do let us know. We'll be in touch."

In a flash, Sarah's left the booth and headed for the door. It takes me a little longer to get out, and Walker's standing in my way when I stand.

"That girl is trouble," she says, still holding up the card. "Don't let her take you down with her."

We stare at each other for a moment. Her eyes are

light and intense. Finally, I take the card and slip it into my pocket then push past her. On the way out, our waitress rounds the corner with our steaming pizza.

"Hey, where are you going?" she asks, clearly ticked off.

I shrug and point to Agent Walker.

"Red's taking care of our lunch," I say. And then I'm gone.

CHAPTER
SEVEN

SARAH'S WAITING FOR ME ON THE SIDEWALK A few stores down. When I get close, she starts to walk away quickly, and I have to jog a few steps to catch up to her.

"What was all that about?" she asks.

"You're going to have to be a little more specific," I say.

"All that stuff about Sam, for starters."

"I was just trying to cover my ass if they didn't already think he was with John after I stupidly said his name. Trying to throw them off the trail."

"Okay, then what about holding my hand. What was that?"

I stop and turn to her. We're on the corner. The wind whips her hair back and forth across her face, and she looks like tears might fall from her eyes at any moment. I have no doubt that the agents are still watching us, so

I step to the side to make sure that they can't see her face from inside the pizza place.

"Sarah, if they think you're his girlfriend, they're going to keep watching you," I say softly. "You know that. I was just trying to throw them off *you* as well."

"I can look out for myself," she says.

"I know you can. But you shouldn't have to. John shouldn't have—"

"I know." She cuts me off in a huff. "Trust me, I know. I'm well aware of how messed up this situation is. All of it. And if there was some way I could fix everything, I would. I half wish John *would* get arrested because at least that way I'd know where he is, and that he's safe."

The wind whistles a little as we stand, not talking to one another. I want to hug her—to touch her in any way—and it takes a good amount of my willpower to remind myself that if I freak Sarah out, I lose the only person I care about, and the only person I can talk to about everything that's happening. Other than a bunch of random people online who are probably old dudes living in their moms' basements and surviving on caffeine and corn chips.

Besides, I've already pushed her as much as I can today.

"Sam doesn't believe in Sasquatches," Sarah finally

says with a faint smile. "We talked about it before. No Bigfoot hunting for him."

"At this point I'm not sure that *I* don't believe in Bigfoot," I say.

This gets a little laugh out of her, which makes me smile.

"I don't know. I think I'd trust Sam on this one. He was way ahead of us on all this alien stuff. He probably knows more about John's history than John does."

This is true. It's something I file away for the future. What did Sam know? How did he find stuff out? And did he leave any records?

"I've got to get out of here," Sarah continues.

"Okay, where do you want to go?"

She shakes her head.

"I just need to be alone for a little while," she says, digging for her keys in her purse.

"Are you sure that's a good idea?" I ask. "I can come over if you want. Or we can stay out in public where no one can get to you."

"Thanks, but I'll be fine. Besides, my brothers are home this weekend, and there's nothing they love more than trying to act tough and protect their little sister. We'll talk later, all right?"

"Yeah," I say.

I watch her walk away and make sure she gets to her

car okay. She's just a speck down the road when my senses come to and I start putting things together about our weird encounter at the pizza place. Agent Noto was sitting behind me.

Does that mean I'm being followed too?

I walk around our tiny downtown for a little while, half to clear my head and half to keep an eye over my shoulder and see if I've got some kind of tail watching me while pretending to read a magazine or something. But there's no one. At least not anybody I can see.

The card Agent Walker gave me gives me absolutely no info—it's blank other than a phone number, which goes straight to voice mail when I call it from the only pay phone I know of in Paradise. I don't leave a message. Instead, I pull up the "Aliens Anonymous" blog on my phone and message GUARD, telling him that I've had a really weird run-in with the FBI and that this is the contact number they gave me. GUARD is good with computers and stuff, so maybe he can use it to find some new information or something.

When I'm walking back to my truck, I run into Kevin, an offensive lineman from school. He's a giant of a guy, with patches of red hair all over his face that almost make it look like he's capable of growing an actual beard. Almost. A few of the younger members on the team are with him, but they hang back, letting him lead. I briefly wonder if that's what I looked like when I was always running around town with my own posse.

"Duuuude," he says when he sees me. We do an elaborate series of handshakes and fist bumps. "We were grabbing burgers and saw you talking with Sarah on the corner. Looked pretty intense. What's going on with you two—you hitting that now that Bomberman is gone?"

Fire rages in me, and I can feel my face turning red with anger.

"Look, man," one of the younger guys says. "He's blushing."

"Don't talk about Sarah like that," I say. My jaw is clenched.

The whole pack "*Oooooooo*"'s as if they were a studio audience.

"Sorry, man, I didn't realize you two were a thing again."

"We're not," I say, trying to smile. "But I'm working on it."

"Must be hard being sloppy seconds to a terrorist," Kevin says with a smirk. "Gotta make you wonder what she saw in a dude like him."

I move before I think. In a flash I've got Kevin up against a brick wall, holding him by the arms of his letter jacket. He may be a giant, but I'm fast, and after years of strength training and weight lifting, I'm not exactly a lightweight.

It feels like one of my veins is going to pop out of my head. It's been a while since I was in a fight—a *real* fight. Since the Mogs took over the school. And even then, I spent half the time hiding in a classroom with Sarah. Part of me wants to unleash on Kevin, just whale on him until I feel better about all the shit that's gone down. But I don't. He may be kind of a douche bag, but even if everything's changed for me, nothing is different for him.

Kevin's expression morphs from surprise, to fear, to something else—something friendlier. Something like recognition.

"Check it out, you guys," he says, turning his head to the others, who are waiting for his instructions. "Mark James is BACK."

My pulse slows a little, and I suddenly start to feel a little high. I smirk.

"John Smith had *my* sloppy seconds," I say. "I'm just reclaiming what was mine to begin with."

The guys laugh and jeer at me. Someone yells, "It's Mark James, bitch!" a little too loudly, and we get disapproving looks from other people on the street.

"We're heading back over to Alex's to try and finish off what's left of his keg before it goes flat. You coming or what?" Kevin asks.

"Yeah, man," I say, not even thinking about it. It feels

surprisingly good just to be standing around being bros again.

Then I feel a buzz in my pocket.

"In a little bit," I say. "Tell Alex I'll be over later."

"Right on," Kevin says, and after another elaborate series of high fives and shakes, they're gone.

I pull my phone out. There's a message from GUARD:

Have you ever heard of an Agent Purdy?

CHAPTER EIGHT

I SPEND THE REST OF THE AFTERNOON AT HOME on the computer, talking to the blog editors. Saturday afternoons must be a lazy day for conspiracy theorists, because GUARD and this other editor named FLYBOY are both online and wanting to talk. FLYBOY seems cool but is much more of a skeptic about the stuff that GUARD and I talk about. Which is good, I guess— sometimes I think we need a rational person to keep us from totally going off the deep end.

It turns out that GUARD called the number Agent Walker gave me and got the same voice mail but didn't leave a message. A few minutes later, his phone rang— even though he'd purposefully blocked his number. GUARD answered because he's not the type of dude to let a chance like that go by. The person on the other end of the line kept asking him how he got the number, but GUARD played it cool and kept saying he knew what was going on in Paradise and demanded to talk to someone in charge.

Finally, he got on the line with an FBI guy named Purdy.

According to GUARD, Purdy was a huge hard-ass who sounded really annoyed and anxious to get off the phone until GUARD said he knew about the Mogs. This, apparently, got Purdy's attention. Only then GUARD didn't want to talk anymore, and Purdy wasn't giving him any info about what the FBI knew or didn't know.

FLYBOY says this doesn't mean anything, but I think otherwise: if this Purdy guy works for the FBI and recognized what GUARD was talking about, it proves that the FBI here know what's *really* going on.

The only question then is how much they know. And who they're trying to help.

We chat online for a few hours as we try to dig up anything we can on Purdy, but all we find is a picture of a piggish-looking man standing in the background at some government ceremony. It's not much to go on. Not *anything* to go on.

My phone buzzes constantly with messages from my teammates over at Alex's. There are more and more typos in them as the hours wear on. Finally I give in and head over once my brain is so full of government conspiracies and half-formed conclusions that I feel like it might just leak out of my ears. When I tell my dad I'm headed to Alex's to hang out with the guys, he gets a wide grin on his face.

"Good to see you getting out of the house and being a high schooler again," he says. "I thought you were turning into some kind of loner."

I shrug and force a laugh, then head out before the conversation gets any deeper than that. I'm almost out the door when he yells to me.

"My truck's parked behind yours. Just take mine, if you don't mind." He tosses me his keys.

"Sure," I say. Dad's truck—the thing he likes to drive when he's off duty and wants to get away from the police cruiser—is a small, single cab. Kind of a piece of crap, but I'm not going far.

I keep an eye out for any cars following me, but I don't see anyone. Plus, it's all back roads from my grandmother's place to Alex's, which is about as clandestine as you can be in Paradise.

I think about calling Sarah and seeing if she wants to come, but I know she'll say no. Especially since the FBI's got eyes on her. (Would the FBI bother with busting a bunch of underage drinkers?) Besides, I know the guys well enough to guess that they'll start talking about either me and her or her and John, and the last thing she needs is to be harassed by a bunch of drunk football players.

As expected, everyone at Alex's is pretty buzzed.

Half the team is there, and for a while it feels like it could be any Saturday night out of the last few years. Still, I spend the few hours I'm there sipping on the same warm beer just in case I need to keep my wits about me. No one seems to notice that I never need a refill as long as I've got a red plastic cup in my hands and mime drinking every so often.

When it starts to get a little late, I sneak out the back and to my dad's truck. I don't bother saying good-bye to anyone—tomorrow morning no one will remember what time I left, and I'll get a text or two talking about hangovers and asking if I got home okay. I'm about to start the truck when I realize there are extra keys on Dad's ring. One for our old house. One for my grand-mother's. And a few more with rubber around the tops: the keys to the police station.

The hair on the back of my neck stands on end as I consider the possibilities of what this could mean.

From what my dad's told me, the FBI is basically working on-site at the school. That means at this time of night there are only a couple of officers at the station. Maybe a few agents too. But I know my way around pretty well up there. If I were to drop by, I could prob-ably figure out a way to sneak past the front desk and get into my dad's office, where all kinds of files might be kept. Even if the FBI's taken over, there must still be initial reports at the station. Whatever it was that my dad and his officers saw when they arrived on scene that night.

If I could get my hands on some of those, maybe they could shed more light on the investigation.

I drive towards the police station before I can talk myself out of it.

CHAPTER
NINE

TODD'S THE ONLY OFFICER ON DUTY. I THINK I'm the luckiest guy alive until he rolls his eyes and gives me a long, drawn-out sigh as I walk in.

"Go home, Mark," he says curtly.

"Todd, man, what are you doing here all alone?"

"Someone mentioned that I was talking to civilians while on duty yesterday, and I got switched to the graveyard shift. That's what."

"Oh," I say. *Oops.*

"Plus there's been some kind of electrical fire on the outskirts of town that everyone was raring to get to." He inhales and wrinkles his nose a bit. "Jesus. You smell like a bar."

I'm not exactly surprised. Alex's house smelled like it had been sprayed down with cheap beer. Still, this electrical fire is great news for me.

"I was just at a party," I say with a shrug. "Someone must have spilled something on me. You know how it is. You've told me about the epic ragers you guys used to throw when you were on the team."

Todd gets a wide grin and goes into a story I've heard a hundred times from him about how he drank the entire special team's roster under the table out in the woods on his eighteenth birthday. I smile and nod and tell myself that I'm never going to be this dude when I get older. If humans aren't the alien workforce or something by then.

Finally he's done.

"Man, that sounds so hard-core," I say, forcing a grin. "I'm super jealous. Anyway, I just came by to pick up some stuff my dad left for me in his office."

Todd nods and gestures to my dad's door, still grinning from his memories.

I unlock the office with Dad's keys and quietly close the door behind me. The place is a mess of files strewn about the desk and seemingly random sheets of paper stacked on every surface. I start digging through the piles, but after a few minutes of searching, all I've come up with are weeks-old traffic violations and endless paperwork on stuff not at all related to John or the Mogs. Then I realize that *of course* that stuff's not going to be lying around, and I use one of the small keys on the key ring to open the filing cabinet by my dad's desk.

After flipping through a few hanging folders, I come to the one I'm looking for: PARADISE HIGH SCHOOL.

Yes.

The first file I pull out is full of initial incident reports and nondisclosure agreements from the first responders. I toss it on the desk to come back to later. The second file's a jackpot: full-page photos of the destruction at the school. The trenches dug through the football field and the huge divots I recognize as actually being footprints. Shotgun shells littering a classroom we holed up in for a while. The trashed auditorium. All signs that point to the fact that this was maybe something *other* than the work of a teenager with a vendetta against the school.

My pulse pounds as I take out my phone and start to snap photos of the pictures. I can upload them all to the blog later. GUARD and the others will flip when they see this shit. I rifle through the pictures as fast as I can, recording each one. My brain is buzzing, and I can hear my blood thumping in my ears.

Maybe that's why I don't hear anyone come in.

Someone yanks the back collar of my shirt and jacket, choking me. I'm swung around, and the surprise causes me to drop my phone. The file photos scatter across the floor. I expect to be staring into the face of a Mogadorian, or one of the agents.

But it's worse.

It's my father.

"What the *hell* do you think you're doing?" he bellows.

"Dad, I was—"

"Do you have any idea how much trouble you'd be in if someone else caught you in here? How much trouble *I'd* be in?"

"Dad, let me—"

"This is a matter of national security, Mark. I mean, *Christ.*"

He pushes me backwards with a strong shove. I stumble over my feet and hit the ground hard just as Dad's picking up my phone. He taps on it, systematically deleting everything I've taken pictures of, cursing the entire time. It's only then that I realize how weird it is that he's here in full uniform so late. Whatever happened with the fire tonight, it must have been important enough to call him in.

When he's done deleting things, he just stands there staring down at me for a minute.

"Go home, Mark," he says, emphasizing every syllable he can. "And stay there."

He starts to hand my phone to me when my text message sound goes off twice, so instead he turns the screen to see what's on it.

That's when his face goes white.

"What?" I ask.

He doesn't respond, only reaches down and pulls me up to my feet, half dragging me out of the office.

"Todd!" he barks, and then Todd is standing by the front door. "Outside, now."

"Dad, what's going on?"

He's still pulling me behind him. I could fight back, but I can tell he's furious. Something's wrong. Something bad has happened.

When we get to Todd's police car, Dad pulls open the back driver's-side door and shoves me inside. I manage to rip my phone out of his hands as I go in, and Dad slams the door before he realizes I've taken it. He yells at Todd.

"You take him straight back to my mother's house. If he puts up any fight, arrest him."

Todd looks at me, shaking his head as my dad runs to his patrol car, yelling something into his radio.

It's only then that I look down at my phone. There are two texts from Sarah.

OMG John is here.

Don't come but if something weird happens I'll txt u.

Shit.

My mind starts to race as I figure out what to do next. I call Sarah immediately. When she doesn't answer, I text:

DAD SAW THIS. HE'S COMING 4 JOHN. GET OUT.

And then I realize what this means. Dad's calling in the FBI, the police—hell, the fire department.
Everyone's about to converge on Sarah's house, and she
doesn't know. She's probably making out with a fucking alien, and the FBI and weirdo Agent Walker are
going to find her.

I start banging my fist against the metal separating
the front and back seats in Todd's car, shouting as he
gets in.

"NO! We have to go to her. Todd, man, take me to
Sarah's. You have to take me to Sarah's right now. Go,
go, go."

"The only place I'm taking you is home."

I keep beating on the metal until blood starts to
trickle from my knuckles and Todd slams his own fist
against the grate, yelling at me to shut up, then mutter-
ing profanities to himself. I'm frantically texting Sarah
as he says: "And I thought the explosion at the Goodes'
place was going to be the highlight of the night."

The Goodes' place. Explosion.

My head tries to put everything together, ignoring
the pain in my hand and the blood beating in my brain.

John's here. He's in Paradise, probably with Sam and
Six. There was an explosion at Sam's house. All the
cops were called out to it. If there was an explosion,

that must mean there was fighting. And the only people John would be fighting . . .

The Mogs.

The Mogs are here. They're after John. And John's
with Sarah.

CHAPTER
TEN

I STAY HOME FOR THE REST OF THE NIGHT. I don't really have a choice. Nana sits in a chair at the bottom of the stairs, with one eye on my door and another on my truck outside—Dad's personal sentry. I have no doubt that if I take one step outside the house, there'll be an officer ready to pick me up before I even make it to the street. The last thing I need is to get thrown into a holding cell—even though it's possible that would actually put me *closer* to Sarah.

Sarah. She's all I can think about. In the upstairs office, I drive myself crazy pacing back and forth, hoping that she's all right and that if things got bad, John at least was able to keep her safe. As much as I hate it, I have to believe that no matter what, he'd protect her. I text GUARD and tell him that shit's going down in Paradise, but he doesn't text me back. Of course this is the one night he's not glued to one of his screens.

I text Dad about a thousand times, at first apologizing and then asking what's happened. He doesn't respond, until finally I ask him just to tell me that Sarah is okay and he replies with a single magic word: "yes."

At least there's that.

As I pace, I listen to my dad's old police scanner, which I grabbed from his room. There's so much yelling and chatter that I can barely make anything out. There's something about a suspect being in custody, then a lot of static. I hear Sarah's name and someone mention the Paradise station, and then someone says something about a "Dumont" facility. After that all the messages stop. Radio silence.

Someone must have realized that the police radios weren't secure enough. I imagine Agent Walker pulling a giant plug that disables the entire radio system, even though I know that's not how any of this actually works.

An internet search of "Dumont facility FBI" brings up some articles about some huge, strictly off-limits FBI compound in Dumont, Ohio, about two hours away.

If Sarah has been taken in, I have to believe that she is being detained in the station jail and not being shipped out to some secret FBI prison. And so at dawn I take a chance and head downstairs and out into the front yard. Nana's no longer at her post, so I guess her orders were just to make sure I stayed in through the night. I jump in my truck and head into town. Dad's phone's going straight to voice mail by now. I park across from the station, watching, trying to get a look at Sarah or anyone else coming in or out. Every time the front door swings open, my chest pounds, only to be disappointed when someone other than Sarah walks out. Each time this happens, I get a little more worried.

It's a little past 8 a.m. when Sarah comes outside, and I feel so supercharged with happiness and relief. She's still here. They've let her go. Maybe this will end up all right after all.

Sarah looks a little scared, and it's my first instinct to jump out and sprint straight to her. Instead, I drive along beside her as she walks down the street.

"Sarah," I say as I pull up to the curb. The whites of her eyes are red, like she's been crying recently. "Get in."

"My parents are coming," she says. "They came to the station when they realized I wasn't at home and stuff was going crazy outside, but the agents at the front desk made them go back home—threatened to have them arrested if they stayed around asking questions about what happened. I told them to pick me up at the grocery store down the street so they wouldn't have to come back in. They're going to have so many questions."

"Tell them I'm taking you home."

"My cell phone's gone."

"You can use my mine," I say, leaning over and opening the passenger-side door.

After a short phone call—lots of "I'll explain in five minutes when I'm home"—she hands me back my phone and lowers her head into her hands.

"What are you going to tell them?" I ask.

"I don't know. I'll figure something out. Maybe I can tell them I need some sleep before we talk."

"Are you okay?"

"No," she says through her fingers. "John came back. I got super emotional and weird with him because I was feeling so crappy about everything before he just magically showed up, and then the FBI tackled me. I don't know where John is now, and I am officially pegged as a person who is somehow connected to all this. I've been sitting in an interrogation room for the last three hours."

"What'd you tell them?"

"Nothing," she says. "It was that Walker agent and a few other people. Noto. And some guy named Purdy."

I note the name—the agent GUARD talked to on the phone. Is he the one in charge of everything going on in town?

Sarah continues.

"They wanted to know why John came to see me, and I told them it was because we made out a few times before he went crazy and he probably thought that I'd do it again if he showed up and threw pebbles at my window like we were in some kind of rom-com. I just pretended to be dumb."

"And they believed that?"

"No, I don't think so. But they let me go, at least. They have John. I think that's all they really cared about. They just told me to make sure I didn't leave town or there'd be trouble." She shakes her head. "I'm on a freaking *no fly* list they said, as if I'd try to skip the country or something."

"Shit."

"I know." Sarah pulls the edge of her gray sweater over her fingertips. "I feel so stupid. This is my fault."

"No, it's mine. My dad saw the text you sent. I shouldn't have let that happen."

She looks surprised about this for a second—even happy that what happened last night might not have been her fault. Then her face falls.

"They were probably watching me anyway. I should have told him, but instead I just ran outside. I was so happy to see him."

"You don't know that they had eyes on you."

"I don't know what they've done with him," she says. Her voice is about to crack. "John . . ."

"I think he's in Dumont. There's some kind of FBI facility near the state border."

"What?!" she practically shouts, jumping in her seat and straining against the seat belt. "We have to go. I have to talk to him. I have to explain to him that I didn't—"

"No way, Sarah. You were just held and interrogated for being caught with him. You may not realize this now, but they could have arrested you for helping a criminal. The dude is on the *most-wanted* list, Sarah. I'm not taking you to an FBI prison so you can get yourself in more trouble. It's not what he would want."

The words come spilling out of me. Suddenly I'm hearing John's voice in my head. That I have to make sure she's kept safe. And right now, that means keeping her as far away from the Loric and the Mogs as I can.

"Besides," I say, softening up a little. "He has superpowers. Do you really think he's going to stay locked up for long?"

"I guess you're right. Sam was with him, but Six wasn't. She'll track them down if he's in trouble, I bet."

"I'm sure. She's one girl I'd hate to have mad at me."

Sarah scowls a little, but I can't decipher what the expression means.

"I've got to buy a new phone," she says. "Or try to get mine back from the FBI." She gets quieter. "Like that'll ever happen."

"You should buy a burner phone."

"A what?"

"You know," I say. "Like they have in shows about drug dealers and stuff. A prepaid cell phone. You know the FBI's going to be tracking every text message and call you get on your old number."

"God. Are we like drug dealers now?" she asks, staring out the window of my truck like I've watched her do a thousand times. "How is this our lives?"

"Don't blame me," I say. "Blame the impending war for our planet between the humanoid aliens and shark-faced bastards with magical swords."

When I drop her off, her parents are waiting on the front porch. I watch as their expressions run the gamut from worried, to relieved, to furious, then some weird mixture of all of them. I stay in the truck, but her dad makes sure to shoot me a glare that tells me in no subtle way that he's blaming me for whatever happened to his daughter. After all, I'm the party-loving ex they had to pry her away from over the summer to begin with. My chest falls a little. Maybe dropping her off wasn't the best idea. Her cell phone's gone. If I'm lucky, she'll be able to keep her computer for "study purposes." Otherwise, there's no way the Harts are letting me see or talk to their daughter.

It's late in the afternoon when I finally hear back from Dad, who's been at work since he caught me in his office. He calls while I'm deep into researching a series of crop circles a few counties west of us, though I'm pretty sure that they're just hoaxes and have nothing to do with actual aliens.

"Hi," I say when I answer the phone. I'm not sure whether to expect to be yelled at or apologized to. Probably the first one.

Instead, I hear a long sigh on the other end of the line.

"Oh, thank God," Dad says.

He sounds so relieved—what did he think had happened to me?

"What is it?" I ask.

"Where are you?"

"At home."

"Good. Have you talked to Sarah?"

"Not since this morning."

"Listen." He pauses for a moment and then starts talking quieter. "Stay where you are. You can't leave the house. I assume the agents took Sarah's phone away from her for evidence, but if you can, get her a message telling her to stay put too. She's a good girl. I always liked her. She shouldn't be wrapped up in all this."

"Dad, what's going on?" My imagination is suddenly going wild and picturing Mogadorian ships landing all over Paradise—though I have no idea what they would even look like.

"I can't really say. But something's happened that's

causing the FBI to go crazy. It's possible there might be one or two people we recently detained who are now unaccounted for. Seems like some weird stuff is going on over in Dumont where they were taken. I just want to make sure neither of you kids got any bright ideas of running away with your classmates if they wandered back through town."

John and Sam. They've escaped.

That didn't take long.

"I'll stay here, Dad."

Even as I say my good-byes, I'm on my computer, emailing Sarah.

Her response is an entire page of exclamation marks.

GUARD is the next person I contact. I've told him that one of my friends was brought in for questioning and that one of the Loric has been taken into custody. He's happy to hear that John has escaped.

> GUARD: AWESOME news. We need more good
> aliens out there.
> JOLLYROGER182: DEF!
> GUARD: I guess this means we know who the
> Feds are working for.
> JOLLYROGER182: what do u mean?
> GUARD: If the FBI was working with the Loric,
> he wouldn't have had to escape, right?

I lean back in my chair. He's right. Of course he's right. If the FBI took John into custody and interrogated Sarah after the fact, they definitely aren't working on our side.

> JOLLYROGER182: shit
>
> GUARD: You said it was Agent Purdy who was in on the investigation?
>
> JOLLYROGER182: and some others. a woman named Walker too
>
> GUARD: Sounds like it's time for me to amp up my investigation into Purdy.
>
> JOLLYROGER182: i thought u said u found everything you could
>
> GUARD: There are other ways.

CHAPTER
ELEVEN

SARAH AND I GET OUR FIRST CHANCE TO TALK together at school the next day. The FBI—in a rare moment of kindness—didn't inform Sarah's parents about the events of Saturday night, so for all they knew, Sarah had just been out way past her curfew and got caught up in the attempt to catch wanted-criminal John Smith. As part of her punishment, she's on a strict schedule: one that includes bus rides to and from Helena High and no more quality time with me. It's a bummer, but it'll pass.

I'm waiting near the entryway of the school pretending to be interested in reading a book for English class when she arrives. We lock eyes, and I motion my head towards the deserted hallway that leads to the back of the school's auditorium.

"Hey," she says. She seems in good spirits, which is a vast improvement over the last time we spoke.

"Hey yourself," I say. "How you holding up?"

"I'm on complete parental lockdown right now, but other than that I'm okay." She looks away from me. "No word from You Know Who."

"I wouldn't worry about that. From what I can gather, they made a clean getaway." And then I realize what she means. John escaped but didn't contact her. He didn't come back for her. "Oh, but . . . I'm sure he's thinking about you?"

It's by far more of a question than a statement.

"It's cool. I've had a lot of time to think it over while barricaded in my room. Of course he didn't come for me. It's not like I can just leave my family and go gallivanting across the world fighting aliens—or whatever it is he's doing. And dropping by again to see me just puts me in danger. I'm sure when the time is right, he'll come back for me."

Great. It's possible that a part of me was hoping that this whole "questioned by the FBI about my arrested boyfriend" thing would snap some sense into Sarah. Looks like I've got more waiting to do.

"I just wish there was some way we could figure out what their next move is."

Something clicks in the back of my head. I see a way for me and Sarah to spend some time together.

"You've got no absences in art after lunch, right?" I ask.

"Right." Her voice has a hint of suspicion in it. "It's only our second week here."

"Good. We're going to try to gather some intel." Her face scrunches in confusion. I smirk. "An explosion at the Goodes' house the same night John's in town. Can't be a coincidence, can it?"

"Of course not," she says. Her lips start to morph into a mischievous smile.

"That's not something you sleep through. I bet Mrs. Goode saw some stuff. Maybe she even got to talk to Sam. I mean, you know she's been worried about him. Maybe he gave her some idea about where they were going."

"And what do we do about art class?"

I shrug. "We had a flat tire at lunch. You're allowed a few unexcused absences. Where's your sense of adventure, Sarah Bleeding Heart?"

She lets out a laugh.

"Don't you dare tell me I'm trying to lead a boring life."

At lunch, we leave hell and travel back to Paradise.

Sam's house is on the outskirts of town, and I stick to all the back roads I can—the last thing I need right now is to run into my dad when I'm supposed to be lifting weights twenty minutes away.

We ring the doorbell a few times and loiter on the

porch, but no one's around. I peer through the front windows and some lacy curtains, but there don't appear to be any lights on inside.

After five minutes, we make our way around the back of the house, where I see exactly why the police rushed out to the Goodes' place. Half the backyard is scorched. It looks like a little well or something has been blasted to pieces. There's a huge window that's been blown out and covered with some kind of plastic tarp. It gives me sudden flashbacks of the way campus looked during the Mog attack.

"They were definitely here," Sarah says, coming up beside me.

"There's no evidence of this being other than a fire, though. No weapons or anything like that. Everything must have been taken away."

"The cleanup crew is thorough."

I nod, and we walk over to the truck, defeated. I'm ready to drive back to Helena when Sarah sees it.

"Mark," she whispers.

She's pointing at something in the passenger-side mirror. We turn in tandem, and I immediately see what's caught her eye. There's a black car parked in the middle of the road about a football field away. Unmoving. The windshield is so tinted that I can't even tell if anyone's inside or not.

"That car . . . ," I start.

"Doesn't look friendly." Sarah finishes my thought.

I put my truck in gear and start driving, my eyes locked on the rearview mirror, hoping that the car will stay put.

It doesn't.

"Mark," Sarah says.

"I know." My foot presses harder on the gas. I tell myself this is just a coincidence, but there's no way I can talk my brain into believing that.

"It's gaining on us," Sarah says. She's completely twisted around in the seat, her hands gripping the headrest.

I glance down at my speedometer. I'm already going sixty in a thirty, but I speed up even more.

"SHIT!" Sarah shouts, and I look in my rearview mirror again just in time to see the front bumper of the car disappear under my tailgate.

The car gives me a fairly light love tap—probably not enough to cause any damage but enough for me to feel it, and to rattle me pretty hard. It lets up a little, but it's still trailing me by only a few feet. Instinctively, I speed up. The car does the same.

"Get back under your seat belt," I yell at Sarah, who's wiggled out of it to keep her eyes locked on the car.

"What do we do?" she asks.

My mind races. I can't slow down. Luckily, the street we're on is fairly straight, but there's a curve coming up

I'll never be able to take at this speed.

"I don't know," I mutter. I'm pushing ninety and rising, but the car's not letting up. I can barely make out someone behind the wheel—just a big black blob vaguely in the shape of a human. I wonder for a second if it's a Mog or an FBI agent or some new type of alien we didn't even know existed, because that's a very real possibility at this point.

"What do they want?" I ask.

"Obviously to murder us," Sarah shouts. She grips her seat.

We're approaching the curve in the road when the car suddenly zips into the oncoming traffic lane and revs up beside me until we're speeding along parallel to one another. The tinting on the car windows make it impossible to see anything but the reflection of the outside world—like the car is some sort of automated machine out for blood without an actual driver inside.

Sarah gasps. "Crap! Is it going to—"

I see what she's guessing at a split second before it happens. I slam on my brakes. Sarah screams. The black car whips into my lane, missing the hood of my truck by what looks like inches. I can feel my antilock brakes pumping beneath my foot as the bed of my truck starts to slide to the right.

"HOLD ON!" I shout, bracing myself with one hand on the wheel and one gripping Sarah's arm—as if I'm going to be able to hold us in place if we start to roll. I can feel the truck start to fall over.

But we don't roll. The truck tips, then shudders, and finally comes to a stop after spinning a quarter turn. Smoke from my tires drifts through the air around us, filling my nose with the stench of burned rubber. Every muscle in my body is contracted, and I can already tell that I'm going to have some kind of bruise where my body's been thrown against the seat belt.

There's no sign of the black car. It's disappeared around the curve.

"Are you okay?" I ask Sarah, who looks at me and nods. Her hair's been thrown over her face, and her eyes are wide. She wriggles a little, and I realize I've got a viselike grip on her. I let her go. My fingers feel stiff.

I put the truck into park and start to shake a little, adrenaline rushing through me.

Ahead of us, the black car appears, stopped at the head of the curve in the road.

"Mark," Sarah says. "Get us out of here."

And then there's smoke coming from the car's wheels as it peels out. It careens straight for the passenger side of my truck.

I flip the truck into reverse to try and get us off the road, but I'm too slow. There's no way we're getting out of the way in time.

And then, at the last second, the car swerves to the

right and misses us completely, then continues to barrel down the deserted road as I stomp on the gas and back up as fast as possible. I end up slamming into a thin, tall tree. It falls over with a crack. Splintering.

We watch as the car disappears from sight again, this time miles and miles away. I'm breathing like I've just played the most intense scrimmage of my life. Sarah's hands are shaking.

"What the fuck was that?" I ask.

"I think that means we were poking around where we weren't supposed to."

"That car just tried to kill us."

"No," Sarah says, shaking her head. "It was just trying to scare us. To warn us about what would happen if we keep digging. If we get more involved."

I glance at the clock. The period after lunch is starting in Helena. Shakily, I put the truck in gear and head towards our new school. There's nothing else for us in Paradise right now.

CHAPTER TWELVE

MY DAD'S ALREADY HOME BY THE TIME I GET back from school that night, which is strange, because he's recently been getting home about an hour after I do. I back my truck around the side of the house—there's a good-size dent in my bumper and some scraped paint on my tailgate that I'd like to hide from him as long as possible. Stupid tree.

I can hear fighting when I walk inside. I rush to the dining room, where Nana's reprimanding Dad about something. There are several cans of beer on the table.

I walk in on him midsentence.

". . . bastards have no right to kick me out of my own damned office."

"You may be an adult," Nana says, "but you won't use language like that under my roof."

They notice me at the same time, and Nana moves to

usher me out of the dining room while my dad swigs back a beer.

"What's going on?" I ask.

"Apparently the FBI has completely taken over your father's station," Nana says, pushing me into the kitchen and pointing at a plate of cookies. I shake my head.

"What?"

"He's less than pleased. Apparently a man named Perty or Purdy or some such kicked him out of his own office."

Purdy.

"How can they even *do* that?" I ask.

Nana just shrugs. "I wouldn't ask him right now if I were you. Let's give him some space."

I nod. I've seen my dad drink beer all my life, but I'm not sure I've ever seen him day drinking like this. Or even actually drunk. So I head upstairs to put my stuff away and check in on what I've missed online during the drive home from Helena while trying to figure out why the FBI might have taken over the police station. The logical part of me says that it's just because John's escaped and they're concerned he's going to come back here, but there's also a nagging thought in the back of my mind: Does this have anything to do with the fact that I was digging around at the Goodes' today? Is this another FBI warning—one more subtle than a car trying to run me off the road but definitely more personal?

I shake my head. This has got to be about the search for John and Six. That's what I have to believe.

I'm bummed Sarah's not online to chat with. I want to tell her about these new developments, but now that her cell is gone and her parents are wardens of the landline, the internet's my only way of communicating with her. When I see she's not there, I email her, telling her I've got some news she'll want to hear but don't actually mention anything specific.

Later that night—when my dad has passed out watching reruns in the recliner downstairs—I get a text from a weird number I don't recognize:

Hi. Have you heard of any sightings of John?

I guess Sarah got a new phone after all. Hopefully a burner. I text her back:

No I think that's good tho.

A few seconds pass and I get a response:

Yeah, I guess. I just wish we could help more

I sigh and text back.

We're doing all we can. Can you call me?? I have stuff 2 tell u

And then nothing.

I lie on the foldout couch with my phone on my chest, waiting to feel it vibrate as I stare at the ceiling. I try to work things out in my head. The FBI has basically taken over Paradise. They're working for the Mogs, or at least aren't on the Loric's side of things. And earlier today, some crazy person tried to kill me and Sarah. Or just scare us badly enough that we'd stop poking around.

But I can't stop digging—can't just go back to the way things were before everything went nuts at the school. Which means that things could get even more dangerous for me, and for Sarah.

I start to wonder what my family would do if I just disappeared one day. If the FBI or Mogs took me. What would the editors of the blog think?

Would all the research and fact-finding I've tried to do have been for nothing?

After a while I pull my computer to the bed and start typing up everything I can remember about the Mogs from the attack on the school. It's part eyewitness account, part profile on the evil aliens. I don't want to forget any details, and it may come in handy one day if we ever have to try to explain to people what really happened that night—or how to fight the Mogs. Or if I get in over my head and suddenly disappear.

I leave the document saved as a private draft on the blog, unsure of what to do with it. Posting it will just send the FBI after me—or the Mogs. They'd probably show up in the middle of the night and gut me with their glowing weapons. It's not a pleasant thought, which is probably why I have a terrible dream once I finally go to bed. It starts off great—one of those dreams where it seems so mundane at first that there's no question that what you're seeing is reality. Sarah and I are in an old cabin that my family used to vacation at up in Michigan—one that I don't think I've been to since I was twelve years old. We're sitting in the room I always used to claim as my own, the one with two twin beds that were covered with these amazing electric blankets that I'd refuse to get out from under on cold mornings. But it's not cold in the dream. In fact, it feels like spring, everything bathed in this peaceful golden light.

Sarah's on one of the twin beds and I'm on the other, and we're just talking. She's saying something about an upcoming cheerleading competition, and I'm telling her she'll be perfect. And she's smiling so much. We're both so happy. The dream is filled with happiness, like it's in the air we're breathing.

And then there's a noise outside. I look through the window and see a huge beast—one of the creatures that attacked the school. A Mog monster, all yellow eyes and claws and horns. It's coming right for us.

I turn away and go to grab Sarah, but she's gone. Mog soldiers have poured into the room, their swords glowing different colors. They're all grinning this sick grin, showing off their gray teeth.

One of them has Sarah.

She reaches out and calls my name. I step towards her. And then something juts out of her chest, right where her heart is. Something long and sharp and glowing.

Sarah screams. Her eyes go wide, and then her body goes slack. And then she's gone. Her body turns to ash and blows away as if she were an alien.

It's my own shout that wakes me up, sweating in the upstairs office. I text Sarah on the new number, but she doesn't answer.

She must be asleep.

At some point I must pass out again, because the next thing I know, light is filtering in through the windows and I can smell bacon cooking downstairs. I'm a little disoriented but head to the bathroom and brush my teeth and stuff before meeting Nana in the kitchen.

"Your father's still asleep up in his room," she says with a bit of an edge to her voice. "Probably will be for a while. And he'll wake up in a crappy mood." She smirks a little. "Serves him right."

I grab a slice of bacon from the ever-growing stack she's got going beside the stove and devour half of it in one bite.

"He'll be okay, right?" I ask.

"Oh, of course. The James men have always just been a stubborn brood." Nana raises a white eyebrow towards me. "You're no exception."

I act hurt, as if she's wounded me with some imaginary bullet. She chuckles to herself. Then there's a knock on the door. She gives me a questioning look, but I just shake my head. She sighs.

"They'll be for your father, I bet." She looks down at her apron, which is smudged with grease.

"I'll stall them," I say. "You go get him up. He won't yell at you as much."

She pats me on the shoulder and walks away. I shove the rest of the bacon slice into my mouth and head for the front door, expecting to find Todd or one of Dad's deputies.

Instead, I open the door and see Agent Walker. At the foot of the porch, Agent Noto stands tall, with his hands clasped in front of him.

My face must register my surprise, because Agent Walker raises a hand in front of her chest as if to calm me down.

"What do you want?" I ask, not trying to hide the anger in my voice. For all I know, it was these two who tried to run me and Sarah off the road yesterday.

"Calm down, Mr. James," Walker says. She frowns. "We're only here to ask you a few questions."

"I'm sure you are."

"Mr. James—Mark—it's imperative that you tell us anything you know about what Sarah Hart was doing after school yesterday."

"Why should I tell you anything?" I ask.

"Because Sarah never made it home last night," Walker says.

There's a silence that settles over the porch. I can't tell if I'm imagining it or if it's just being caused by the sudden pounding in my ears.

"Wh-what do you mean?" I manage to stammer.

"Her parents filed a report last night," Walker explains. "Since Ms. Hart is a person of interest, we're bypassing the normal waiting period required to declare someone a missing person and jumping straight into the investigation. So I ask you again, Mark: What did Sarah do after school yesterday?"

I shake my head. None of this makes sense. I talked

to her just last night. She texted me. She—

The text. From a number I didn't recognize. It could have been anyone.

A voice keeps repeating in my head. *Sarah's gone. Sarah's gone.*

"Nothing," I say. "I mean, I don't know. I haven't talked to her since lunch yesterday. She took the bus home."

Agent Walker nods. She seems satisfied with this answer. For a moment her face changes—like some kind of mask slips away—and she looks at me with concern. Maybe even pity, as if she wished she could do something for me. Maybe even give me a hug. But the moment passes, and her steely expression resurfaces, her mouth with a glued-on smile.

"We'll be in touch," she says, turning away from the door. And then she's gone, into one of the ubiquitous black SUVs that have flooded our town.

Sarah's gone.

I failed to protect her.

What am I supposed to do now?

No, that's an easy question to answer. I find her.

But how am I supposed to do that?

CHAPTER
THIRTEEN

IT TAKES A WHILE FOR ME TO REALIZE THAT
John might have come for her, and so I sit glued to my
computer and check my phone every two minutes, hoping that she'll send me some sort of message telling me
she's all right. She must know that I'm going out of my
mind, and she'll let me know she's safe.

Days pass without any word from her, and I realize I'm holding on to unfounded hope. If she was with
John, she would have found a way to contact me. She
wouldn't have just left me behind.

It's so easy for me to look at the day she disappeared
and see the things I should have done. When she—or
whoever it was—texted me from that strange number. I
shouldn't have ever even left her alone after what happened at Sam's house with the black car. I feel like an
idiot. I feel useless.

I have to do something.

I'm practically glued to the blog, but there's only so much research I can do online. I can't just sit around and do nothing. I'll go crazy.

Something dings in the back of my head. Sarah saying that Sam probably knew more about what was happening with the Loric and the Mogs than any of us.

His backyard was a battleground. His mom is probably scared, not staying at the house. The back window has been blown out, covered only by a sheet of plastic.

It would be the easiest thing in the world to climb through it. If Sam had a better idea of what was happening between the Mogs and Loric, maybe he left behind some clues I can use.

It's almost 2 a.m. when I sneak downstairs dressed in all-black clothes, cringing at every creaking step. No one wakes up to stop me except for the dogs—but I've prepared for them. A few pieces of beef jerky, and Abby and Dozer are as quiet as can be.

I keep my headlights off until I'm already on the road. I drive past Sam's house a few times to see if I can spot anyone around it, but it doesn't look like someone's home. I park a few houses away just in case. There's no car out front, and a quick peek in the garage tells me there's no car in there either. I knock, just to make sure that no one answers. It's dead quiet inside.

Bingo. Empty house.

I take a deep breath and psych myself up. I've snuck

in and out of a few houses in my life, but I've never actually done any breaking and entering. I tell myself it's no big deal. And I need to do this. Any info I get helps us. Any info I get helps me get closer to finding Sarah.

I push in the plastic and climb through the window in the backyard and end up in the dining room. It's not hard to tell which room is Sam's: the one with a sign that says ENTER AT YOUR OWN RISK. I cross the brown carpet covering the hallway and slip inside.

Sam's room is covered in posters that remind me why we all thought he was a weirdo at school. *Star Wars*, *Alien*, *Starship Troopers*, and at least two different NASA flags. I imagine that wherever he is right now, he's wearing the same old ratty NASA T-shirt.

After bumping my head against a bunch of painted balls hanging from the middle of his ceiling, I start looking around. I'm not sure where to begin my search, so I just kind of start moving things on his desk. The problem is, I could point anywhere in Sam's room and my finger would land on something "out of the ordinary." I sift through action figures, blurry pictures of the sky, and a telescope it looks like he was trying to repair. I accidentally break the arm off a model robot and feel bad for about a split second before I remember that Sam's off somewhere with John and probably doesn't even remember that the model exists. Finally, I come across something that gets my attention.

I take a seat in Sam's desk chair and open up a copy of a little magazine called *They Walk Among Us*. It looks like a photocopy. It's full of alien conspiracies, lizard men, and other crazy-sounding articles, like how the Loch Ness monster is really an extraterrestrial sea horse. I thumb through a few issues before I read a headline that causes me to shiver.

THE MOGADORIAN RACE
SEEK TO TAKE OVER EARTH

The article is little more than a teaser of a bigger story that's going to run the next month, but I can't find the next issue anywhere. I take a picture of the article and front cover of the magazine and send it in a message to GUARD. He's going to flip out when he sees it. Maybe he can help me track down the people who wrote it—people who might know more about what's going on and how I can find Sarah.

GUARD responds quickly.

GUARD: WHOA.
JOLLYROGER182: i know. can u find anything else out about the mag?

I grab a few loose CDs lying around the desk just in case they've got files of interest on them. Unfortunately,

I don't see any kind of computer. Either Sam took it with him, or someone else has already made off with it. With a stack of magazines under my arm, I head out of Sam's room and through his house, glancing at pictures of his family that line the walls. Sam's dad is in some of them, staring back at me through thick glasses that look a lot like the ones Sam always wears. I barely remember Malcolm Goode from school parties and stuff when I was a kid. I look down at the pile of crap I'm technically stealing from his son's room.

"Sorry," I murmur, and then head to the backyard—through the back door this time.

Outside, I freeze: there's movement in the woods near the end of the yard. I think about running, but if there isn't anything there, that'll cause me to look more suspicious. Just as my palms start to sweat nervously, an owl flies out of the woods. I exhale, telling myself that's what I must have seen.

The side of the house casts a shadow that I disappear into, pressing myself up against the vinyl siding. I stand there for what feels like a long time watching the road, trying to see any movement or lights—anything that might suggest that there's a black sedan ready to run me down. But there's only the breeze and the sound of birds and insects somewhere out in the woods. Finally, I start back to my truck. I'm silently congratulating myself on a job well done when I realize the only thing that means is that the crazy person who was after us the other day *was* in fact after Sarah. That she's probably being held captive by them right now.

Or worse.

CHAPTER
FOURTEEN

I STAY UP MOST OF THE NIGHT SENDING PIC-
tures and scans of the magazines to GUARD. He works
his internet magic and comes back to me with several phone numbers for the people who publish *They
Walk Among Us.* He asks if I want him to call, but I
take responsibility for it. I'm the one who's now pored
over every column in every issue Sam had, hoping that
something—*anything*—will give me a clue as to where
the people holding Sarah might be. Or if not them,
where John and Six and Sam might have escaped to.
If I can find them, they can use their superpowers to
rescue Sarah, no problem.

No problem. I repeat this over and over in my head,
hoping that eventually I'll believe it.

I buy a burner phone after school the next day and start
in on the numbers GUARD came up with as I drive home.
The first three I call have all been disconnected—not

a good sign. The fourth and final number connects, though. Actually, it rings forever, with no voice mail. After about twenty rings, I hang up and call back. I count twenty more, and then I hang up and call back again.

I've never been one for subtlety.

After the third ring, someone hangs up the phone. I can hear the muffled sound of a split second of connection.

So someone's there.

I take a chance and call back. This time the pickup is immediate.

"What do you want?" The voice on the other end of the line is shaky and high-pitched. It's a man's voice. By the rate of his breathing, it sounds like he's hyperventilating.

"Hi, this is . . ." I fumble for a second before landing on a name. "Roger."

"Whatever you want, Roger, you've got the wrong number. Don't call back."

"I'm just trying to get some info on *They Walk Among Us*. Are you one of the writers or editors or whatever?"

"I said, you have the wrong number."

Click. The voice on the other end is gone.

I slam my fist on my dashboard and try to figure out what to do next. Then I say, "Screw it," and dial back. This time the man sounds pissed when he answers.

"Don't. Call. Again."

"My friend is in trouble," I blurt out. There's silence from the other dude, so I continue. "She's missing. It has something to do with the Mogadorians. I just want to find her. I just want to know that she's okay."

I sink back into the driver's seat, letting my head hit the rest behind me.

"Please," I say.

There's a long sigh on the other end of the line. When the voice comes back, it sounds like the guy is crying.

"We don't publish the newsletter anymore. They've taken everything. What more do you want from us? What more do you want? They've taken everything."

"Who's 'they'?" I ask, but I can guess. "The Mogs? Did they get to you?"

There's no answer on the other end. I take the phone away from my ear and stare at it for a moment before hanging up. I shouldn't be surprised that this was the fate of the magazine. Hell, I'm surprised anyone was left alive at all.

I message GUARD about the conversation. Then I make a proposal.

JOLLYROGER182: the people who subscribed to They Walk Among Us knew about the Mogs. it was in their mag

GUARD: Right. We know that.

JOLLYROGER182: we should change the name of our blog. make it easier for true believers to find

GUARD: You want us to become the new TWAU?

JOLLYROGER182: i think it might help us find some new recruits. and the more people in on this the more chances I have of figuring out what happened to Sarah

GUARD: It'll make us even bigger targets if the Mogs shut down the old TWAU.

JOLLYROGER182: but u r a computer whiz. untraceable addresses and IPs. im not worried.

GUARD: Let's do it. I'm emailing you an encrypted file. Password is a sea monster's planet.

I know exactly what he's talking about—this morning before I left for school, we'd made fun of an old article I found in *They Walk Among Us* about how sea krakens come from the planet Schlongda. It was maybe the first time I'd ever got a hint that GUARD had a not-so-serious side. Now that Sarah's gone, he's kind of the only person I can talk to about everything that's going on. I know I haven't met him in person or even talked to him on the phone, but he seems like the smartest person I've ever met. The things he can do with a laptop and internet connection blow my mind.

And when I get home and open the file he's sent me on my computer, I am nothing less than astonished.

I'm staring at a text file that lists a ton of information on Agent Purdy. Not things like his bio or what he's working on, but numbers that hold a much different power. Telephone numbers. Bank accounts. Passwords.

I message GUARD.

> **JOLLYROGER182: how the hell did you get all this????!**
> **GUARD: I'm an internet wizard.**
> **GUARD: Oh, and I'd print that out and then delete that file. IT WAS NEVER HERE.**
> **JOLLYROGER182: can you get into his email and stuff?**
> **GUARD: I'm trying, but it's all intranet stuff. Heavy, heavy firewall. Lots of stuff off-line too.**
> **JOLLYROGER182: what if we had his work computer?**
> **JOLLYROGER182: would 1 of these passwords open it?**
> **GUARD: That's a different story.**

GUARD: Wait. Are you about to do something really stupid?

I've been dying for a way to take action. I guess I just found it.

CHAPTER
FIFTEEN

BEFORE I LEAVE NANA'S I PUT A FEW NOTES ON my desk. If I'm caught, there's a chance I'll be shoved into a black van and never see the light of day again. That's how the FBI and Mogs work, right? If that's the case, I don't want my family thinking that I ran away because of them or something. I want them to know that I didn't just abandon them for no reason.

And if possible, that they should probably get out of Paradise too. This town is getting too dangerous. I leave a separate note addressed to Mom, telling her I'm sorry I haven't called and that she should bring Dad and Nana up to Cleveland. That way they'll be together, and out of Mog central.

I hope they don't have to read the notes.

I set up an automatic blog post too with my draft from earlier on what had really happened at Paradise High. If I don't log in and adjust the post time—if I get taken away—it will go live in a week. Maybe others can learn from what I knew. Maybe they'll be able to find Sarah if I can't.

I park my truck in an alley near the station where I can just see the front doors through a chain-link fence. There are a couple of agents milling about inside, but that's all I can see. I message GUARD, who is acting as a diversion for me, calling one of the phone lines the FBI has commandeered and reporting to whoever answers that a teenager with glowing hands and the power to move things with his mind just entered a truck stop outside of town. Whatever he says, it must be convincing, because the agents fly out of the station, jumping into their black SUVs and disappearing down the dark streets. I wonder briefly if Dad's being called in. I hope he's in good enough shape to put himself together, if he has.

An agent stays at the front desk, but I've figured out a way around that already. There's a window in the men's bathroom with a latch that's been broken since I was a kid. I remember once a rookie cop locked himself out of the station and got stuck climbing through it. But I'm more athletic than he was, and after crossing the street and skulking around to the side of the station, I'm bracing my arms against a porcelain sink as I pull the rest of my body inside, careful to close the window as softly as I can with my foot.

I'm in. Now I just have to stay hidden.

I walk out into the hallway where the bathrooms and some closets are and peek around the corner. There are a few rows of desks between me and the agent at the front, who seems glued to a computer screen. Dad's office is across the station, twenty yards away. *Just two first downs,* I tell myself. *It's a cakewalk.*

I'm halfway across the station when my dad's office door opens.

It takes half a second for me to slam onto the floor and roll under a desk, where I hold my breath and try to fight off the trembling in my hands. I must have been fast enough, because the two men who walk out of the office don't stop talking.

"I'm telling you, the situation here is under control," a man's voice says with a slight wheeze. "My agents are—"

"If things were really under control, Four couldn't walk in and out of this backwoods town as if it was his own private warship," the other man bellows, his voice like a bass drum. "I never should have left Paradise to someone who couldn't handle it. From now on my soldiers will be taking over here."

I flatten myself on the floor and press my face up against the bottom of the desk, which offers me an inch or two of room to see through.

"That's not necessary," the wheezy man says. His face

is pink and piggish, with a big, busted nose that looks like he's been tackled one too many times. I recognize him from the photo GUARD and I had found online: Purdy. At least that means Dad's office is empty if they leave. If they stay—well, I'm completely screwed. The other man is a behemoth. He's at least seven feet tall, with jet-black hair pulled back into a ponytail that disappears beneath his black coat. From the back, he's a wall of a man. A mountain.

"Your usefulness wears thin, Purdy," he says. "Don't let it wear out completely."

The giant of a man takes a step forward, then pauses. He turns his face to the back of the station, towards me, as if he's heard something. The man's eyes are almost completely black. They reflect the buzzing fluorescent lights overhead.

I'm looking at a Mogadorian. I'd recognize those terrifying black eyes anywhere. I don't breathe. If I could stop my heartbeat, I would in order to keep him from discovering me.

But he turns away, barking at Purdy.

"Take me to Number Four," he says.

He means John, I think. *I've only got a few minutes before they realize the report is a sham.*

As soon as the station door shuts, I roll out from under the desk and tiptoe across the room. Fortunately, the agent at the front desk is trying to make himself look as busy as possible, and he types loudly on the keyboard, giving me at least a tiny bit of noise cover.

Luck stays on my side: my dad's keys still work.

Once I'm standing in Dad's office, I allow myself a second or two to exhale and get my shit together, though the fact that I almost got caught and probably just saw a high-ranking Mog is hard to get past. The office has changed quite a bit since I was in it last, when Dad was dragging me out the night John was taken in. There are a few big boxes sitting in one corner that look like they're full of all the files and papers that used to litter the place when it was my dad's. The desk is tidy now—compulsively so—which is great for me because it means less to sort through.

I take a seat in the chair behind the desk and rifle through some of the papers and files. They don't tell me anything. It's all memos and bulletins that are the kinds of things that go up on the FBI website—public information. I'm looking for something a little more secretive than that.

Purdy's laptop is sleek and black, like something out of a spy movie. I open it up while removing a piece of paper from my pocket that's got all the things GUARD found written on it. Sure enough, the computer is password protected. I type in the one GUARD pegged as Purdy's main access code and, just like that, I'm in. I'm on an FBI computer.

"God bless you, GUARD," I whisper.

The desktop is littered with files. At the bottom of the screen are a few applications. I open up Purdy's email, figuring if anything, it might be the easiest way of getting info on Sarah. The first password GUARD handed over is a bust, but the second one gets me in.

I type Sarah's name into the search bar so fast that I misspell it twice. Finally, it goes through, bringing back over fifty emails containing her name. I shudder to think how many times *my* name might pop up in these emails, but that's not what I'm here to find out. I sort through the newest ones first until I hit the jackpot.

Detainee Hart has been transferred to the facility at Dulce.

Dulce. I recognize the name immediately from back issues of *They Walk Among Us* and old posts on the blog. It's a name that pops up all the time—a secret government base where weird stuff is supposedly always going down. A small-scale Area 51.

Sarah is being held in Dulce. New Mexico. Half a country away.

I have to go to New Mexico.

I start looking through other emails when I hear the station door slam shut, followed by a string of curses from what sounds like Purdy's voice.

Shit. Sitting in front of me is a wealth of information— maybe enough to change the tide of the battle between the Loric and the Mogs. A battle that will decide what happens to Earth. I was hoping to have more time on the computer, then just to sneak out and let Purdy think I was never there. If I leave now, I can try to find Sarah and figure out what else is going on between the FBI and the Mogs on my own. But if I take the computer, if I *steal* this FBI laptop, maybe I can be the hero. With GUARD's help, I can crack everything on the hard drive. Who knows what all we might learn. Sarah can help, once I've saved her. If this laptop has good intel on it, maybe I can save everyone.

And wouldn't Sarah be impressed by that?

"Fuck it," I say, pulling the power adapter out of the wall and taking the computer under my arm.

As Purdy berates the agent at the front desk, I unlock one of the windows to Dad's office and slip out. In a flash, I'm in my truck, shooting through the alley. I take one last look at the station as I drive away. Purdy's still in the front. Good. Maybe I'll have a while before he realizes what's happened.

Just enough time to leave Paradise.

CHAPTER
SIXTEEN

I HAVE BREAKFAST IN A DINER A FEW HOURS outside of Paradise: a steaming pile of pancakes and two sides of bacon. I was never a big coffee drinker, but I'm on my third cup. I need to stay alert and awake. I've got a long drive ahead of me.

Between bites of pancakes, I spin my burner phone on the table. My actual phone is sitting somewhere on the side of the road outside of Paradise, completely wiped clean of all my personal files and run over by my truck. All the info I need is on my burner now. I'm concerned about Sarah not having my number if she tries to contact me, but I can't risk anyone tracking me. Besides, I still have email, and I plan on emailing her every day until I see her again. I'll have GUARD figure out how to block my IP address or bounce my emails off a satellite or something.

I've already cancelled the automatic blog post. It

will remain in my drafts folder for now. I'm not ready
to come out with all this information. Something tells
me I need to save it for later, when it can be used more
strategically.

I thought about calling my family and trying to
explain myself further, but I can't risk it. They won't
understand, and giving them any info about where I'm
going or what I'm doing is dangerous for them. I just
hope that they aren't too upset. With any luck, Sarah
and I will be back in time for prom. Assuming there is
still a prom. Assuming there is still a Paradise.

The diner's pretty empty—the sun is only just starting to rise in the distance—but I'm still cautious. I wait
until the old man in the booth behind me leaves before
I pull out the laptop and open it up. I'm not even sure
where to begin. Maybe it'd be best if I just mail the
damn thing to GUARD. . . .

No. If anything on here will help me find Sarah, I
need the info now. More than just the town she's in. I
need to know how I can help her.

I flit through some emails, mostly full of termi-
nology I don't recognize. I tell myself that over time
I'll analyze every word in these correspondences.
There seems to be problems between the FBI and the
Department of Defense, and I rack my brain to try and
remember anything from my American government
class about what it is the Department of Defense does

other than something vaguely related to keeping the country safe. There are also a bunch of references to a secretary who's helping out the Mogs, but I don't know why Purdy's so interested in some office assistant.

After a while I take a break from emails and start looking around for information in other places. I start clicking around the computer's desktop. One folder stands out to me: MogPro.

Mogs.

I double click the folder, but instead of opening up like it should, a password terminal flashes on the screen. No username request, just a password field floating on top of the desktop. I try to escape from it or click on one of the other files, but it blocks me from doing anything else. I pull out the list of passwords GUARD sent me and try out the one that got me into the computer. A small red "X" appears below the password field.

Okay.

I try the next one and end up with another red "X." As I hit Enter on the third one, it dawns on me what the "X"s probably mean.

"Oh no, no, no, no," I whisper. But it's too late. I've fucked up. A third "X" appears, and suddenly there's a whirring from inside the computer as the hard drive spins into overdrive. In the background I see files disappearing from the desktop. Finally, the screen goes black. The power button is unresponsive.

"No!" I shout. "Son of a bitch!"

I slam my fist on the table, rattling my dishes. The sparse customers at the diner all turn to look at me. My waitress hurries over.

"Everything all right over here?" she asks, with a little more annoyance in her voice than worry.

"Yeah," I say, pulling out my wallet. "I just . . . lost my homework."

I start to hand her my debit card but pull back before she can take it. I've seen enough crime shows to know I shouldn't be leaving a trail. Instead I hand her a twenty and wonder if it's already too late for me to hit up an ATM—if doing so will bring a hoard of FBI agents choppering in from the sky.

I'm fuming at myself when I walk outside and think about chucking the laptop in the air and kicking it into the parking lot. But it may be useful still. I'm only just learning about all this computer stuff. Maybe GUARD can still get something off the hard drive. Maybe even info that'll help the Loric and the rest of the world if the Mogs one day decide to invade on a massive scale.

I get in my truck and pull onto the highway. There are hardly any cars in sight. The sun's at my back. My eyes are bloodshot from all the coffee, but I'll be fine. Better that than to be falling asleep on the road. After all, it's another twenty hours until I'm in New Mexico.

I AM NUMBER FOUR

THE LOST FILES

FIVE'S BETRAYAL

CHAPTER ONE

THERE WAS ONCE A PLACE THAT WAS BEAUTIFUL and lush and full of life and natural resources. Some people lived there for a long time, but then others came along who wanted or needed the land and everything on it. So they took it.

There is nothing special about this story. Open any history book on Earth—and probably every other planet—and you'll see a version of it play out continuously, on loop, over and over again. Sometimes the land is taken in the name of spreading a better way of life. Or for the sake of the native people. Occasionally the takers seize it based on some intangible reason—some divine right or destiny. But all of these reasons are lies. At the center of every conflict is power, and who will wield it. That's what wars are fought over, and why cities, countries and planets are conquered. And though most people—especially humans—like to pretend that gaining power is just an added bonus on top of whatever a conflict is *supposedly* about, power is the only thing that anyone is really after.

That's one great thing about the Mogadorians: they don't really bother with pretense. They believe in power. Even worship it. They see its potential to grow and serve their cause. So when you're someone like me who has extraordinary abilities, you become one of two things to the Mogs: a valuable asset, or an enemy who will eventually be destroyed.

Personally, I like being alive.

The Mogs don't pretend that they took my home planet of Lorien—which I barely remember—for any reason other than because they needed its resources. It's the same reason they're on Earth now. A planet as big as Earth will serve the Mogs well for decades— maybe even centuries—before they have to go looking for another home. And the humans . . . well, it's not like there's anything really special about *them*. They're pretty weak for the most part and are only barely managing to keep the planet alive as it is. One day soon there will be a full-scale invasion, and all their petty problems won't mean anything, because suddenly there will be some incredibly powerful extraterrestrials lording over them. Showing them how to live. Giving their lives purpose.

And I'll be one of their new rulers. Because the Mogs

have seen the potential in me. They've promised me a spot as a commanding officer in the Mog ranks, with North America as my kingdom. My personal play-ground. And all I have to do is fight alongside them and help them capture the other Garde remaining on Earth. Then I can help the Garde see that there's no way the Loric are ever going to defeat the Mogs. I'm assuming they were spoon-fed the same stories Rey, my Cêpan, told me when I was growing up: that the Mogs were our enemies.

But that's not true. Or at least it doesn't *have* to be true. Not if we join them.

After sitting around training and waiting for almost my entire life, it feels good to finally have an actual mission. To have a purpose. To not just be hiding and waiting for something to happen to me. It makes me actually *want* to train and study and get better, because what I'm working towards now isn't some fairy tale Rey fed me over dinner on the island, but a future I can see.

I've learned a lot about the reasons why wars are fought and won in the last few weeks since I've been living in a Mog compound somewhere in the middle of West Virginia. In fact, most of my "research" hours are spent in an interrogation room that's been converted into a study for me, where I learn about famous battles and conflicts or read the Great Book, which is the story of the Mogadorians and how their intellect and abilities outgrew their planet and forced them to seek other worlds to rule and guide. About how the Loric refused to share their resources or listen to reason when it came to adopting the Mogs as rulers. It's a book written by Setrákus Ra, the unstoppable leader of the Mogs, and, well, let's just say if I'd read it earlier, I would have had a much clearer viewpoint of the fight between the Mogs and the Loric than I did when I was hiding in a lean-to shack on a deserted island. I've begun to wonder if all my memories of being so young and happy on Lorien are just because I was too dumb and little to know what was really going on. I mean, any civilization that puts their last hope in a bunch of toddlers on spaceships has got to be a little bit out of whack, right?

Ethan's helped me see these things. He's helped me realize that I have a choice in this war, even though the Elders didn't want me to have one. It was strange at first to find out that my best friend was working for the Mogs—and that I'd technically been under Mog care for the better part of a year without knowing it—but I can't blame Ethan for keeping things a secret from me at first. I'd been so brainwashed by my Cêpan's stories of the Garde triumphing over the armies of the Mogs and returning Lorien to its former glory that I probably wouldn't have seen reason if he'd been up front with me at the beginning. Ethan is what some of the Mog commanders here have called a rare example of a human who has the intelligence to side with the winning team.

Still, it's so strange to be here underground. I'm technically an honored guest of Setrákus Ra, but I haven't proved myself yet. All they have is my word that I'm now loyal to them, but words don't carry a lot of weight with the Mogs. They believe in action, and results. And so I study and train and wait for the day when I get the chance to show them I am capable and ready to lead in their name. I follow orders. Because even though someday in the future I'll become invaluable to the Mogs, right now I'm just a former enemy living under their roof.

I'm buried in a book about the founding of America—particularly the expansion of European empires across the country—when Ethan comes into my study, flashing the toothy grin he always has plastered on his face.

"Good afternoon, Five," he says.

"Hey," I say, closing the book in front of me. Ethan's arrival means study time must be over. As much as I'm looking forward to being in charge of Canada and the United States, reading about the endless cycles of wars they've been caught up in can be monotonous. At least once the Mogs take over, war will be a thing of the past. There'll be no armies capable of standing up to them.

"How did you find today's reading?"

"There was some pretty dirty biological warfare going on back when Columbus and other explorers were first coming over. Smallpox blankets? It's kind of insane."

Ethan's grin doesn't flinch.

"The beginning of every great empire is stained with a little blood," he says. "Wouldn't you say it was worth it?"

I don't answer immediately. Ethan's eyes shift almost imperceptibly, but I catch them. He's glanced at the one-way mirror at the other end of my desk. It's easy to see what he's getting at. Others are watching. Here in the Mog compound, someone is *always* watching.

I tense up a little. I'm still not used to being under constant surveillance. But it's necessary, as Ethan's explained, so that the Mogs know they can trust me. It makes me only want to say things that will impress whoever's watching, or show off how smart I am. I'm getting better at keeping my brain focused on that.

"Definitely," I say.

Ethan nods, looking pleased. "Of course it's worth it. Keep reading that book tomorrow, and write down a few positive things about the conquerors' tactics."

"Whatever our Beloved Leader requires of me." I say this almost as a reflex. The first few days I was here, I heard it so many times that I just kind of adopted it. I probably say it ten times a day now without even realizing it half the time.

"Did you read the assigned passages from the Great Book?" Ethan asks.

"Of course. Those are the best parts of the study sessions." This is completely true. The other books are boring and make me suddenly understand why teenagers like me were always complaining about homework on TV shows I saw before coming to the Mog compound. But the Great Book is, well, great. Not only is it written much simpler than the other books, it also answers a lot of questions I've had throughout my life. Like why the Mogs went after Earth even though they had Lorien, and why they started hunting down the Loric once they got here, even though there were so few of us. The book explains that the Loric were weak but sneaky, and the Mogadorian belief that leaving even one enemy alive gives them the power to recruit others and multiply, gain power and one day rise against you.

Also, it's really bloody and violent, which makes it much more fun to read. I can see it play out in my head like one of the action movies I used to love to go see when I was still in Miami.

"And what did you learn about today?" Ethan asks.

"About how Setrákus Ra bravely fought our Elders. How they tried to trick him and poison him, but our Beloved Leader was courageous and bested them, anyway."

"*Our* Elders?" Ethan asks, slight concern on his face.

I correct myself. "I mean the *Loric* Elders. It makes me even more excited to meet our Beloved Leader."

I have not had the pleasure of meeting Setrákus Ra in person yet. Apparently someone higher up thought it wasn't a good idea to give a superpowered guy like me an audience with the future ruler of the solar system until I've proved myself.

Ethan grins and pulls something out of his pocket. He tosses it on the table, and it bounces heavily a few times and then rolls. I stop it with my telekinetic Legacy and lift it in the air: a steel ball bearing almost as big as a Ping-Pong ball.

"What's this?" I ask.

"Consider it a gift. Use your power on it. See how it feels."

I float the ball over to the palm of my hand. With a little focus, my body suddenly takes on a metallic sheen. I drum my fingers on the table in front of me, and the sound of metal meeting metal fills the air. Ethan calls this Externa, the ability to take on the properties of whatever I touch. It's the newest of my abilities and the one that probably needs the most work.

I shrug as I crack a metallic knuckle.

"It feels like I'm made of steel. But I could have just touched the table and gotten the same kind of effect."

"But the table's not going to be with you all the time.

From now on, this ball bearing should be. I don't want you to find yourself in the middle of a fight with nothing but sand or paper to turn into."

"Thanks." I smile. It's definitely not the flashiest or most expensive thing Ethan and the Mogs have given me, but I can see how it might end up being useful. I shove the ball bearing into my pocket, where it settles beside a red rubber ball I've carried with me for a long time—a trinket from a kid's vending machine.

Ethan tosses me a rolled-up sheet of paper. I push some books out of the way and spread it out in front of me. It's a map of the Western Hemisphere.

"What's this for?" I ask.

"I just wanted to make sure we had all the information correct on it. For record keeping and stuff like that."

The map includes a thick red line that zigzags across the United States and down into the Caribbean. There are dates printed along the markings.

"This is a map of all the places I lived growing up," I say.

"Correct. Just give it a once-over when you have a chance. I guessed on a lot of the dates based on stories you'd told me."

"But what good is any of this information?"

Ethan shrugs. "Just in case the Garde somehow caught your trail or tried to track you down, we'd know where they might be searching. We'll want to put a few scouts in those locations, just in case."

I nod, looking over the map. It's weird to think of myself as being young and powerless with Rey in all these places. Ethan comes up behind me and looks over my shoulder.

"Where was it that you said your guardian started to get so ill?" he asks.

I point to a place where the line dips into Pennsylvania.

"Around here somewhere. I'm not sure where exactly. We were camping in the mountains."

Ethan scowls.

"There are some of the finest hospitals in the country in that area. You know, if your Cêpan hadn't forced you to stay hidden on the island for as long as you did, he probably would have lived," Ethan says. "It's a shame he was so shortsighted that he couldn't see the inevitable future of Mogadorian progress."

"He thought the warmer air would help him."

"What he probably needed was a shot of antibiotics." Ethan shakes his head and crosses his arms. "I'm just glad you were able to get off the island before you ended up going crazy and talking to the pigs. I still can't believe someone as powerful and smart as you was expected to raise those slop-covered animals."

I laugh a little. Over the last few weeks I've told Ethan

basically everything I can remember about my life. All about the tiny little shack and the pigs I raised and how I trained myself to use my telekinesis on my own. He and the other Mogs seemed really impressed by that part. Like I managed to become something great even when every card in the deck was stacked against me.

When I look at Miami on the map, my mind flashes with memories of the time I spent there before Ethan took me in. When I was just a punk-ass street rat wasting my powers on petty stuff like picking pockets, totally oblivious to how much authority I should have been wielding. There was a girl. Emma. My partner in crime who turned on me when she saw what I was capable of. Who was afraid of what I could do instead of respecting my abilities. I frown at the memory, and my stomach drops a little because it's been a while since I've thought of her. There had been a time when she was my only friend in the world, but she was just using me too, wasn't she? I was the one with the real talent. She was just riding on my coattails.

There's a knock on the door, and then a Mog enters. One of the vatborn messengers and servants in the compound. I straighten up in my chair. This is a reflex. Even though I've been here a few weeks, I'm still getting used to seeing Mogs every day. More than that, I never know what they're going to ask me to do when they show up in the interrogation room that's been turned into my study or track me down in my bedroom. For all I know, they could be telling me that I've failed some test of theirs I didn't even know I was taking.

"You weren't responding to your radio," the Mog says to Ethan, clearly a little ticked off.

Ethan points to the little earpiece that's hanging out of his collar.

"Of course not," he says. "All of your superiors know that I never wear my earpiece when I'm with our guest." He motions to me. "It would be rude."

"Commander Deltoch requests your presence in the detention wing," the Mog says.

"I'll be there at once." Ethan nods.

"You *and* the Loric."

I tense up. What do they want from me in the detention wing?

"Is that how you would address an honored guest in this base?" Ethan asks. "How about 'sir'?"

The Mog seems a little apprehensive but nods his head to me.

"Sir," he says.

"Dismiss him," Ethan says to me.

"What?" I ask.

"You're going to have to get used to giving orders at some point."

I look at the Mog, who's got a full-on grimace now. I suddenly feel awkward. I hate it when Ethan does this. He's always trying to make everyone on the base treat me like their king or something. And while I'll be leading them one day in the future, I'm still unproven potential, and the last thing I want is anyone stirring up animosity against me.

"Five," Ethan says.

"You're dismissed," I say.

The Mog hesitates a moment. I assume his orders were to escort us to the other side of the building. I can almost see him trying to figure out who outranks whom in his head before Ethan clears his throat and, in a flash, the servant is gone.

"Conflicting orders, I'd imagine," Ethan says as if he could read my brain.

"Do you think I'll get him in trouble?"

Ethan's face goes serious.

"You can't worry about that. Don't forget who you are. When the Mogs take Earth, you'll be one of their officers. A leader. You may be new here, but you are the powerful Number Five. Show them mercy now, and they won't respect you when you're in charge."

"I need a chart to keep the ranks all straight in my head."

"Just always act like you're at the top of the food chain. Now come along," Ethan says, motioning towards the door. "Let's see what Commander Deltoch is up to with the prisoners this afternoon."

He doesn't give me time to react, only turns and heads out the door. I can't help but glance to the wall across from my desk, where a photo is taped up. It's a guy who looks like he's a few years older than me, with long brown hair. He's built like an athlete—way fitter than I've ever been in my life. He looks smug. He's jogging in the photo and seems to be unaware that his picture is being taken. I haven't met him yet, but I know he's here on the base with me. Locked up. They've tried to torture him, but that doesn't really work. He's protected by magic, like I am. By a charm put on us when we were kids that keeps us from being hurt until our number is up.

He is Number Nine.

The Mogs want me to kill him. His is the blood that must be spilled for me to advance.

He is my proof of loyalty.

CHAPTER
TWO

FOR A LONG TIME, THE THING I WAS MOST
afraid of was being left out. Alone on an island in the
Caribbean. Left behind as the other Garde banded
together without me. That wasn't exactly helpful when
I was also afraid of getting too close to anyone for fear
of them finding out my secret: that I'm not human. I
had a really crappy life because of all this.

Until I met Ethan. Until the Mogs took me in. Now
I have no worries of ever being left out. And I'll definitely never feel alone. It would be impossible to: there
must be thousands of us living together on the West
Virginia base.

The compound the Mogs have here is maybe the
most incredible structure on Earth, even if few humans
will ever see the inside of it. It's hidden in a hollowed-
out mountain, and is so vast and full of trailing tunnels
and caves that I doubt anyone has seen every corner

of the place. I've spent a lot of my free time floating around the corridors and rocky hallways, and I think I've seen only a twentieth of it.

It's almost all Mogs here—the vatborn soldiers and servants and the trueborn higher-ups—but there are a handful of humans. Most aren't here by choice, though Ethan's an exception, as are the men and women in dark suits and military garb whom I pass in the halls on occasion.

And there's one other Loric. Nine.

I follow Ethan through the cavernous main hall, floating a few feet above him because flying is good practice and Ethan says it reminds the others that I'm powerful. I don't mind, really, because it's easier than walking. There are dozens, maybe even hundreds, of Mogs who we pass as we head towards the detention cells. They stop walking and step aside as I go by, staring at me. Some of them nod in respect, knowing that one day I'll be a powerful force in the Mog ranks. Others look at me with skepticism. I can feel their eyes on me as I fly over them.

The only really annoying thing about the base is the scalding-hot green stuff that flows throughout it and pools in the main chamber. It's some sort of energy source for the Mogs, Ethan said, but if you touch it, it'll eat through your skin like acid (or a least that's what I hear—I haven't been dumb enough to actually test that theory out). Whatever it is, it smells like sulfur and rotten coconuts. As we pass through the main hall, the scent is heavy in my nose, and I grimace.

"Why do you think we've been summoned?" I ask Ethan.

He shrugs.

"Maybe Commander Deltoch thinks it's time for you to take your place in the leadership."

As a commander, Deltoch is the highest-ranking Mog in charge of the base. He reports to a General Sutekh and sometimes our Beloved Leader directly. He's also become my de facto keeper—the person Ethan reports to and who I assume is on the other side of the one-way glass watching me in my study half the time. He's an aggressive, trueborn Mog—I've come to learn that's something to be proud of around here—and takes exquisite delight in telling me that I don't *look* anything like a soldier. He has never explicitly said that I'm maybe a little on the heavy side, but it's almost certainly what he's thinking.

I'm always a little on edge around Deltoch. I can't help but want to impress him every time I see him.

For my part, the detention area is the one place I'm not allowed to go on the base. I've seen only the first few cells. Ethan says it's because they don't want me to hurt Nine just yet. They're still trying to figure out a way to force him to spill everything he knows about the Garde—and besides, since his death will be so important, it must be ceremonious. I've wondered what it would be like to be imprisoned here, like Nine. To spend all day in a cold stone cell. It sounds terrible. But then, I don't have to worry about it. I chose to join the Mogs—to serve their cause in order to elevate myself. I'm sure the others here had the same chance. They just threw it all away. And for what? Do the imprisoned humans really think their own resistance to the Mogs means a damned thing in the long run? That they're anything other than a speck of dust in what will be the vast empire of the Mogadorians? Maybe I would have thought that once, but not after seeing their resources and strength with my own eyes.

We pass row after row of containment cells in the detention wing, the entrances barred and pulsing with some kind of blue energy field. I keep my eyes darting back and forth, trying to catch a glimpse of Nine, to no avail. Inside are the weak and unrepentant enemies of the Mogs. Most of them are humans who got a little too close to figuring out what was happening around them on Earth and refused to quit snooping, or who disobeyed orders. The traitors are being taught an important lesson about crossing their superiors—one they won't forget when they go back out into the world after they've served their time, which is what Ethan says happens to most of the ones who realize the error

of their ways. A few are test subjects or people somehow related to the Loric cause—I hear there are even
a few Greeters in captivity, those whose job it was to
introduce the Loric to the human ways of life on Earth.
Not all of them were as smart as Ethan was. It's hard to
imagine that he might have been in one of these cells
had he not foreseen the Mogs' inevitable victory.

Deltoch stands in the middle of the hallway. He's
at least two heads taller than me and built like a
giant wrestler shoved into an ominous black officer's
uniform. His skin is pale, and his hair is gleaming
jet-black and pulled into a tight ponytail. Dark tattoos
peek out around his hairline, above eyes like big black
marbles.

"So thrilled you could join us," he says flatly as I
approach. He glances at Ethan and sneers slightly—
despite Ethan's role as my recruiter and mentor, I don't
think Deltoch has been a big fan of having a human
roaming around his base with so much authority.

"Whatever our Beloved Leader requires of me," I say.

"Our afternoons are usually spent expanding upon
Five's powers for the good of Mogadore," Ethan says,
which I recognize as his way of asking why we've been
ordered to come to this side of the compound.

Deltoch narrows his eyes a little. "I assume you must
have been in the middle of something very important
since it took you so much time to get here."

I start to stammer a response, but Ethan speaks on my behalf.

"He was just reading from the Great Book," he says, grinning. "What could be more important than our Beloved Leader's words?"

Deltoch smirks in a way that bares all of his gray sharklike teeth. It's not exactly a happy expression.

"You're here because the all-wise Setrákus Ra is *anxious* for Five to prove himself loyal to the Mogadorians."

"We're looking forward to him taking his rightful place as a high-ranking member of the Leader's forces as well," Ethan says. "But these things take time, as I'm sure—"

"Five," Deltoch says, ignoring Ethan. He steps aside and points a long, thick finger at one of the cells. "Do you wish to see the power of the Garde?"

Ethan starts to protest, but I nod.

"Yes, sir."

I step up to the blue force field and stare. There's a prisoner inside, stretched out on a dirty slab of rock serving as a bed. The guy is shirtless, his muscles glinting under a sheen of sweat. Long, dark hair is spread out around his head. His eyes are closed, and his lips move slightly, as if he's meditating or saying some sort of prayer.

Number Nine.

"He doesn't speak when he's conscious, but he talks in his sleep sometimes," Deltoch says. "That's how we figured out his number."

Something within me stirs as I look at Nine. Not pity or brotherhood, but something unsettling. A sort of fear. When the Mogs first recruited me, they gave me a folder with Nine's picture inside it. He's to be my victim, the blood offering that proves my loyalties to the Mogadorian progress. The only thing is, I've never killed anyone before. I had a hard time even killing animals back on the island with Rey. And so deep down I'm afraid that when the time comes and I'm finally given the order to end Nine's life, I won't be able to do it.

Thankfully, whatever magic the Elders of Lorien worked on us when we were kids is still in effect, because there's no way I can kill Nine out of order. At least, not that the Mogs or I know of. If there's a way to dispel the magic that protects us, that knowledge probably died with Rey or the Elders. I have no idea how to break the charm.

"What do you think?" Deltoch asks. "Is the hunger for power rising up inside you? Are you ready to take the next step and ascend into power among us?"

My stomach drops. They *have* brought me here to kill Nine. I swallow hard and try to steel my churning guts.

Deltoch lets out a little laugh.

"You look pale all of a sudden, Five," he says, his voice a low bellow.

I don't answer. I can't take my eyes off Nine. Another Garde. It's the first time I've seen him in person instead of in the photograph pinned up in my study. He's thinner now than he is in the picture—a side effect of whatever they have or haven't been feeding him I assume—but he's still built like a Greek statue. Strong looking. Deltoch has obviously noticed this, because he's quick to mention it.

"He's managed to stay in incredibly formidable shape despite being a prisoner," he says, very pointedly not looking at my less-than-athletic build. "I'm told he spends most of his waking moments exercising in his cell."

I change the subject.

"Why doesn't he use his powers to escape?" I ask.

"He's tried. Many times." Deltoch motions to the pulsing blue shield. "But we've learned to keep him under control."

"Maybe he's just waiting for the perfect time to lash out," I say.

Deltoch bares his teeth.

"Come with me," he says, turning and heading deeper into the detention wing. Eventually we come to some kind of cell that looks like it's part interrogation room and part laboratory. There are chains hanging from the ceilings and silver gurneys on one side, and a few tables on the other. The room smells of bleach.

"What is this place?" I murmur.

"This is where many of our prisoners' fates are decided," Deltoch says. "Where they choose to give themselves over to the Mogadorians and offer us their intelligence, or they condemn themselves to a cell indefinitely."

I glance at Ethan, but his eyes are fixed on Deltoch. Usually Ethan knows everything that's going on at the base—or at least he does when it involves me—but he seems to be as confused as I am as to why we're here.

"Many brave soldiers gave their lives in this room when Nine first arrived, as they tested the strength of the Loric magic that protects him," Deltoch says, running his finger over a tray of shiny scalpels. "That's how *they* proved themselves loyal to the Mogadorian empire."

"And you were okay with wasting soldiers like that?" I ask.

"We do not consider it a waste." The commander has an angry edge to his voice now. "It is the highest honor to die for the Mogadorian cause. Besides, the Loric charm is not something we wholly understand. We weren't sure if it was possible to weaken the charm so much that it broke completely. It was a possibility we could not ignore."

"But you couldn't get rid of it." It's more a statement than a question that comes out of my mouth.

"No." Deltoch frowns. "No matter how hard we tried. And Nine didn't say a word. He just laughed as some of our finest men died in front of him." His expression changes and becomes almost pleasant. "But his Cêpan did talk."

"What?" Ethan asks. Apparently this is news to him as well.

"This is confidential information," Deltoch says, shrugging towards Ethan.

"What about his Cêpan?" I ask. "Do you have him too?"

"We did," Deltoch says. "But Number Nine murdered him."

My mouth drops open.

"He *what*?"

"His Cêpan was smart. We were still trying to negotiate and give Nine and his guardian a chance to join our cause. The Cêpan was going to talk—to cut a deal with us—and when Nine found out, he murdered the Loric in cold blood."

Deltoch takes a few files off one of the lab tables and hands them to me.

"See for yourself," he says.

I open the top folder and am greeted by a stack of

photos—stills from a security camera in the very room I'm standing in. Only in the photos, there are two figures. One looks like an older human. He's hanging upside down from the ceiling with thick chains wrapped around his ankles. There's blood everywhere. Nine stands beside the man, a dagger in his hands.

"It's my own fault, really," Deltoch says. "I left the two of them in this room together and assumed that Nine had a sense of loyalty. Obviously I was wrong. The Garde used his powers to break through his containment field and attacked the brave Mogs guarding him. It took a few minutes before we were able to get into the room, but that's all he needed."

I flip through the photos. They're like a slide show, and I watch as Nine steps closer and closer to his Cêpan, raising his weapon. And then finally, he buries the blade in his guardian's chest. In the next few pictures, Mogs show up and drag him away, but the damage has already been done. Nine struggles against their grip, gnashing his teeth, and then he's gone. The last photo is just the Cêpan, hanging upside down. Alone. Lifeless.

My memory jumps back to Rey, dying in our little hut on the beach. Sure, we didn't get along a lot of the time, and he was probably a little crazy, but I can't imagine I could ever have killed him. He was the person who raised me.

I'd always been taught to think that the Garde were these saintlike people—that we had to be perfect in order for our planet to have a chance at being resurrected. That the Loric were a peaceful, inherently good race while the Mogs were evil incarnate. It dawns on me that this was just more Loric propaganda. That the Loric and Mogs probably don't have that many differences between them, other than the fact that the Mogs don't pretend to be anything that they aren't. Ethan always says that history is subjective, and that the history I knew to be true was just the Loric side of things. Besides, now that I've felt the power that comes with my Legacies and how good it feels to have people see the potential in me, I can't imagine that Lorien was the utopia Rey made it out to be.

"Have you brought me here to kill him?" I ask.

"Not yet," Deltoch says. "Not until we figure out a way to break this charm. There's no way of knowing what would happen if one of the other Garde tried to inflict death upon him, and we don't want to lose our secret weapon: you."

"Your most valuable asset," Ethan says to the Mog.

"Exactly," Deltoch says. He motions to the photographs. "But when the time comes, be careful. He's unhinged. He's hardly even an intelligent life-form anymore. Just an animal. I imagine he wouldn't think twice about killing you if given the opportunity."

I turn back to the photographs. *An animal.* Staring at the crazed look in Nine's eyes as he howls—his Cêpan's blood on his hands—I believe it.

All I can think is what an idiot he is to willingly choose murder and imprisonment instead of the opportunity I've been given. How stupid Nine must be.

And how one day this chained-up animal will be my ticket to the top of the food chain.

CHAPTER
THREE

AFTER SEEING NINE IN ACTION—AT LEAST IN photos—Deltoch insists that I take the rest of the files the Mogs have on him so that I can study them well. "Know your enemy," he says, and then he cancels my afternoon training with Ethan while I retreat to my room on the other side of the compound. The place they've made for me here in Mog central isn't as nice as, say, Ethan's beach house in Miami, but it's pretty plush. I wouldn't even know I was half a mile inside a mountain if it wasn't for the fact that all the walls are made of smoothed-down stone. I've got a big king-size bed, a *giant* TV, and an arsenal of gaming consoles and games I've never even heard of before—Mogadorian battle simulators that have graphics any next-gen console would kill for. The Mogs had them arranged for me because Ethan told them how much time I'd spent playing games in my downtime back in Florida. These are unlike anything I've ever played, though—a weird combination of military and governing missions. It took me a while to get the hang of them because I was so used to playing games where you got points deducted every time you caused collateral damage or civilian casualties. But I'm getting a lot better.

With Nine's files in hand, though, I ignore all the electronics and stuff that the Mogs gave me and go straight to my bed. There, I spread out the papers and reports on Nine. Ethan had told me that Nine lived in luxury in Chicago, but it turns out that's pretty general speculation based on what they pieced together from Nine and some former girlfriend of his who was working with the Mogs for a while. They don't actually know where his place is in the city.

One of the things included in the files is a transcription from an interview with Nine's Cêpan that the Mogs have typed up for me. He says that Nine lived a charmed life. He never wanted for anything, and went and did whatever he pleased. On one hand, I'm not surprised that he ended up in a Mog cell, but on the other, my jealousy of how he got to grow up compared to how I lived burns somewhere deep in my chest. They even have quotes from his Cêpan about how Nine was a popular kid in school who had girls following after him wherever he went and lived like a miniature king on campus. Meanwhile I was eating coconut meat for lunch and sweating half to death in the Caribbean.

At the end of the interview is a brief section where the Cêpan discusses how the Elders decided on our numbers:

It wasn't random. They were given that order for a reason. The Elders judged who they thought were the strongest and brightest—those with the most potential— and saved them for the end. The first few were hardly anything more than cannon fodder. Their Cêpans were instructed to keep them hidden no matter the cost to their well-being so that the higher numbers would be kept safe. After all, the Garde couldn't very well die if their order wasn't up. I always considered myself lucky to have been assigned to the highest number. Nine rarely thought of anyone lower than him unless it was from a tactical standpoint: it was always assumed that if the Garde ever did come together to fight, Nine would be the one who would command them.

I have to stop reading. My head pounds, and with one brisk surge, I send the files flying across my room in a telekinetic wave. I throw open my Loric Chest that sits on the nightstand beside me. My favorite thing inside it—the only thing I've really learned to use—is a concealed blade inside a gauntlet. I use my powers to send it sailing through the air, popping out the knife hidden inside. It skewers the sheet of paper with the Cêpan's interview on it and embeds itself in the stone wall of the room. I start to rummage through my Chest, which usually helps me focus and calm down, but it's no good. I'm too wound up. Then I throw myself down onto the bed and crack my knuckles as anger boils up inside me. So that's what Nine thought of us—of *me*. That I was worthless. That I'd be someone he could command one day. Well, the joke's on you, Nine. Because now you're the one hidden away, and I'm the person with all the power. I'm the one who's going to control everyone else.

Over the course of the next few weeks, I continue my daily routine of studying, training and learning more about Mogadorian culture. Every time I see the picture of Nine in my study, I get frustrated and pissed off as I think about the files—of him and his Cêpan regarding the lower numbers as being weak. I try to channel this into my training, like when Ethan takes me into an unused room in order for us to do a little training on my Legacies. Ethan sets a box down on the metal table in the middle of the room while I use my telekinesis to straighten all the chairs and get them all pushed in and out of the way.

"Your ability to move things with your mind has really progressed both in terms of strength and finesse," Ethan says. "The Mog leaders and I are all very impressed."

"Thanks," I say with a grin. "I *have* gotten pretty

good at moving boulders around in the tunnels."

"True." He nods. "So today I want us to focus on your Externa. In particular, the quickness with which you can change forms and the length of time you can stay in them."

This sounds easy enough. I've gotten good at taking on the properties of the things I touch. I reach into my pocket, where my fingers find the red rubber ball. My skin stretches, and my fingers take an elongated form, like the kind of fingers people who have never actually seen an alien would expect me to have.

"Let's do it."

Ethan starts to toss things at me left and right from the box he brought with him, hardly giving me time to change before my body has to reset and transform again. I hold a leather-bound book, and my skin grows tough. I catch a smooth white stone, and I'm a moving statue.

"Excellent," Ethan says. "But can you do it while flying?"

Without answering, I float up in the air and continue to change as Ethan tosses more and more objects at me. We keep it up for a few minutes, and then suddenly I start to get tired—I've never overworked my Legacies like this before. But I don't show any weakness. I think about Nine's Cêpan and how he thought the higher numbers were better than me, and I power through the fatigue, gritting my teeth and imagining myself standing over Nine as he begs for mercy.

Ethan tosses me something small and shiny that I catch with my telekinesis and float over to my hand.

"Do the stone, not the band," he says as it travels through the air. I don't understand until I realize that I've got a diamond ring in my palm.

"No problem," I say, touching the gem with the tip of my pinkie. My skin hardens and takes on a brilliant shine. The tips of my fingers are completely clear. I float over to the steel table and drag one of my fingernails along the top of it, engraving the numeral "5" into it.

"Now *this* could come in handy," I say.

"Sure," Ethan says. "If you want to be the target of every weapon on the battlefield. Your skin is too shiny. It would be impossible to be incognito. But keep this form for now. Let's see how long you can hold it."

I wave my arms around in front of me and watch the light bounce off them, sending reflections all around the room.

"I think I met some people down in Miami who would have me chopped up into pieces and sold off for millions if they could see me now."

The harder I concentrate while I touch the stone, the clearer my body gets and the harder my skin becomes. But it takes work. And the more I focus, the more my head starts to pound, and I start to feel like I'm losing control of my body. When I first developed the Externa ability, I was terrified that I'd never be able to revert back to my normal form again. Suddenly, that same fear attacks me, and my heart rate and breathing go through the roof.

I must look like I'm afraid, because when Ethan says, "Five, calm down, buddy," his voice is steady and low. He sounds like that only when he's concerned.

So I take a few deep breaths, close my eyes and let the ring fall to the ground as my feet find the stone floor again. I tune out the world for a few seconds and just concentrate on my normal body and how much I want to be back in it. When I open my eyes again, my fingers are pink and soft. I'm back. But my head is still pounding.

"Ow," I say, raising a hand to my right temple.

"Headache?"

"Yeah."

"We'll get you some aspirin," Ethan says. "But, hey. That was great. This is where we'll start focusing our training from now on."

I think of Nine, and how Deltoch doesn't think I look like much of a soldier.

"I'm fine," I insist. "I can keep going."

"I don't want you to hurt yourself."

Ethan must think I'm weak too.

"I'm not some *kid*, Ethan," I say. "I'm a superpowered

Loric and the guy who's going to be the Mog officer in charge of this country. If I say I can keep going, I can."

Ethan looks a little taken aback. Before he gets a chance to say anything, the door bursts open, and Commander Deltoch enters. A flash of annoyance crosses Ethan's face as he turns to his superior.

"Commander," he says with a little nod of a bow, "to what do we owe the pleasure?"

"You're needed, Ethan," the Mog says. "Report to Central Command."

Ethan waves at me. "Come along, Five. You should go back to your room and get some rest."

"The Loric stays. I have a surprise for him."

There's a moment when Ethan and Deltoch just stare in defiance at one another. Deltoch must win in the end, because Ethan shrugs, gives me a fleeting glance and then turns on his heel. Just like that he's gone, and I'm left alone with the Mog commander. I don't realize how accustomed I am to Ethan always being there until he's gone.

I wonder if today is the day. If they're taking me to try to kill Nine.

"Five," Deltoch says through his sharp, dark teeth. "How is your training going?"

"It's good," I say, nodding fervently, which only makes my head hurt more. But I ignore that. "I can show you if you want."

I blink, and in the course of doing so, the chairs all fly out from under the table, spin around the room and then go right back to where they began. Whatever Deltoch has in store for me, I know I need to impress him. To show him that I'm doing well and that I'm ready to take the next step.

Deltoch chuckles a little, but it doesn't sound like he's actually amused.

"A good trick," he says. "I'm sure our enemies will cower in fear when they see our great army of chairs and tables laying siege to their cities."

"I can move something else," I say, feeling stupid. "Something bigger. Or a bunch of swords or something."

"What I have in mind for you today is a little more interesting. A true treat. Come, follow me."

We move in silence through the compound. I fly, he walks. We head towards the front entrance that leads out into a wooded area that's fenced off from the rest of the world. I'm not forbidden to go outside by any means, but for caution's sake I have to get approvals and a tracker and all kinds of boxes checked off if I want to spend the day in nature, so I hardly ever do. Besides, I'm much more of a beach person, and it's cold up here in West Virginia. I've grown used to much warmer climates.

The entrance to the compound is camouflaged and

well guarded. Soldiers salute us as we pass by, and then we're just hiking through the woods, and I'm completely lost as to what we're doing. I can't even fly here, with all the low-hanging branches—I'd have to be above the tree line—and soon I get a little short-winded as we hike along, which I try to mask by breathing as quietly as possible.

"Where are we going?" I ask, clouds of white escaping my lips in the cold.

"I told you, it's a surprise."

I try to figure out why Deltoch would go through the trouble of arranging something for me. Is this some sort of ploy to get me to exercise more, or is he leading me out into the woods to teach me some new kind of Mogadorian fighting that requires the open air? Is he leading me to Nine? I slip a hand into my pocket and let my fingers close around the metal ball, just in case.

But I discover that it's none of these things as soon as we come to a clearing. Standing in the winter sunlight is the last person I'd ever expect to see here.

Emma.

CHAPTER
FOUR

IT TAKES ME A SECOND TO REALIZE THAT EMMA is actually there and not some sort of hologram or android or something. But it really is her. I can tell because holograms don't leave footprints in the dirt as they shift their weight back and forth nervously on their feet, and androids don't cry.

Emma looks terrified.

I can't really blame her. She probably *should* be scared.

She's grown up a bit in the year or so since I last saw her, when she was swinging a metal pipe at my head the night of the botched job—the night Ethan took me in. When we were running the beaches as small-time crooks, her black hair was always pulled back into a short ponytail, but it's around her shoulders now, hanging messily halfway down her back. She's wearing pink pajama bottoms and a white tank top, which leads me to assume that she was taken in the middle of the night. Someone thought to give her a trench coat like all the Mogs wear, which practically swallows her.

She must not have been expecting to see me, because when I step out of the trees and into view, she freezes, her face twisting in shock.

"C-Cody?" she stammers through shivering lips. I'm not sure if she's shaking because of the cold or something else.

It's been a long time since I went by that name, and it takes a second for my memory to catch up with what she's saying and to realize that she means me.

"Hi, Emma," I murmur.

I don't know what to say or do, or even how to feel—why has this girl been plucked out of Florida and brought up to West Virginia? My first instinct is to go to her, but there's a look in her eyes that stops me. I recognize it as a mixture of confusion and hatred. The same look she had in Miami when she called me a freak. Right before she tried to bash my brains in.

I turn to Deltoch, who is emerging from the trees now. When Emma sees him, she cowers a little and takes a few steps back. Obviously she's had a bad experience with Mogs over the last day or so.

"Good. We *did* find the right girl," he says. "You'd be surprised how difficult she was to track down. After that unfortunate night at the warehouse, she and most of her family practically disappeared."

"What's going on?" I ask.

"Before you are able to begin your new life as a champion of the Mogadorian cause, you'll have to put everything from your past behind you."

I don't say anything. Just turn to Emma and stare at her. She still looks scared, but her hands are clenched in fists at her sides. I know her well enough to guess that right now she's trying to figure out how to escape from this situation. She's a fighter. Hell, the last time I saw her she gave me a concussion.

"How do you even know about her?" I ask.

"Ethan's reports on you have been incredibly thorough, even now," Deltoch says. I must look surprised by this, because he lets out a snort of a laugh. "The two of you may have a close relationship, but the reason that Ethan found you in the first place is thanks to our Beloved Leader's guidance and enthusiasm to recruit you. You would be incorrect if you thought for one moment that your future was given to you by Ethan and not the all-powerful Setrákus Ra. Ethan is your friend because he was ordered to be."

I know Ethan works for the Mogs, but I guess I never really think of him as reporting back to them about me. At least not about nonessential stuff like who I hung out with back in Miami. But I've read the files the Mogs have on Nine, so I guess I shouldn't be surprised.

Still, it somehow seems like a betrayal of trust, and I wish Ethan were here to tell me that it wasn't true. I know he lied to me back when we first met, but that was for my benefit. I guess I'd assumed he wouldn't *still* be reporting on me now that I'm at the base.

The thought pisses me off.

"At the end of the day," Deltoch continues, "Ethan is only human. That's his greatest weakness. The humans don't have our discipline or sense of loyalty. It will do you well to remember that. The humans are here to serve us, but he is holding you back."

"How?"

"He doesn't think you're ready to become an officer."

My mouth drops open a little—Ethan doesn't believe in me? That can't be true.

"Why is she here?" I ask, turning back to Emma. I still don't understand what's going on.

"Please," Emma says, "I just want to go back home. I don't want to be here. I'll give you whatever you want."

"For you to have closure and to focus completely on your future as an officer of Mogadore," Deltoch says with a grin. "Ethan said this girl was the only other person in the world who you had any sort of friendly relationship with."

"I guess so," I say quietly. When he puts it like that, it makes me sound like a total loser.

"Well then, what happened?"

The memories course through my head. A bunch of thugs trapped me in a warehouse on a job for Ethan. The only way out had been using my telekinesis. I'd never used it on other people before, and it felt so good to slam them into shelves and walls after they'd been beating up on me. But Emma had seen—one of the guys had been her *brother*. And she'd turned on me in an instant.

"She called me a freak," I say, staring at Emma in the forest clearing. "She asked me if I was possessed when she saw what I could do."

"Please," Emma says. She just keeps shaking her head, her eyes darting around to the edges of the tree line. She was standing there alone when we came out, but I'm guessing there are Mog soldiers in the woods around us, making sure she doesn't escape.

"She scoffed at your abilities?" Deltoch asks. "Even though you'd been friends?"

"We'd been more than friends," I say, taking a step towards her. "We were partners."

"The humans will fear you when you are unveiled as their leader. You can use that fear and turn it into respect. Some will cower and hide or try to fight you, but the smart ones will bow at your feet. You can't hesitate when it comes to taking action. You have to know when to show mercy and when to be ruthless."

Ruthless? My palms start to sweat as I begin to imagine what Deltoch has brought me out here to do.

"Why did you bring her here?" I ask again.

"She was frightened by just a taste of your abilities. She fought you. Disrespected you. Why don't you show her what *true* power is?"

I stare at Emma. She's shaking, her eyes now fixed on me as her fingers tremble. The Emma I remember from the beach—before things went bad between us—was cool, confident and my partner in crime. I'd wanted her to think I was like her. But now I see her for what she really is. Just a scared girl who has no idea what's happening in the world around her. A pitiful, naive ant. Human. Part of me has always been angry about the shitty things she said and did to me at the warehouse, but I don't know that she deserves to be hurt because of that.

I don't know that I *can* hurt her, as pathetic as she looks.

"She's not worth it," I say as I turn back to Deltoch and start towards him.

"Please!" Emma screams. She must be afraid of what will happen once the only familiar face here disappears. "Just let me go home. I don't want anything to do with you monsters!"

Monsters.

Something in me snaps.

I whip around to her, holding my right arm outstretched. She lets out a short gasp as she rises off the ground. My telekinesis is wrapped around her body, squeezing her tightly. As I raise my hand, she goes farther up.

I rise too until I'm floating just a few yards in front of her. We have to be thirty feet in the air. Her eyes are wide as they stare into mine. She keeps making little gasping noises, even though I'm not squeezing her all that hard. I can barely hear her ragged breaths over the repetition of the word "monsters" in my head.

"If you want to call me a monster, I can *be* a monster," I say.

"No." She shakes her head.

"I could crush you with a single thought," I whisper, and the look of horror on her face makes my blood race and my ears pound. That part of me that has festered with anger and wants revenge for the way she turned her back on me feels so satisfied that I can hardly breathe. It's not just her; it's all the times I've felt weak or lost or like the Loric had forgotten about me or forsaken me. All of it courses through me, fueling me.

I know Nine is supposed to be my symbolic first kill, but maybe Deltoch has taken me out here to see if I really have what it takes. Maybe I *should* squeeze her a little tighter with my Legacy. Or let her drop back to the hard ground below us.

But then another voice joins our little party and interrupts my thoughts.

"Five," Ethan says. "Put her down." He turns to Deltoch and speaks in an angry whisper that's loud enough for me to hear. "No one told me about this. What the hell is going on out here?"

"I'm observing the future of the Mogadorian cause," Deltoch replies.

"Five, come back to the ground."

"You are *not* in charge here." Deltoch's voice is calm but booming. I can see his nostrils flare a little bit. "Do not stand in the way while he proves to us that he is capable of making tough decisions."

"He's not ready for this," Ethan says.

Deltoch turns to me with a smile that says "I told you so."

"I am too," I shout.

"You don't know what you're—"

"Do *not* talk to him as if you have any idea what he is or what he is capable of," Deltoch says. Then he adds a single, damning word: "human."

And for the first time since meeting Deltoch, I'm on his side. Ethan is my friend, but he's never been in my position before. He's the one who tells me I need rest when I know I can keep training and can push myself harder. The one who tells me to act like I'm on top of the food chain and then tries to tell me what to do.

Ethan looks at me, breathless. "Do you really want your first kill to be this worthless girl when it could be Nine?"

I shift my eyes back to Emma, who has tears running down her face. She's staring at me, waiting for my decision. I can see the pleading in her eyes, and even though I don't want to, all I can think of are the good times we had back in Miami. I know that she's not the only one holding her breath. That Deltoch, and Ethan, and the Mogs all around are watching to see how I act. And I suddenly feel like there's so much pressure in my brain that it might explode, because I don't know what I'm supposed to do. I can't disappoint the Mogs. I can't show weakness. Deltoch *obviously* brought me out here to kill this girl.

Unless there's some other way . . .

"Is your brother still a wannabe gangster in Miami?" I ask Emma.

She looks confused.

"Answer me!" I shout, more out of frustration with the situation than with her silence.

"Y-yes," she says. "The rest of us left after what happened, but he stayed."

Both of us descend to the ground. When her feet touch, I release her from my telekinetic grip. She crumples to the earth. I turn my back on her and walk to Deltoch and Ethan.

"Her brother might be of use to us," I say to them. "He was small-time when I was in Miami, but he may have gained some kind of influence—connections we can exploit. We should use her to leverage any information out of him that might be valuable in tracking the Garde, the same way we're using FBI resources. Maybe nothing will come of it, but she's definitely no good to us if she's dead."

"Five . . . ," Ethan starts.

"I've been reading book after book on how wars are fought. Information can be just as powerful as armies. You should take her to the detention wing, Ethan. After all, she knows you. You're part of the reason she's here."

Ethan doesn't say anything, but I can tell he's clenching his jaw. He's not used to me talking to him like this, but I can't help it. My adrenaline is pumping out of control. Taking charge, I feel like a leader.

"If you need to know what happened before you got out here for your reports," I say, lingering on the last word, "I'll be happy to fill you in."   ·

Ethan stares at me for a few seconds as if he's trying to figure out where all this is coming from. Then he throws a spite-filled glance at Deltoch and grabs Emma's arm, dragging her into the woods. She doesn't put up much of a fight.

"A wise decision," Deltoch says.

"Was this some sort of test?" I ask.

"All of life is a test. You of all people should know that."

"Did I pass?" I ask.

Deltoch's lips spread wide.

"With flying colors."

CHAPTER FIVE

A FEW WEEKS GO BY, AND THEN EVERYTHING happens very quickly.

The Mogs track one of the Garde to a place called Paradise, Ohio, but *two* end up being there. At least, that's what survivors of the battle say. Not that many Mogs are left standing after they try to apprehend the two Loric fighters. From what the commanders can gather, one of them was Number Six, who used to be in Mog captivity but managed to escape before I was brought on board. Practically all of our forces are reassigned to track the two across the country, leaving less pressing matters like my history lessons ignored.

Something impossible also happens: I get hurt.

Four is still alive—I know that because there's no new scar on my ankle—but when one of the Mog soldiers I'm sparring with hits my arm with a sword, I get cut. Blood actually runs out of my shoulder, and the soldier is left completely unharmed.

The Loric charm has been broken.

I am vulnerable.

It's a weird thing to suddenly be able to die, or get hurt. To know that there's not another number standing in the way of me and nothingness. It's kind of terrifying at first, but it just reminds me that I've made the right decision. I can't imagine facing the Mog armies without a charm protecting me. The Garde don't stand a chance if they can't be convinced of their idiocy.

Ethan freaks out about my sudden mortality and demands that Deltoch stop any training that involves actual fighting. He says I'm not ready for fieldwork yet—of *course* he does. But Deltoch agrees enough to put my fight training on hold. Instead, I make myself useful by scouring the internet for anything that might be helpful. That's how I stumble onto a website called "Aliens Anonymous," and while it's full of a bunch of stuff that sounds like total bullshit, it also has articles about what went down in Paradise. The posts sound like they're written by someone who knows about the Garde and the Mogs—someone who might have an idea as to where Six and the other Garde ran off to after the battle. So, using a little bit of persuasion, I manage to get in tight with some of the editors and contributors on the blog. They know me as FLYBOY.

There's one idiot who goes by JOLLYROGER182 who

claims to have been involved in the battle in Ohio. He's hesitant to talk about it at first, but when I feed him a made-up story about seeing some guys with black eyes and head tattoos chasing after some sad-looking teenager who ended up flying through the air, he starts to ask me a ton of questions—questions I'll only answer once he tells me what *he* knows. So he spills. He says his former classmate was one of the Garde, a guy named John Smith. But more important, the backwoods ass hat tells me something else: John is Number Four.

When I give this news to Ethan, he says he's sure the Mogs already have someone watching the blog and that I probably shouldn't get in too deep with the editors there in case I accidentally let something slip. I tell him that's ridiculous and that he doesn't know what a good liar I am, and we get into an argument that ends with me going to Deltoch myself and telling him about what I've discovered. I swear it's the first time I've ever seen the Mog look like he's happy with me. He tells me to keep doing what I'm doing—that Setrákus Ra is pleased with me.

After that, I start to see more and more of the Mogs and less of Ethan. I think maybe he's jealous of me, even though I'm really just behaving the way he always said I should act—like I'm a big shot here. Mostly I see him only when he briefs me on how things are going in the Mogs' search for the Garde or at meals. Deltoch takes over my training.

We track Four and Six across the country—from Ohio to Tennessee and then to Florida. Somehow they always stay a step ahead of our forces or end up taking out our scouts. But our big break comes when Four makes a stupid move. He returns to Paradise, where the Mogs are obviously still sniffing around.

And now he's in our custody.

I was kind of hoping Four would be someone I could talk sense into easily, but based on what the Mogs and JOLLYROGER182 tell me, it sounds like he's a total idiot. I mean, you kind of have to be if you go back to the place the Mogs found you to begin with. I'm surprised his mark wasn't burned into my ankle months ago. He might still listen to reason. If so, maybe Setrákus Ra can give him Europe to rule, or Africa or something.

But there's one person who definitely won't be getting his own continent. Things are moving fast here in the compound, including my promotion to commander over the Mog forces. The Loric charm is broken. I don't have to worry about some strange magic hurting me if I try to harm another Garde. Nine's time is up, and our Beloved Leader, Setrákus Ra, is coming to personally oversee me execute him. The thought of finally taking my rightful place as a leader within the Mog forces blacks out practically all hesitation I have about Nine.

When the time comes, I'll just have to remind myself of the files the Mogs had on him and power through it.

I can bleed now. That means Nine can bleed too.

My time has come.

The morning of my ascension, I'm called into one of the Mog science labs. There's apparently been some sort of big discovery they want my help with, and while I'm flattered, I already have a lot on my mind thanks to what's going to happen that night when Nine is dragged into the Great Hall in chains and I take my spot as a commander of the Mog forces.

It doesn't help that they keep me waiting in the lab. As time ticks by, I grow bored, and find a notepad and pen.

I start to draw.

I haven't had a chance to draw stories or anything like I used to in the sand on the beaches since I've been at the Mog base. But now, in the labs, I remember how much I used to like to do this.

I draw Nine. He's held to the ground by heavy chains attached to a collar around his neck. He's frail and weak. I, on the other hand, look like a superhero. I float above him. Nine is so insignificant that I don't even dirty my hands with him. Instead, I have a monster— an attack dog of sorts—that's going to dispatch him. The beast is like nothing that's ever walked on any planet (probably). It's got three lizard-like heads and a furry body, with razor-sharp talons. And wings. It's the most badass hell-beast I can imagine. All of its mouths are wide, and poisoned saliva drips from pointy teeth. Its gnarled arms . . .

"Five," someone says from behind me.

I turn around. I've gotten so caught up in my drawing that I didn't even notice one of the Mog scientists come in. He wears a long black lab coat and white rubber gloves. In his hands is something I recognize. I almost leap off my stool, because I think for a second that someone's been in my room and taken my Loric Chest, but then I realize it's not mine. The gleaming symbol on it doesn't belong to me.

"We recovered this Chest from one of the Loric in Ohio," the scientist says, gently placing it on a workbench. "We thought maybe you might want to try to open it."

"What makes you think I can?" I ask.

The scientist shrugs. "We believe this Chest belongs to Number Four. We're hoping that higher-ranking numbers might have unbridled access to the Chests of those beneath them."

I think of Nine's file and the mentality that he is the most powerful among us because of his number and clench my fists. I know I haven't been great about figuring out how to use things in my own Chest, but the thought of him being able to rifle through *my* stuff makes my pulse pound.

"All right," I say. "Let me try."

I do everything I can think of. The Chest doesn't react to my touch. I pry at it with my telekinesis until I have a splitting headache. Finally, I use my Externa to turn to metal and start banging on the side of the damned thing.

The scientist is not thrilled about this last bit.

"If you *would*, sir," he says, trying very politely to step between my super-strong metal body and the Chest, "maybe we should call it a day. We'll keep the Chest under close watch until after the ceremony tonight, and then you can give it another try later."

I allow my body to revert back to normal.

"Sure," I say. "Is that all?"

The scientist nods. I'm almost out of the lab when he speaks again.

"Sir? You forgot your drawing."

I turn back. He's holding up my doodle—my one-page story. I suddenly feel stupid for having drawn it.

"Keep it," I say. "After today I will have no more need for childish things."

"Hmmm." He stares at the notebook. "Perhaps this can be of some inspiration in my work."

I shrug and then leave.

Ethan meets me in the hallway outside. I'm a little

surprised to see him and wonder how long he's been waiting outside.

"What's up?"

"Just trying to help out the scientists a little," I say. "What are you doing here?" I ask.

He pushes a carefully folded stack of black clothes into my hands.

"I wanted to be the one to give you this," he says.

"What is it?" I ask.

"Your ceremonial uniform," he says. "What you'll wear tonight when you ascend to your new position." He nods at my jeans and T-shirt. "From now on you should start wearing a Mogadorian officer's uniform. It'll remind everyone who sees you of your position."

"There won't be any need for that," I say. "After tonight everyone will know me as their superior regardless of what I wear."

Ethan smirks a little and nods, but there's a sadness in his expression I can't place. Maybe it's just because he doesn't have his usual painted-on grin.

"I wanted to apologize for the whole thing with Emma," Ethan says slowly. "I know I should have done so earlier, but then everything got crazy. I never should have questioned whether or not you're ready for this. Obviously you are."

"Thanks," I say.

He leans in close.

"They never should have brought her here," he whispers.

"Well, at least she's alive."

"Is that what they told you?" he asks, his eyebrows knit together.

"Deltoch said she was sent to another base somewhere closer to Florida," I say. My thoughts start to race. Ethan makes it sound like she's not actually in Florida, so where *would* she be? I shouldn't be concerned with Emma, but I am. And if the Mogs are lying to me about her, then . . .

But Ethan smiles and reassures me.

"I'm sure that's where she is then," he says. "I haven't heard anything myself."

We start the long walk back to my side of the compound, and even though I try to forget about Emma, thoughts of her keep nagging at the back of my mind. I wonder if I should ask Deltoch about her. No, *obviously* I can't. That would show weakness.

But I forget about Emma when we enter the cavernous main hall and I see figures like I've never seen on the base before. Mog women, dressed in long gowns in deep purples and reds. Their heads and faces are heavily tattooed. Most of them have gleaming black braids or ponytails jutting out of their shaved heads. Unlike the soldiers I'm used to seeing, they're thinner and more snakelike in their movements, long arms rippling at their sides as they walk.

There are others who I've never seen before too. Only a few of them. Young-looking Mogs about my age if I had to guess. They're dressed in expensive-looking uniforms that aren't unlike those that the Mog commanders wear.

"Trueborn Mogadorian children," Ethan says, noticing where my eyes are. "And several women from high-ranking families. They've come to see you take your place among the officers."

I smile ear to ear. I can't help it. It feels so incredible to have all of these people here for me. To cheer me on.

I realize that Five is kind of a weird name for the newest Mog leader. It's just so . . . Loric. I wonder if I should go back to one of the other names I used in the past. Bolt. Maybe Cody? I know Cody doesn't *sound* very Mogadorian, but I was him for a long time. That's who I was when Ethan first met me.

As we round the corner to the hallway my study is on, a question comes to my mind that I've never thought to ask before.

"How did you know I was Number Five?" I ask.

"What do you mean?" Ethan's eyebrows scrunch together.

"When I found you in your study talking to Commander Deltoch—before I knew what was going on—you both referred to me as Number Five. But how did you know that's who I was? There were only two dead, and the Mogs had only captured Six and Nine before."

Ethan looks at me as if this is the strangest question I could possibly ask.

"When you first got to the beach house, you used to draw in the sand all of the time," he says in his calm, smooth voice. "Pictures and stories and strange symbols. The tide always washed them away, but I got to see some of them from the house."

Of course. He was probably always keeping an eye on me.

"The only symbol I could ever make out was the numeral five."

I feel stupid. How easily I gave myself away. I'd gotten into the habit of drawing in the sand back on the island with Rey, but I'd always watched as the water destroyed anything I created. I thought I'd been so careful, so *clever*.

So they didn't know what number I was when they first recruited me.

I must look unhappy, because he places a hand on my shoulder.

"Is everything okay, Five?"

I shrug.

"I guess I'm just wondering if the Mogs were

bummed I was a low-ranking number and not, like, Number Eight."

Ethan's face scrunches up.

"Five, we wanted you for *you*, regardless of what number you were. I saw your potential the moment we first met on the beach. I could see the hunger for this in your eyes."

I smile a little. "Thanks, Ethan."

"Is this about Nine? Are you worried that you're not ready to take the next step?"

A couple of Mog soldiers run by us. There must be a fire somewhere that needs to be put out, some prisoner who needs to be taught a lesson or a high-ranking commander who needs an entourage.

"Of course I'm ready," I say.

"Five, listen to me. You have to do this. You have to do whatever it is the Mogs ask of you as long as it means you'll ascend to the highest levels of their ranks on Earth. You're not just doing this for yourself, you know. I'm counting on you to let me live in the beach house again once you're running the planet."

"You should follow your own rules," I say with a smirk. "The way you argued with Deltoch—"

"Was stupid." He grins that grin, ear to ear.

"Let's go then." I say. "I'm ready to do this."

More Mogs run by, and then suddenly the hallways are teeming with soldiers. Some of them are yelling, but I can't make out what they're saying—the noise echoing off the stone walls and floor turns everything into a roar of sound.

"What the hell is going on?" Ethan shouts.

And then there's an explosion somewhere inside the base, and everything goes insane.

CHAPTER
SIX

AT THE END OF THE TUNNEL, A WALL OF FIRE blows past, and I instinctively push against it with my telekinesis to try to keep the flames from engulfing me, Ethan and the Mogs rushing through the hallway. Either I'm successful or the fire was already going to pass us by—whatever the case, we remain unscathed.

The same can't be said for the people in the adjoining hallway.

Has there been a prisoner uprising? Did our Beloved Leader's ship crash into the mountain? Or could this just be some sort of horrific accident?

The steady sound of gunfire from somewhere in the compound counts these last two possibilities out.

We're under attack.

"We should take cover," Ethan says. "We can retreat deeper into the mountain."

I pause. My ceremony has been ruined. Everything

I've been working towards has been crapped on by whatever's happening in the compound right now.

I won't let that happen. This is my chance to show the Mogs what I'm made of. That I really am worthy to lead them. Screw killing a single Garde—I'll take out whatever army is attacking us with a wave of telekinetic power. Setrákus Ra might even see me in action. Hell, I might be able to fight alongside him.

"No," I shout to Ethan over the noise of weapons and yelling and boots hitting the ground. "I'll fight. *You* take cover."

Ethan starts to argue, but I'm already tossing my ceremonial uniform to the ground and running down the corridor, my hand reaching into my right pocket to touch the steel ball bearing. My skin takes on a metallic sheen, and my footfalls get heavier—I could fly, but I don't want to be a floating target for whoever it is that's managed to infiltrate the base.

I'm steps into the next corridor when a wave of hot air hits me, heavy with the scent of char. It's hard to see through all the smoke and ash, but then I realize where that smoke and ash has come from. The Mogs in this hallway must have been completely annihilated. Whoever's attacked us isn't pulling any punches and is obviously trying to inflict as much damage as possible.

I follow the shouts and gunfire as I jog through the tunnels, but the combination of my metal form and my being used to flying everywhere keeps my pace pretty slow. By the time I make it to the vast main room, it's easy to see the route the intruders have taken; there are piles upon piles of ash strewn about the big hall. The space has devolved into utter chaos as the injured cry for help and the monstrous beasts that have escaped from their pens trample Mog soldiers who've been caught completely by surprise. I pause to try to figure out which direction the attackers went, then realize that there's an easier way than trying to follow the ash trails: there are tons of pikens running, crawling, and flying towards one side of the compound, chasing something. So I fall in alongside them, rushing towards the detention cells.

Detention cells. Is this some kind of rescue attempt?

I take a chance and fly up to the corridor that leads to the cells. I think I hear someone shouting my name behind me, but when I look back, it's just a mass of feathers as birdlike creatures flap past me. So I continue on, and there, turning a corner at the end of the detention hallway, is Nine, followed by someone I've seen before. Someone I recognize from Mog reports about the incidents in Paradise.

Number Four.

The two Garde run out of view, and there's a distant rumble of rock cracking and falling. I clench my fists at my sides. Of course they've screwed everything up.

I spent years—*years*—on a deserted island without so much as a hello from any other Loric, but I come to the one place the Loric should be steering clear of—the home base of their sworn enemies—and I meet two of them.

A part of me wonders if they know I'm here. If they know what today meant for me. And if they've ruined all of it on purpose, as one final joke on pitiful Number Five, who they all thought would rot on a beach somewhere.

There's a squad of Mogs reaching the top of the stairs to my right. They run after me as I jet through the hallway, but the path Nine and Four disappeared down is now blocked, collapsed in on itself—no doubt due to Four's or Nine's Legacies. My mind races as I try to remember other ways that the tunnels connect and where we might head them off. Behind me, a dozen or so Mogs from all over the compound regroup. I listen to their conversations as I try to figure out my next move. They've managed to capture one of the intruders. He's a human. A teenager. Reports are that Four is the only other assailant, not counting Nine.

The prisoners.

I turn to the Mogs and immediately start barking orders. This is my time to shine.

"You three," I say, waving to a small huddle of soldiers. "Find any other escaped prisoners. The rest of you, come with me. We're going to cut the intruders off at the pass."

There's hesitancy in their faces.

"Look around you," I continue. "We are under attack, and I am the only person even close to being a commander in sight. If you don't move immediately, you'll be answering to our Beloved Leader for your treason when he arrives."

They all nod to me at once. Several salute.

Ethan approaches from the corridor. He's out of breath but looks pleased with what I'm doing. As the Mogs move out, he tosses me an earpiece communicator, pointing to another one in his ear.

"In case we get separated," he says.

"I thought you were going to take cover."

"Nah." He shakes his head. "I want to see if all that training has paid off."

I grin and then shoot through the air over the heads of the Mog soldiers.

"This way!" I shout. "We can't let these Loric bastards escape!"

A few of the tunnels we go through have partially collapsed from whatever it is Nine and Four are doing, but it's no matter. The adrenaline in my system sends my Legacies into overload. I'm moving boulders left and right and jetting through the tunnels. The Mogs do their best to catch up to me, but I'm moving too quickly for them. I shoot from corridor to corridor, my mind trying desperately to remember, from my downtime spent exploring, how these passageways all fit together, until I come to a fork in the tunnels that I don't remember. Time is of the essence. If we're going to stop Four and Nine, I have to take action.

But I don't know where to go.

My troops start to catch up behind me. I split their ranks down the middle with one hand as I float in front of them.

"Half of you that way, the other half follow me. As fast as you can. They can't be far ahead of us now."

They don't hesitate this time—just charge onward. Ethan follows the other group, again tapping on his earpiece. I know he'll alert me if they come across anything on their side.

And of course, that's what happens a few minutes later.

"We've spotted them," Ethan's voice crackles in my ear. "They're headed for a bridge. We're going to try to cut them down."

"Shit," I mutter. I halt the Mogs who followed me. We race back around, into the other tunnel. The sound of Mog weapons firing bounces off the corridor walls. We're almost to the bridge when I hear Ethan screaming in my ear in a way I've never heard before: primal and full of pain.

I speed forward until I think I may go supersonic. When I fly out into the cavern where the bridge is, it's a madhouse. Half the team I sent has been reduced to ash. The other half is missing limbs or is in other ways wounded by the acidic green lava that pools under the bridge. Nine or Four must have used their powers to somehow turn it into a weapon. I feel stupid for never realizing what powerful offensive capabilities the lava could have when paired with my telekinesis.

But I forget about all of that when I see Ethan. He's staring at his right hand. Or, rather, the place where his right hand should be. Now it's just a stump, charred and cauterized by the green ooze. He looks up at me, one eye wide and full of desperation. The other is hidden by a smoking patch of green gunk. Then his good eye rolls back in his head and his legs give out, and he's falling back, plummeting towards the lake of deadly green sludge below.

"No!" I shout, and before I know what I'm doing, I'm flying after him, diving and catching him right before he hits the surface of the bubbling green lake.

I float back up to the bridge with Ethan's body in my arms. He's still breathing, at least. Maybe he's in shock. The Mogs from my half of the group stare at me, awaiting orders.

"Why are you standing there?" I shout. "Go get them."

And then they're off over the bridge and into the tunnels after Four and Nine. I should be going with them. But I can't leave Ethan behind like this.

I fly us both back through the tunnels the way we came. Towards the central hall, where there's a med lab that's probably swarming with injured Mogs already.

It's in the grand hall that I see him. He's tall—maybe eight feet. It's hard to tell exactly from my place floating above him. The surviving Mogs back away from him, bowing. His hair is short and black. His skin is pale. Something about his face reminds me of a gargoyle— maybe it's the grayish tint to his skin or the way his sharp teeth are bared behind dark, snarling lips. He's got a thick purple scar on his neck. Three pendants shine on his chest.

"Our Beloved Leader," I whisper.

He turns his head, and his eyes bore into me. He raises one hand. There's a crackle of blue across my vision, and then suddenly I'm falling, rapidly. My Legacies aren't working. All I can do is hold on to Ethan and try to position him so that I take the brunt of the fall.

I hear my head bounce off the stone floor the second before everything goes black.

CHAPTER
SEVEN

I WAKE UP IN MY BEDROOM STILL WEARING MY dirty clothes from the attack. There's blood on me, but I don't know who it belonged to. For a second, I think I might have dreamed the whole thing, but one touch to the sore lump on the back of my head proves otherwise. I glance at the clock. It's a little after noon, but I have no idea if I've been out for hours or days. It takes me a few minutes to put my thoughts in order and realize two things: I don't know what happened to Ethan, and Setrákus Ra is here.

Before I can even begin to make sense of it all, a Mog scout enters my room.

"Our Beloved Leader will see you now," he says. I wonder how he knew I'd woken up, but of course there must be cameras somewhere in my room. The Mogs are always watching.

"Ethan," I say. My head aches as I speak, shock

waves radiating from the lump on my skull.

"Our Beloved Leader will explain everything," the Mog says. "But I wouldn't keep him waiting if I were you. He's in Central Command."

I suddenly remember how I got the injury on the back of my head. I fly off the bed and float in the air while at the same time using my telekinesis to clear the top of a dresser in my room.

Well, at least my powers are back. But what did our Beloved Leader do to me that caused me to fall?

I don't waste any more time as I jet through the hallways towards the room where Setrákus Ra awaits. My thoughts are tinged with worry. What exactly happened at the base? Did Nine and Four manage to escape? How is Ethan?

And what of my place in the Mog ranks?

I half expect a gloom of mourning or depression to be cast over the compound because of all the casualties we suffered—they had to be in the hundreds, at least. But it's as though nothing has changed apart from the scorched walls and destroyed doorframes in some of the hallways. My side of the compound doesn't seem to have any cave-ins, at least, though I don't know how the rest of the place fared with Four and Nine ripping through it. The Mogs go about their jobs dutifully, nodding to me or saluting as I pass. Some are fixing the things that were damaged in the assault; others are cleaning up the ash that litters the corners and floors. Sweeping up their dead.

Two soldiers move out of the way as I approach the base's Central Command room. I burst through the doors, and for a moment everyone inside freezes. There are several commanders all standing in front of digital tabletops displaying three-dimensional maps. On huge screens around the room, news reports, security footage and various other videos and images are displayed. Several humans in dark suits stand at the consoles, pointing at files they bring up on the screens. They're comparing photos of Four and Nine escaping to a few candid shots of people in restaurants and gas stations.

And in the center of it all is the single most powerful person in the galaxy. Setrákus Ra, our Beloved Leader and the Mogadorian ruler who will lead his people to continued prosperity. He leans on a gold staff with a black orb in its handle. His sheer physical presence is staggering, but there's something else about him that intimidates me. When he looks at me, it's as if he's assessed my every flaw and has passed judgment on me before I've even said a word. I wish I could tell what his verdict is.

I bow to him. I don't know what else to do.

"It is an honor, my Beloved Leader," I say.

He simply stares at me. Everyone remains quiet as all eyes drift to him, wondering what his response will be.

"Clear the room," he bellows, and before I know it, it's only the two of us and the slight hum of computers and electronics.

He motions to a big chair in the center of the room—one that looks like it's reserved for the person in charge—as he walks towards one of the computer terminals.

"Have a seat," he says.

I do, because his orders are the only ones that matter. Somehow I manage not to ask a thousand questions as I wait for him to speak. He takes his time, studying a monitor with Four's photo on it.

"It feels good, doesn't it?" he finally asks.

"What?" I don't know what he's talking about. All I feel is a pulsing pain in my head and nagging confusion in my mind.

He turns to me and grins, showing off his pointy teeth. His hand waves, and my chair spins a little, turning a full 360 degrees until I face him again.

"Being in the seat of power. It suits you. You look comfortable in it."

I stare at him as a few seconds tick by, trying to soak in what he's just said to me. Our Beloved Leader thinks I look comfortable with power.

"Thank you," I finally manage to say.

There are so many questions shooting through my brain that I don't even know what to ask first. How did the Garde manage to attack us? Where is Ethan? What does this mean for my future? And so I try to ask one question that will encompass all of them.

"What happened?"

Setrákus Ra pauses briefly, allowing a small grimace before he launches into his explanation.

"Number Four," he says, his voice a low rumble. "It appears that he and a human conspirator were able to sneak into this compound. Our best guess after reviewing security footage is that they were able to use a Legacy to make themselves invisible during their infiltration. They stole a few items we had in lockup—slaying several pikens in the process—and then proceeded to slaughter countless Mogadorian soldiers, scouts and trainees as they made their way across the compound to the detention cells. They killed without discretion. Many of our visiting guests were murdered."

I swallow hard as I think of the elegant women and young-looking Mogs I'd seen passing through the main hall before everything went nuts. They were in the compound for the ceremony. *I* was the reason they were here.

"I believe that's where you caught up with the Garde, am I correct? As the prisoners escaped?"

I nod. "I led a small group of Mogs. We tried to stop them."

"And what happened then?"

"The tunnels were blocked, so I chased them through an alternate route. Eventually we had to split up, and the group I wasn't leading found them. By the time I got there, most of that team had been annihilated."

"And?" Setrákus Ra asks.

"Ethan was still alive. He fell. I caught him and brought him back to the main hall. Where I saw you. And you ... ." I shake my head, touching the back of my skull. "I fell. What happened to me? What happened to Ethan?"

"Your Legacies are gifts that can be taken away by those with the power to do so. I blocked your use of them in the chaos because we were unsure of what was happening."

"You can just cancel out my abilities?" I ask. This seems impossible—losing my powers is a nightmare I've never even imagined.

"It is within my ability," Setrákus Ra says. "There's little that is not."

Without my Legacies, I am as normal as a human. Even if I'm not from Earth.

Do the Garde know about this? Did Rey? Or was this some cosmic joke we were all supposed to find out about as we got our asses kicked? I almost laugh at the idea of the Garde, confident in their superpowers, discovering that their enemy can strip them of their abilities with little more than a wave of his hand.

"And Ethan?" I ask again.

Setrákus Ra begins to pace around the room. My chair turns so that I am always facing him. He must be using some kind of telekinetic ability to twist it. I wonder what other powers our Beloved Leader can command. Are there any limits to what he can do? He's conquered planets. My Legacies, while powerful, are probably nothing compared to the scope of his talents.

His pace is slow as he walks. I stay silent. Finally, he stops in front of a computer terminal. He pushes a few buttons, and Ethan's face shows up on one of the screens. Setrákus Ra turns back to me, a scowl on his face.

"Ethan is still alive," he says, and a wave of relief washes over me.

"Good," I say.

"Is it?" Setrákus Ra asks. "Two of the Garde escaped, and Ethan lives. We lost valuable assets, and our enemies gained a powerful weapon in Nine. I don't consider that a victory. Do you?"

I pause. I haven't really processed anything that's happened, or what the repercussions of my actions might be. I know fundamentally that I chose incorrectly when I saved Ethan—I've been around the Mogs long enough to realize that. But this is the first time I've ever had to wonder about how important Ethan's position is to the Mogs. I shake my head. "I'm sorry. I know. It was a dumb thing to do. I might have been able to capture Four and Nine if I'd left Ethan behind."

"So why didn't you?"

I've hardly had time to think about this myself, much less provide any sort of convincing answer to Setrákus Ra.

"I don't know. I mean, Ethan's always been there for me."

"Ethan does what he is told," Setrákus Ra says, leaning on his staff. "I'm sorry you have to hear it like this, but all of Ethan's kindness and mentoring to you stems from me. He was following orders as my proxy when I could not be there with you myself. Do you understand that?"

I nod. He continues.

"Despite being held prisoner on this base, Nine's true identity was known to very few. Mostly only officers and a few of our top scientists."

"How could the Garde have known Nine was here then?" I ask.

"We don't know," Setrákus Ra says. His eyes narrow a little, and his face grows grim. "The most obvious answer would be that someone within the compound told them. Someone who had access to that sort of confidential information."

I start to shake my head immediately. I see what he's getting at.

"It wasn't me," I say. Words start spilling out. "I would never. I know I'm technically one of the Loric, but I've never had any communication with any of the others. I've been trying to help track them down for you! Check my room. Check all the security tapes and electronics I own. There's no way I'd even begin to know *how* to get in touch with them, much less—"

"Relax, Five," he says, and his voice leaves no room for argument or further comment. "I'm not suggesting it was *you*."

He lingers on the last word, staring me down.

"You think it was Ethan," I say.

"The humans are a tricky sort."

"I can ask him," I say. "He'll tell me. Where is he?"

"Would he really be honest with you?" our Beloved Leader asks. "The Mogadorians have never been anything but up front with you, Five. But Ethan deceived you for a year. We wanted to take you in immediately, but he convinced us you weren't ready. That you weren't clever enough to see reason. We've been wanting you to play a more active role in our conquering of this planet, but he has always said you've needed more time."

My thoughts flash back to when I had Emma in the air. Ethan saying, "He's not ready."

I shake my head again.

"But we've seen the security footage from the attack," he says. "I've seen how well you can lead. I *know* you're ready to move forward. I think it's time you were assigned a mission, don't you?"

"Yes," I say without hesitation. "What can I do for you?"

"You know of the krauls that live in the pens here, yes?" Setrákus Ra asks. "Or *lived*, rather. Many of them were killed in the attack, and others still roam in the tunnels of this complex."

"I do."

"When a kraul is injured, do you know what happens to it?"

I shake my head. I've never given much thought to the gross little creatures, other than to make sure that I stay away from them. The tunnels leading to their pens smell awful.

"It's devoured by the rest of the pack. It's a simple evolutionary instinct that's helped keep the species alive through the years. Many Earth creatures do the same sort of thing, both literally and metaphorically. An injured animal in the pack is a vulnerable point, a chink in the armor. This is even truer when it comes to more evolved species. Those who can think and act with intelligence. Those who have information that can be exploited when they are weak."

I try to convince myself that he's not about to propose what I think he's going to propose, but I can't. My Cêpan may have raised me to be a liar, but I'm not *that* good.

"You're going to kill Ethan, aren't you?" I whisper, and after the question comes out, I immediately wish I could take it back, as if by speaking the words I've put this idea in his head. Even though I know this isn't the case.

"I am not," Setrákus Ra says. "You are."

I stop breathing as I try to deal with what he's just said. My fingers tighten on the armrest of the metal chair, and I am made of cold steel—my Externa acting out of control.

It doesn't last long. Setrákus Ra waves his hand at me, and suddenly I'm made of normal flesh again.

His power is terrifying.

"You must show your allegiance to the Mogadorians with an offering of blood. You've known this since your first day among us. That has not changed."

I feel sick, but I try to steady my stomach as best I can with sheer willpower. The last thing I need to do is show weakness in front of him.

"You do want to rise in power, don't you, Five?" he asks.

"Of course I do," I say.

And it's true. I've come too far now. I can't go back to hiding. And now that I've seen the extent of the Mogadorian forces, I know there's no way the Garde stand a chance against them. Nine and Four might have mowed down a lot of our soldiers here, but that's nothing. A speck of the Mogs' power.

"You've been studying the Great Book," my Beloved Leader says. "What does it say about anyone who is suspected of treason?"

"That they must be destroyed," I say reflexively. I try to backpedal. "But I don't think he would have done this."

"Can you say that with one hundred percent certainty? Would you stake your life on it?"

And I realize that I don't know for sure.

"No," I murmur.

"Ethan is a problem for you. He is a weakness that the Garde can exploit. And they *will*. Make no mistake about that. Would you rather have him die nobly at your hands or fall into the clutches of the Garde? Who knows what they might do to him—you've seen what an animal Nine is. Do you really wish that upon Ethan?"

"No, of course not," I say.

My head is a complete mess as I try to process everything Setrákus Ra is saying. It all makes sense. Each reason abides by the things I've been studying—that Ethan himself has been *teaching* me. But I wish there was another way.

I look up at him. He's peering back at me with those judging eyes, as if he knows that a big part of me doesn't want to harm Ethan—my one friend. But then, I don't even know if he *is* my friend. Maybe he has just been working under orders. And if he had anything to do with the attack . . .

"Do you know what I planned to do at the ceremony before the Garde laid waste to so many of our forces?" Setrákus Ra asks.

"You were going to make me an officer," I say.

"In a manner of speaking." His lips spread a little when he sees that this confuses me. "Deltoch offered you North America—your beloved Canada—when you first made the decision to see reason and join us. But I've read the reports on you. I've watched you grow from afar. When this planet falls, I want you to be the one I can count on to rule under my guidance. I was going to name you as my right hand, Five. My disciple."

"You want me to rule alongside you?" I ask. My head spins.

"The moment you carry out this mission, you will become the second most powerful person on this planet. There is no need for a ceremony, only action." He walks closer to me, crossing behind my chair and putting a hand on my shoulder. "Ethan is a liability, Five. He must be dealt with if you are to ascend."

And that's all there is to it, really. I have endless potential. I will rule alongside our Beloved Leader. I'll finally get to go back to Canada, which I liked so much when I was young—only this time I won't have to be afraid. I will be the one who everyone loves and respects. Or fears. But in order for that to be a reality, I have to do one thing. This one small thing.

I have to.

"I agree, my Beloved Leader," I say, but in the back of my head, I'm wondering if I can find another way around this. Like I did with Emma. I just need some time to think.

Setrákus Ra smiles.

"You have forty-eight hours," he says. "Since we were unsure of his true loyalties, we moved him back to the Mog safe house in Miami. You should know where it is—you lived there for a year. We have eyes on the place. You shouldn't meet any outside resistance. If you cannot kill him, you are nothing more than another injured kraul."

It's not hard to get what he's implying. Fail to do this, and I'm the problem. I'll end up in a cell like Nine did. Or worse. They'll kill Ethan, anyway—probably in front of me. Or draw it out, slowly bleeding him dry to show me the error of my ways.

But I am not weak. I am not the problem. I am endless potential and power.

I am the future ruler of this forsaken planet.

And as much as I owe to Ethan, our Beloved Leader has made up his mind. Ethan no longer has a place here. The best thing I can do for him is make sure his death is quick and painless.

"I'll ready a ship for you," Setrákus Ra says. He comes back around to the front of my chair and offers me his hand. I take it, and he pulls me to my feet.

"That's okay," I say. "I can get there on my own."

CHAPTER EIGHT

THERE ARE ALMOST A THOUSAND MILES BETWEEN West Virginia and my destination in Miami. I could take a plane or a ship—I actually can't wait to see what kind of warships and transports the Mogs have that I haven't seen—but I choose to go alone. To fly myself. Partly because I know long-distance flying will be good training for me, and partly because I need to clear my head and focus on the task at hand, and I know that's not something I'll be able to do if other people are around.

Besides, I've been living in the compound with thousands of other people for months now. Always under scrutiny. I could use a little time to myself.

Setrákus Ra agrees to let me go out unaided and doesn't even make me wear any kind of tracking device or communicator. Instead, he wishes me luck and has one of the scientists give me some kind of light suit that fits me like a second skin. I wear it under my clothes in order to fight against the cold air of the high altitude. I'm not sure what exactly is going to happen next, so I shove my Loric Chest in a duffel bag and strap it to my back. I don't want to leave it behind.

And then I'm off.

I stay above the clouds so no one on the ground has the chance to see me and so there aren't bugs constantly smashing into my face. I spot a few airplanes now and then, but I just swerve one way or the other and put some distance between us. Otherwise, it's just me and the sky. And my thoughts.

I have almost a thousand miles to talk myself into killing Ethan. Because, as much of a front as I put up for my Beloved Leader, there is still a big part of me that needs convincing.

The conversation with Setrákus Ra keeps playing over and over again in my head as I constantly try to remind myself that going to Miami is what I have to do—that I can't just take a right turn and head out into the Midwest or up to Canada. I *want* to be the right hand of our leader. I want to rule. I don't want to go back into hiding, where I never feel safe and can't show off my power. Especially now that the charm seems to be broken.

I'm mortal. I can be hurt and killed. Even if I wanted to betray the Mogs, there's no way they'd let me live.

The route I take to Miami is close to the one I took through the Appalachian Trail with Rey when I was just a kid, when his cough started getting bad and we moved down through the states and to the islands. I probably wouldn't have realized this if Ethan hadn't shown me a map of that journey recently. But when I was a kid on those trails, we were moving slowly, and I was scared the whole time that at any moment the Mogs might show up and take me away. It's almost funny looking at it from where I am now, flying like a jet, not from the Mogs but for them.

I think of Rey in earnest for the first time in what seems like weeks. Already that part of my life feels so distant and far away, like it was a weird dream I suddenly woke up from one day. I wonder what he would say if he knew what I was doing. It's not like Rey wasn't a murderer. I think about all the animals he slaughtered for us to eat and survive on when we lived on the island, or even the snakes that he beheaded just to make sure they didn't attack us. And I realize for the first time that Rey killed other things too. People. Mogadorians. When the Mogs came for me in Canada— when I'd hidden in a tree scared out of my mind that the boogeymen Rey always talked about had come to take me away—he killed them. Turned them to ash right in front of me. And I'd never thought about it as being anything bad because he'd always told me they were evil. He killed them without a second thought because he thought they were a threat.

That's sort of what I'm doing, right? Maybe Rey would completely understand the mission I'm on. I wonder if he might even have seen reason if he hadn't gotten sick and had actually sat down and *talked* with the Mogs instead of just blindly follow the Loric orders to destroy them.

I stop somewhere in Georgia to rest and refuel myself with a couple of burgers. The Mogs gave me a fat stack of cash to use in case I needed shelter for the night, but my adrenaline is pumping. So I take to the sky again.

I have to focus.

How am I even going to do what I have to do?

The easiest thing would be to use my telekinesis, I guess. I could just snap Ethan's neck the moment I see him. We wouldn't even have to talk. He'd never see it coming. Or I could send him sailing through the sky and into the sea. Or I could use my Externa and become a walking blade. I realize that there are a million different ways that this could play out—a million different ways to kill—and I wonder how I'm supposed to decide on one perfect end that is humane and painless and honorable. How am I ever supposed to do this?

I wonder if Ethan really was involved in the attack on the base. I don't want to think it's possible, but it could be. And I guess that's all that matters. That tiny sliver of doubt is the kind of thing that has to be eliminated. Just like the rest of Mogadore's enemies. Just like it says in the Great Book.

It's not like this is my decision. Setrákus Ra has determined Ethan's fate. He is going to die whether I kill him or not. If I don't do this, who will? Would they throw him in a cell for a while? Torture him? I don't want him to have to go through that.

I am doing the right thing.

It's almost midnight by the time I reach the beach house, and by that point I'm completely exhausted. The place is just as nice as I remember it. How long ago was it that I first saw it? A year and a half? Two years? I guess I wasn't keeping track of time for a while there. But seeing the house again for the first time in months makes my stomach jump. It's a weird sensation, one I'm not used to.

Something like going home.

I float in the air above the front gate and tell myself that it's not too late. I can turn around and go. But even as I'm thinking this, my shoes are on the ground and my finger is on the doorbell and another voice is in my head, saying, "This is the only way, and when it's done you will rule this place."

A servant answers the door—a maid I don't recall but who must know me because she gasps when she sees me and then disappears inside. There's some kind of commotion in the living room, and then Ethan shuffles out.

He's changed so much in the tiny window of time since I saw him last.

His right arm has been amputated above the elbow and is wrapped in white cotton. He has a bandage on the right side of his face. There's a dark smudge threatening to bleed through from the other side of it. I knew that his eye was bad, but it looks like the green lava must have eaten through half his face. When he sees me and tries to smile, he ends up wincing, and I picture the most grotesque injuries imaginable under all the gauze and cotton.

Do it, I think. *Now is the time. Just get it over with; finish it right here.*

But he speaks. And I can't.

"I know I'm not much to look at," he says.

"I'm just glad you're alive," I say. Even as the words come out of my mouth I know how ridiculous they are, but I can't stop them. It's like my mind has slipped into autopilot and is making me say things that I know a normal person would say. I'm just pretending. Just lying.

"I was worried—I don't really remember much about everything that happened. When I woke up, I was in a Mog helicopter. They'd treated me with something that had counteracted whatever the green stuff did to me, but . . ." He raises what's left of his right arm. "As advanced as their medicine is, the damage had already been done. They told me you were fine, though. That you'd saved me from falling into the green lake."

I nod.

"But the attackers escaped, right?" he asks.

"Yeah. They did."

Ethan laughs a little and shakes his head, even though I don't think anything is actually funny. Then his face gets really serious for a second.

"That's a shame," he says, and his voice is gloomier than I've ever heard it before.

I just nod. He narrows his good eye as he inspects me.

"You've got bug guts on your shoulders, and your hair's all matted down. Don't tell me you flew all the way here."

"It was good training," I said.

"Jesus. Who forced you to do that?"

"No one. I suggested it."

Ethan just nods a little bit.

"You've outgrown all your teachers," he says quietly.

"We're about to start the next phase of my mission," I say. "The endgame is about to begin. I have about forty-eight hours before I'm needed back. Well, less than that now. About a day."

The words keep coming out because part of me

wants to stall. Maybe because I know as soon as I finish my mission, everything will happen very quickly. And as ready as I am to take my place at our Beloved Leader's side, I want to savor my last few hours in the calm before the storm.

Or maybe—more likely—it's because Ethan really is my weakness. And seeing him here in the house where he took me in and trained me is too much, and I can't go through with what I'm supposed to do. Not yet.

"You look tired." Ethan smiles as best he can beneath his bandage. "Your old room is empty. How about we catch up over breakfast. I'm sure there's been a lot going on since the attack. You are staying here, right?"

"Yeah," I say. "Only for one night. I just came to say good-bye."

CHAPTER NINE

EVEN THOUGH I'M OVERWHELMED BY THE NOS-
talgia of being in my old room, I pass out the moment
my head hits the bed, still fully dressed. As good as I
am at flying, it's zapped the energy out of me. But it's
not a restful or deep sleep that I enter. I wake up several times throughout the night in a cold sweat, until
finally, the last time, I say screw it and just get out of
bed completely.

It's dark outside, but there's a hint of light coming up
over the beach. In the bedroom closet, I find a bunch
of my old clothes. I change, slipping on a T-shirt and
oversize light hoodie. I don't want to wake up anyone
else in the house—especially Ethan, who I'd have to
make small talk with—so I open the bedroom window
and slip out. I bring my Chest with me as I float down
to the edge of the water—I need only one thing out of it,
really, but cataloging the Chest's contents always helps

to center me when I need to focus. On the beach, I kick off my shoes and roll up the legs of my pants. There's the slightest chill in the air coming off the ocean. The sand is cold between my toes as I burrow my feet down into it.

It's been too long since I had my feet in sand.

The rising sun feels different in Florida than in West Virginia. Maybe it's just because I've spent so much time underground and haven't really felt it on my skin lately. I plunk my Chest into the beach next to me and open it, rifling through it. I find what I'm looking for inside. Then I let my fingers fall across the other items, until I pull out the file on Nine that Deltoch gave me a while ago. The notes are tattered and falling apart where I've folded them and unfolded them over and over again. I read them to remind myself that though the Mogs recognize me for what I am, the Garde do not. That my future is as a ruler, not as a servant to a bunch of dead old Loric who sent me to Earth with an impossible mission.

I read the pages to psyche myself up. To get my blood flowing and my anger raging. To get ready for what I'm about to do. What I *have* to do. Just this one thing and then the world will be mine. All the power I could possibly want.

Somewhere to my left, seagulls make a racket. Most of my life I wanted off a deserted island. Wanted to be in the action, in the thick of things. In cities. In battles. But sitting here now, for a moment I kind of wish I could disappear and become an anonymous speck on the map again. Not forever, but for a day or two. As much as I hated the island, there was a kind of peace with not having anyone around or anything to do.

But then Ethan shows up and the moment passes.

"Good morning," he says.

"Hey," I answer, pulling the sleeves of my hoodie down over my fingers. "You're up early."

"I wanted to catch the sunrise," he says, staring out across the ocean. "I haven't seen one in a long time. It's more beautiful than I remember."

The bandage on his face looks fresh. The right arm of his crisp white dress shirt is rolled up to the elbow. He notices me looking at it and kind of shrugs.

The wind picks up, and it carries the papers in my hand up the beach. I jump to my feet and chase after them instinctively, until I can focus on the scattered pages and bring them drifting back to my fingers using telekinesis. Even when I have the complete file in my hands again, I keep my back to Ethan. I think of all the things he's done for me over the last year—I can't help it, even though it's the last place I want my mind to go. Helping me understand my Legacies. Training me. Feeding me. He acted like the Cêpan I'd always wanted. Like a friend.

But then, those were his orders.

I hear a click, and when I turn back around, my Chest is closed. Ethan stands over it.

"Didn't want you getting any sand inside on any of those important Loric relics."

I nod.

He grins as much as he can. That tacked-on grin he always has.

I wonder for a minute if there's maybe another way out of this. Maybe I could turn someone else's body over to the Mogs and pretend it was Ethan's. But they'd know, wouldn't they? They're undoubtedly watching now. Besides, where would I get another body?

I have to think of my future. Think of what will happen if I don't do this.

"How do you feel?" he asks. "Excited to be out of the compound for a bit? You're on the threshold of a brand-new life."

"Yeah," I say, trying to muster some feeling into my voice. "I can't wait."

I don't say anything for a little while. I realize that he hasn't asked what I'm going to do now that Nine has escaped and my right of passage has disappeared, or how the Mogs are going to retaliate. He hasn't even asked me anything else about the attack on the compound. Or if I met Setrákus Ra.

"Are you hungry?" he asks.

"Not really."

I think back to the first time we ever spoke alone, over a huge table of food. I stuffed myself full of fancy dishes while he talked all about what a good job I was doing as a small-time crook. He'd told me that I reminded him of his brother, who'd been a thief on the street like me but who hadn't survived. Unlike his brother, though, I had infinite potential and incredible skills. And I'd felt bad for Ethan but also great about myself. About *us*. Like we'd had some inherent bond. So in the same conversation, when he called me "the future," I'd listened.

I realize that the whole story about his past was probably a lie.

"What happened to your brother?" I ask.

"What brother?" Ethan looks puzzled.

And that's all I need to hear. All I need as a reminder of the ways that Ethan has manipulated me, just like Setrákus Ra said. He told me lies from the very beginning to gain my trust and use me. Every word he's ever spoken to me needs to be reexamined and fact-checked.

Ethan is not my friend. He's just some human who wanted to get on the good side of power. He is my weakness. The thing that has to be cut out of me. The insignificant enemy who must be put down so he isn't allowed to fester.

I watch Ethan try to connect the dots in his head.

And suddenly his face falls into a sad smile.

"Oh," he says. And that's all.

I walk over to him, my bare feet sinking into the sand as I trudge along. He's grinning at me now, but it's not the plastered-on smile he usually has. This one is somehow more authentic.

When I'm within a few feet of him, he holds his arms out.

"You're going to be such a good leader," he says. "I'm so proud of you, Five."

I embrace Ethan. His arms fold around me as he pats me on the back. He lets out a long, slow sigh and then starts to say something. I cut him off before he can get the words out. I can't stand to hear him say another thing.

"Ethan, I'm really sorry about this. But it's for the best."

I can feel his body clench as the blade slips out of my forearm sheath and into his back. It slides between his ribs—a lucky shot—then retracts back into my hoodie sleeve. It's over in an instant. I step away from him. He stands frozen, probably in shock. There's a deep spot of red blooming across the right side of his chest where the blade must have broken the skin. Blood drips down from the hidden wrist sheath, running over my right hand before falling from my fingertips to the sand.

"It's over," I murmur, more to myself than to Ethan.

He's probably not paying much attention to what I have to say. Tears are welling in his good eye, but I don't know if they're for me or for himself.

He blinks once and then falls to the beach with a soft thud.

I wish he were a Mog. If he were a Mog, at least his body would turn to ash and disappear.

But this will be the *last* thing I ever wish for. From now on, anything I want, I will have. I will take. Because I've offered the Mogadorians a sacrifice, and now I will rule them. And the humans. This was necessary. It had to be done.

These are the things I think about as I walk into the ocean and wash Ethan's blood off my hands.

Somewhere behind me I hear a helicopter approaching. The Mogs, of course, have been watching my every move.

CHAPTER TEN

I AM NUMBER FIVE: THE RIGHT HAND OF Setrákus Ra.

Commander Deltoch is in the helicopter that lands at the side of the beach house. He's got his normal scowl on, but he salutes me when I approach—something he's never done before. I'm technically his superior now that I've completed my mission. I should feel thrilled about this, but instead I just feel a little numb. It's probably for the best. No one obeys a smiling superior.

I wonder if my expression looks like Deltoch's. I wonder if he had to prove himself in the past too in order to become a commander.

We take the helicopter towards a base in the Everglades that the Mogs have been setting up for me to use at my discretion until I figure out where I want my Central Command to be located. Deltoch tells me that our Beloved Leader would like to have been with us in person but is busy interrogating the human who was captured during Four's infiltration of the base, just in case there is any time-sensitive info that can be gotten out of him. After congratulating me on my ascension, Deltoch presents me with a Mog officer's uniform.

I am officially one of them now.

Over the course of the next few weeks I split my time between briefings on the Mogadorian Expansion and visiting Mog bases in other parts of the country, and in South and Central America. Deltoch accompanies me. It seems that he will be my tail for a while, teaching me how the Mog fleets are commanded and run. Showing me the ropes. At every base, I'm introduced as the highest-ranking officer in the Mogadorian empire, second only to our Beloved Leader himself. I stand onstage in front of thousands of troops who salute me and shout my name—ready to fight for me or defend me or die for me if that's what I ask of them.

I can barely hear myself think over all the cheering. I am power now. Soon, the entire world will know me as its superior.

And the Garde will know me too.

I don't really have any downtime anymore, and when I do, it's usually spent going over the same facts that are already engrained in my brain—I may officially be Setrákus Ra's disciple, but that just means I want to impress him even more. Plus, keeping busy reading files on the Garde and reports from bases around the world means my mind is so preoccupied with strategy and tactics that I don't have time to think about Ethan, or what happened to his body, or the pattern of blood that appeared on the front of his shirt after I stepped away from him on the beach.

I can't allow myself to think of him. I can have no weaknesses.

It's safe to say that Six and Four have been working together. So when our forces in Spain report that Six has attacked them and taken another suspected Garde under her wing, we have to assume it's Seven or Eight. That leaves only one of the Garde unaccounted for, though it's entirely possible that Four and the others have gotten to whoever it is already and have just managed to keep him or her hidden from us. I'm not surprised that they've banded together. That was always a fear—that they would be working as a group without me. I wonder if they've finally made their way down to the Caribbean and found my little shack.

It doesn't matter. I don't have any fears now.

It's not until something happens at one of our bases in the Southwest that Setrákus Ra reveals his plan to me.

It's time I meet my fellow Loric. I'm going to infiltrate their ranks and learn their secrets. Then I'll break up their group so that when the Mogs show up, they'll be weakened and caught by surprise. Whoever is smart will join us and live in paradise. Those dumb enough to turn their backs on reason will die. Divide and conquer. A simple and timeless strategy as evidenced by the books on war I've studied.

The only part of the plan that our Beloved Leader hasn't finalized is how I might get the Garde to split up. But I thought of a great plan on my own. My Chest. It holds powerful items—not that I've figured out how to use most of them. Our Chests are important to the future of Lorien. And so if I say mine is somewhere else and full of all kinds of helpful items—that I had to hide it or risk it being taken from me—I can get a few of the Garde to escort me on a mission to retrieve it.

Maybe I can get Nine to go with me and show him that I am not weaker than he is in any way.

And that's how I find myself floating over the dense vegetation and scummy waters of the Everglades late one night, looking for the perfect secluded place to hide my Chest and bring the Garde. Far enough away that they won't discover the Mog base, but close enough that I can call in reinforcements if necessary. If they turn deaf ears to me when I try to talk sense into them.

I want to take my time and make sure I find a spot that I can locate easily, so I leave my new security detail and spare Mog troops behind. I go alone to bury my Chest.

After circling in the dark for an hour or so, I settle on

a muddy little island that's hidden away but can be easily reached by boat. A single gigantic tree grows in the
center of it. The plant's gnarly roots pop up in various
places around the island and in the shallows around it.
It's a little creepy looking and totally easy to spot from
the air.

I like it.

I land and stretch a little bit before getting to work.
Out of the corner of my eye I see movement. I turn,
outstretching my hand, ready to telekinetically attack
whoever's wandered across me. But it's only an alli-
gator, drifting with its head half submerged in the
water—black eyes staring at me, the intruder.

It occurs to me that this Chest might need a guardian while I'm gone. I wonder if there's a piken I could
have sent to keep it safe. Hell, I hear that the Mog scientists on other bases have been experimenting on
creatures from Earth and Lorien. Maybe they can whip
up some completely new sentry for the place. Maybe I
can design my own creature even.

With a few powerful telekinetic swipes, I've got a
nice big hole in the soft island mud. I open my Chest
to give the contents a final once-over, making a mental
inventory. I keep the blade with me, on my arm, where
it feels like it belongs. Hidden danger completely unde-
tectable from the surface.

And then I see it. Something strange and small

tucked away under all the other items in the Chest. A cream-colored piece of paper folded over into a small rectangle with my name on it. I recognize the handwriting immediately.

Ethan.

The fact that there's something in my Chest that *I* didn't put there doesn't make any sense. There's no way Ethan could have gotten inside of it. The only time he would have been able to was . . .

Out on the beach. The day I killed him. With all the base tours and briefings, I haven't really been through everything inside my Chest since it happened.

I try to put together everything that this means. Ethan's words ring in my head. *They're always watching.* He must have wanted to make sure that I was the only person to see whatever is in the note.

Something else nips at my mind. Ethan had seen me go through my Chest plenty of times before, had helped me to catalog its contents. He surely would have noticed that my wrist sheath was missing the day I killed him. That I was wearing it.

My stomach drops.

I unfold the note and read.

> *Five,*
> *By the time you read this, I'll probably be dead—most likely by your hands. Assuming this*

*is true, I won't embarrass myself by telling you
not to be upset about it. I was living on borrowed
time among the Mogs, anyway. Surely you've
seen what happens to those whose usefulness
runs out. And let's face it—I wasn't really in tip-
top shape anymore. At least by killing me, you've
proved your loyalty, so they won't be tossing you
aside anytime soon. (Please don't think of me
as a martyr. If there'd been any chance of me
escaping the Mogs for good, I'd have done so.)*

*I haven't always been a perfect mentor to
you, but let me leave you with one last lesson:
think for yourself. I know this probably sounds
strange coming from me, but I've got nothing to
lose now. You should question everything the
Mogs tell you. Question everything I've told you.
Everything the Mogs have said to you or given
to you serves one purpose: to keep you fighting
for them. The files on Nine, for instance? I'd be
willing to bet most everything in those notes
came from someone like Deltoch and not Nine's
Cêpan.*

*The best kind of prisoner is one who doesn't
even know he's in prison.*

*Remember that you are powerful and that
your abilities serve only one master: you. I did
everything I could to endure in this world. I*

*hope you do too but end up more successful at it
than me. Survival is everything, Five. Never put
anyone before yourself. Not even Setrákus Ra.*

*Do whatever it takes to stay alive, and regret
nothing.*

Your friend,

Ethan.

P.S. We had a good run, didn't we?

My breathing goes heavy, and I feel like there's a
hole opening up in my chest that shouldn't be there.
Ethan knew. He knew I was going to kill him, and he
let it happen.

I killed my only friend.

I curse him. Because he recruited me, and befriended
me, and made me care about him, and then let me kill
him. Because he's not here anymore to guide me and
probably had nothing to do with the attack on the base
if he sacrificed himself for my ascension. And because
if he'd just told me he knew what was really going on
when I showed up at the beach house, we could have
figured something else out.

I wonder if he was right back in the forest clearing
with Emma when he'd said I wasn't ready for all of this.
For a moment, I question whether I'm ready for my new
place as the right hand of Setrákus Ra.

But there's no other way. My best chance of survival

is with the Mogs. Ethan knew that, and I know that too. There's no way the Garde can fight them. A handful of teenagers versus an army—only a fool would choose to be on their side. And to keep in the Mogs' good graces, I had to kill Ethan. Survival of the fittest.

So why do I feel like my chest is in a vise?

The blade on my arm suddenly feels heavy and constrictive. I rip off the sheath and toss it into the Chest, then throw the whole thing into the ground. Ethan's note goes into my pocket. And then I use my telekinesis to cover everything up, pushing sand into the hole. The act feels so familiar, and then I realize that I've buried things using my Legacy before. Back on the island, when Rey died. Pushing everything down just like I am now. And I think of Rey's final advice. *Do whatever it takes to survive.*

It's strange how similar his words were to Ethan's. Sure, Rey probably meant that I had to survive for Lorien, but the basic principle is the same.

I wonder how I got myself into this situation with two dead guardians. I keep telling myself one thing: *this isn't my fault.* I was just doing what Ethan would have wanted—to survive by pleasing the Mogs. This is *his* fault if it's anyone's.

No, not Ethan's. This is *Nine's* fault. And Four's. If they hadn't shown up when they did, I could have carried out Nine's execution as planned, and none of this would have happened. Nine would be dead and Ethan would be alive and Setrákus Ra would be crowning me as his right hand because I'd killed one of the Loric. But the Garde had to ruin it all for me, and now everything's gone to shit.

The picture of Nine from my study is so burned into my mind that I can envision it clearly, even as I stand sweating over a newly filled hole in the middle of the Everglades. I focus the anger bubbling up inside me on him. He'll pay for what he's forced me to do. Somehow. Someway. The other Garde will hopefully come to their senses, but he won't. And that's just fine with me.

I'll see him dead.

I fish around in my pocket and pull out the metal ball bearing Ethan gave me to practice with. A gift. It's cool in my hand, and I focus on it, trying to turn my brain off as much as I can—to think of anything else in the world other than the fact that I've murdered perhaps the only person who was truly looking out for me. As my body takes on the properties of the ball, I start to calm down a little. My skin gets hard. I'm untouchable. There's something comfortable about turning into steel. Into something cold and unbreakable.

I don't have time to wallow. I don't have time for pity or regret. The next day our plan goes into action.

It starts with a cornfield.

I hover above it. Using my telekinetic powers, I flatten the corn into the shape of my Loric symbol, the one that's engraved on my Chest. I empty two giant gas cans on the pressed-down vegetation. The corn is wet from a recent storm, but that's perfect—it just means that my symbol will burn alone for a while before it ignites the rest of the damp crop.

I take a look around. It's dark out. There's no one here but me and the corn and the farmhouses that will call this fire in as soon as I light it. I slip my hand into the inside pocket of my black Mog uniform and pull out the letter Ethan left for me, along with the folded-up notes about Nine. I can't hold on to the letter. Regardless of its content, carrying around a note that Ethan left behind for me would be a sign of weakness, and I'm not supposed to have any of those. I'm stupid for not having gotten rid of it in the Everglades. Besides, the only way to honor Ethan is to live up to his words. And so I use my telekinetic powers to slip the papers into the gasoline-soaked corn.

Part of me is undeniably sad that Ethan is gone, but I realize that without him around, I have no one to worry about getting hurt. And I promise myself that I won't let someone be my weakness like he was ever again. I won't let anyone get too close to me. Why have friends when I can have troops? I don't *need* anyone.

I am fearless.

From another pocket, I pull out a fancy metal lighter. It sparks and drops through the air, landing beside the notes I've left behind. Suddenly I'm hovering above a flaming testament to my greatness. The sign will be impossible to miss.

I jet through the air and catch up with a ship hovering far above the clouds a few miles away. It's milky white and perfectly round. A small passageway opens on one side as I approach—my entry point.

Inside the ship, I allow myself to relax a little. I pop my knuckles and crack my wrists. I think about my hidden blade, buried with my Chest in the Everglades. I was stupid for getting so emotional yesterday. An idiot. But I won't make that mistake again, unless I want to end up killed. From now on, nothing matters but keeping myself alive, and that means making the Mogs happy.

There's a rumble of thunder from outside as I enter the ship's control bridge. Setrákus Ra stands in front of a giant window flanked by two computer screens that keep refreshing with things written in the Mog alphabet. I'm learning the language, but I'm not nearly good enough to read anything on the screens yet. Our Beloved Leader's eyes are fixed on the fiery symbol that's fading away in the distance as the ship shoots through the sky.

"This is the beginning of the end for the Garde," he says. His voice is low and steady, and there's not a glimmer of doubt in it.

I take my place at his right side.

"Are you worried at all?" he asks. "That you might not be able to blend in among them?"

"No," I say honestly. "I can be an excellent liar when I need to. It'll be simple. I just won't tell them anything true. It'll be like a game I used to play when I was very young. Before the Mogadorians saved me."

"I have no doubt that you'll make an excellent double agent."

He smiles and places a hand on my shoulder.

"They'll be given the same chance I was, yes?" I ask. "I can try to get a feel for who might have the intelligence to join us."

"Of course. You are my right hand, Five. But I have foreseen that another of them will be my left. You will help her come to see reason."

Her?

"What about Nine?" I ask.

Setrákus Ra grins.

"I'll leave that to you when the time comes."

A smile spreads across my face. I wonder what the Garde are doing at this exact moment. What Nine is doing. Are they trying to figure out what the Mogs have planned next? Have they realized yet how powerful their enemies are?

Are you out there looking for me, fellow Loric?

I turn to my Leader and nod.

"I'm ready to meet the rest of my kind."

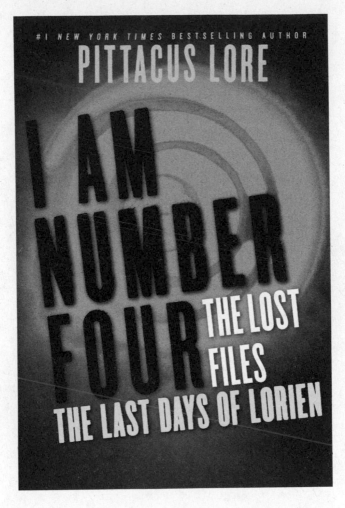

CHAPTER
ONE

THIS IS LORIEN. IT'S "PERFECT" HERE. THAT'S
what they say, at least.

Maybe they're right. Over the years, Lorien's Office
for Interplanetary Exploration has sent recon missions
to pretty much every inhabitable planet out there, and
they all sound terrible.

Take this place called Earth: it's polluted, over-
crowded, too hot and getting hotter every day. The
way the scouts tell it, everyone there is miserable. The
earthlings all spend a lot of time trying to kill each
other over nothing; they spend the rest of their time
trying not to get killed.

Scan through one of their history books—we've got
a bunch of them available in the Great Lorien Information Depository—and you'll see it's all just one pointless
war after another. It's like, *Earthlings, you idiots, get it
together!*

The thing is, other than Lorien, Earth's about the best

place there is out there. I'm not even going to bother mentioning Mogadore. Talk about a dump.

Here on Lorien there's no war. Ever. The weather's always perfect, and there's enough variation in ecosystems that you can find a place with whatever your own version of perfect weather is. Most of the place is pristine forests, perfect beaches, mountains with views you wouldn't believe. Even in the few cities we've got, there's plenty of space to move around and no crime at all.

People don't even argue all that much.

What is there to argue about? The place is perfect, so of course everyone's happy. Like, always. You walk down the street in Capital City and you see everyone smiling like a bunch of happy zombies.

But there's no such thing as perfect, is there? And even if there is, then I have to say: "perfect" is pretty boring.

I hate boring. I always do my best to find the imperfections. That's where the fun usually is.

Although, come to think of it, as far as a lot of people are concerned—my parents chief among them—*I'm* the biggest imperfection of all.

It's positively *un-Loric*.

The Chimæra was packed the night it all finally caught up with me. The music was blaring, the air was full of sweat, and—surprise!—everyone was happy and grinning as they bounced and spun and crashed into each other.

Tonight, I was happy too. I'd been dancing for hours, mostly on my own, but every now and then I'd bump into some girl and we'd end up dancing together for a few minutes, both of us smiling and laughing but not taking any of it too seriously until one of us got caught up in the music and danced away. It was no big deal.

Okay, it was turning out to be a pretty great night.

It was almost dawn before I was out of breath and ready for a break, and after hours of nonstop motion I finally let myself flop up against a bank of columns near the edge of the dance floor. When I looked up, I saw myself standing next to Paxton and Teev. I didn't know them very well, but they were regulars at the Chimæra, and I'd come here enough that we'd been introduced a few times.

"Hey," I said, nodding, not sure if they'd remember me.

"Sandor, my man," Paxton said, thumping me on the shoulder. "Isn't it past your bedtime?"

I should have been annoyed that he was making fun of me, but instead I just felt happy to be recognized. Paxton always thought it was funny that I always found my way into the place even though I was still technically too young.

I didn't see what the big deal about being underage

was—the Chimæra was just a place to dance and listen to music. But on Lorien, rules are rules.

Paxton was only a few years older than me and was a student at Lorien University. His girlfriend, Teev, worked at a fashion boutique in East Crescent. From what I could tell, they both had the kind of lives I wouldn't mind having someday. Hanging out at cafes during the day, dancing at places like the Chimæra all night, and no one giving either of them a hard time about any of it.

I didn't have that long to wait anymore. But it felt like I'd already been waiting forever. I was tired of being a teenager, tired of going to school and obeying my teachers and playing by my parents' rules. Soon I wouldn't have to pretend to be an adult. I would just *be* one, and I'd be able to live my life the way I wanted.

For now, the Chimæra was the one place I could actually be myself. Everyone here was a little like me, actually. They wore crazy clothes, had weird hair; they did their own thing. Even on a planet like Lorien, there are people who don't *quite* fit in. Those people came here.

Sometimes—not often, but sometimes—you'd even catch someone cracking a frown. Not because they were unhappy or anything. Just for fun. Just to see how it felt, I guess.

Teev was looking at me with an amused expression,

and Paxton pointed at the identity band on my wrist. "Aren't those things supposed to be foolproof?" he asked with a smirk. "Every time I see you, you've figured out another way in that front door."

The gates at the Chimæra scan all patrons upon entry, mostly to prevent underage Loriens like me from getting in. In the past, I'd sometimes snuck in a back entrance or shoved through the doors unnoticed with a big crowd. Tonight, though, I'd gone a step further, modifying my ID band's age signature so the machines would think I'm older than I am. I was actually pretty proud of myself, but I wasn't about to give up all my secrets. I just gave Paxton a sly shrug.

"That's me. Sandor, Technological Wizard and Man of Mystery."

"Forget about the door scan, Paxton," Teev said. "What about the Truancy Register at his school? You *do* still go to school, right? You better hurry or you're going to get busted. It's getting late."

"You mean *early*," I corrected her. The sun would be coming up any minute. But she was right. Or, she *would* have been.

Teev had a mole above her lip and a scarlet-colored birthmark high on her cheek, fading back into her hairline. A thin-line tattoo encircled the mole and then curved up into an arrow, pointing at the birthmark. She was shortish and kind of cute and there was something offbeat about her. She was who she was, and she wasn't going to hide it. I admired that about her.

I was tempted to tell her how I'd gotten around the problem of the Truancy Register. It had actually been an easier fix than the door-scan problem—or maybe I was just that good. All I did was borrow my friend Rax's ID band and embed a copy of my own digital bio-signature inside it. Now whenever I cut class, the class register scans me as "present" as long as Rax is there.

I'd figured the trick out after I'd gotten in trouble a few months ago and had been forced to do some time working in the school's front office. There, I'd discovered the flaw in the Truancy Register's system: it doesn't catch redundancies. So when Rax and I both *do* show up, there are no red flags. It's perfect.

"Can't reveal my secrets," I say, giving a little smirk.

"Cool kid," said Paxton, his admiration curdling slightly into contempt. I flushed.

"Thanks," I said, trying to act like I didn't actually care. But before I could think of anything else to say, I froze. Over by the club's entrance, I spotted someone I knew. And not someone I *wanted* to know.

It was Endym, my interplanetary cultures professor at Lorien Academy.

Okay, Endym was generally a pretty cool guy, probably the only teacher I had that I actually liked. But cool or not, if he saw me out at the club, underage and with no hope of making it to school in time, he'd have no choice but to report me.

I grinned at the couple I was talking to. "Teev, Paxton, it's been a pleasure," I said, easing myself out of Endym's line of sight and into a mass of dancing people with a half wave. Under the cover of the crowd, I peered back towards the entrance and saw Endym as he was approached by one of the club's vendors. He took one of the proffered ampules and popped it into his mouth, his eyes scanning the club, and then he stepped forward, onto the dance floor. I was pretty sure he hadn't seen me—yet—but he was heading right in my direction.

Shit. I ducked behind a column to escape his sight.

The Chimæra's a big place, but not big enough. If I stayed where I was, I was going to spend all my time trying to avoid him—and even then, I didn't like my odds that he wouldn't spot me.

I had to get out, and I had to take my opportunity now, while Endym was distracted. He'd just struck up a conversation with a woman in the middle of the dance floor and was flirting with her shamelessly as she danced. I rolled my eyes. The fact that my teacher was at the Chimæra was suddenly making it seem significantly less cool.

The only way out was to go deeper in. I'd never been in the dressing room below the stage, but the performers had to come from somewhere. The only problem was that Endym had somehow positioned himself in the worst possible spot for my purposes: I'd have to go past him to make it to the entrance, but he had a direct line of sight to the back stairwell, too.

I cast around the place, trying not to attract attention by seeming frantic, hoping I'd find a solution to my dilemma. Then I realized it as I spotted them, still standing a few paces away: Teev and Paxton. They would help me. At least, I hoped they would.

"What would you say," I said, sidling back over to them with my conspiratorial smile plastered across my face, "if I told you the guy over there is a teacher of mine?"

The couple glanced over at Endym, then back at me.

"I guess I'd say this place is going significantly downhill," Teev said. "They're letting *teachers* in now?"

"Bad luck, dude." Paxton laughed. "All that trouble to get in here and now you're going to get busted."

"Come on man. Don't laugh. How about helping me out?" When they just looked at each other skeptically, I gave a sheepish shrug. "Please?"

Teev tossed her hair and rolled her eyes amiably. "Okay. You got it, little dude," she said, patting my face. It was kind of humiliating, but what could I do? "We'll take care of you," she promised. "Get your ass out of here."

I watched for a second as Teev and Paxton approached Endym and the woman he was dancing with and inserted themselves between the dancing pair. Teev danced off with Endym; Paxton danced off with Endym's partner.

When I was sure they'd reeled Endym in, I took my chance. I slid through the crowd, keeping my head low to avoid being seen.

I was almost home free when someone shouted at me. "Hey!" I looked back, startled, to see an angry face and a guy shoving toward me. I had accidentally knocked the guy's ampule to the floor as I'd pushed past him, and he wasn't happy.

The last thing I needed was to be caught in a fight on the dance floor. I picked up speed and ran for the edge of the stage, where I groped the dark corner and found a small door.

Of course it was locked.

"Hey! You!" shouted the guy whose drink I'd spilled. He was getting closer. "You're gonna replace that!"

I jiggled the handle furiously. When it didn't budge, I gave up on trying to be cool and began throwing myself against the door, hoping that with enough force—and a little luck—it might give.

The dude was getting closer, still shouting. What a

jerk—making this kind of scene over one spilled drink? All over the room, heads were turning toward me. I'd be caught any minute.

One last try. With all of my force I threw myself against the small door.

This time, it gave.

CHAPTER TWO

THE FORCE OF MY WEIGHT SENT ME TUMBLING blindly into the room on the other side of the door. I tripped across the floor, crashing through layers and layers of fabric. I tripped and fell, my head hitting the ground with a snap.

Then I heard a voice. A *girl's* voice. "Now *that's* funny."

As I lay there, I realized that what I'd crashed into was a rack of clothes. Women's clothes. Now I was lying in a heap of them on the floor. I looked like I'd gotten caught in an explosion of rhinestones and sequins.

Standing above me, a guy in black metallic pants and a collarless shirt was struggling to lock the door I'd just busted through.

"Yeah, funny," he was saying sarcastically. "I love it when underage pipsqueaks come barging into the dressing room."

I stood up sheepishly and tried to gather up the pile of dresses I had knocked loose. This really was not how I'd imagined my night going.

"So. So. *Funny.*" I spun around to see a girl with electric-white hair sitting on a low stool in the corner of the room. She was wearing a tiny pair of shorts and was in a crouching position. She was drawing on herself with some kind of makeup pen, marking her bare calves with an elaborate pattern of swirls and curlicues.

"No," I said.

I probably should have apologized. Or at least explained myself. But I couldn't. I was too starstruck. All I could say was *no*.

"Oh, *yes*," she said, still drawing on her leg. She leaned down closer to the serpentine markings, pursed her lips, and blew up and down her calf, drying the ink.

It couldn't be. But it *was*.

It was Devektra.

Most people on Lorien probably would have had no idea who she was. But I'm not most people, and I'd been listening to Devektra's music for months. For people in the know, she was *the* most buzzed about Garde performer on Lorien. With her striking beauty, her wise-beyond-her-years lyrics—because she was practically a kid herself, only a little bit older than me—and her unusual Garde legacy of creating dazzling, hypnotic light displays during her performances, it was all but certain she was going to be a huge star before long. She was already well on her way.

"What, you've never seen a girl putting makeup on her legs before?" she said with a twinkle in her eye.

I tried to regain my composure. "You must be the top-secret performer," I finally managed to say, stumbling over practically every word. "I'm, um, a big fan." I cringed as I said it. I sounded like a total loser.

Devektra appraised her legs, then stood up and looked at me like she didn't know whether to be angry or to laugh. In the end, she split the difference. "Thanks," she said. "But you know, they lock those doors for a reason—to keep big fans *out*."

Stepping forward, she threw her arms theatrically around my shoulders and pulled my ear right up next to her mouth. "You gonna tell me what you're doing in my dressing room?" she whispered. "I don't need to call security, do I?"

"Um," I stuttered. "Well, see, it's like this . . ." I searched my brain for an explanation and couldn't think of one. I guess I'm a lot better at hacking software than I am at talking to girls. Especially hot, famous ones.

Devektra stepped back and looked me up and down with a mischievous twinkle in her eye. "You know what I think, Mirkl?" she asked.

"What?" the guy I'd practically forgotten about asked in a bored voice. Honestly, he sounded like he was kind of sick of Devektra.

"*I think*," she said slowly, "that this little fellow's *way* too young to be here. It looks to *me* like he was about to get kicked out for being underage and snuck in here looking for a place to hide. We've got a lawbreaker on our hands. And you know how I feel about lawbreakers . . ."

I looked at the floor. Now I was *definitely* busted. This wouldn't be the first time I was in trouble for something like this. Or the second. This time, though, the consequences would definitely be serious.

But Devektra surprised me.

A grin spread across her face and she began to giggle. This girl was sort of crazy, I was starting to suspect. "I love it!" she said. She narrowed her eyes and wagged a scolding finger at me. Her nails were glittering in every color of the rainbow. "Such a naughty little Cêpan."

For the second time in just a few seconds, she'd caught me by surprise. "How do you know I'm a Cêpan?" I asked.

Like the majority of public figures on Lorien—athletes, performers, soldiers—Devektra was a Garde. I was a Cêpan. An elect group of Cêpans were mentor Cêpans, educators of the Garde, but most of us were bureaucrats, teachers, businesspeople, shopkeepers, farmers. I wasn't sure which kind I'd turn out to be after school was finished, but I didn't think any of my choices seemed too great. Why couldn't I have been born a Garde and get to do something actually *fun* with my time?

Devektra smirked. "My third Legacy. The dull one I don't like to mention. I can *always* tell the difference between Garde and Cêpan."

Like all Garde, Devektra had the power of telekinesis. She also had the ability to bend and manipulate light and sound waves, skills she used in her performances and which had made her the rising star she was. That was a pretty rare power already, but the third Legacy that she'd just mentioned, to be able to sense the difference between Garde and Cêpans, was one I'd never heard of at all.

For some reason, I felt self-conscious. I don't really know why—there's nothing wrong with being a Cêpan, and although I'd often thought it seemed like a lot more *fun* to be a Garde, I'd never felt insecure about who I was before.

For one thing, I'm not usually a very insecure person. For another thing, that's just not how it works around here. Though Garde are revered as a collective—a "treasured gift" to our planet—there was a widespread conviction, shared by Garde and Cêpan alike, that the

Garde's amazing abilities belonged not to them alone, but to *all* of us.

But standing there, faced with the most beautiful girl I'd ever seen, a girl who was about to go onstage and demonstrate her amazing talents for everyone at the Chimæra, I suddenly felt so *ordinary*. And she could see it. She was Devektra, *the* Devektra, and I was just some stupid, underage Cêpan with nothing going for him. I didn't even know why she was bothering with me.

I turned to go. This was pointless. But Devektra caught me by the elbow.

"Oh, cheer up," she said. "I don't care if you're a Cêpan. Anyway, I'm just kidding, thank the Elders. What a boring third Legacy *that* would be. My *real* third Legacy is much more exciting."

"What is it?" I asked suspiciously. I was starting to feel like Devektra was messing with my head.

Her eyes glittered. "Isn't it obvious? I make men fall in love with me."

This time, I knew she was pulling my leg. I blushed, suddenly realizing the truth. "You read minds," I said.

Devektra smiled, impressed, as she leaned back against Mirkl, who looked less than amused. "Mirkl," she said. "I think he's starting to get it."

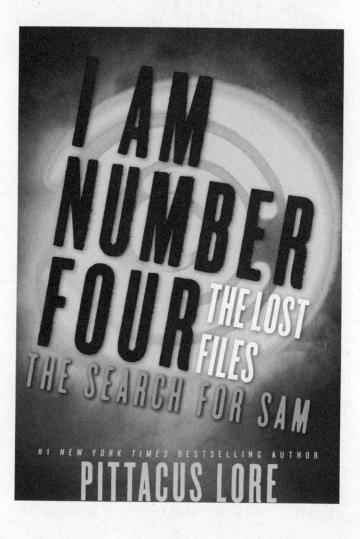

CHAPTER
ONE

I DON'T KNOW IF I CAN.

I'm too weak to speak, so I don't say it out loud. I merely think it. But One can hear me. She can always hear me.

"You *have* to," she says. "You have to wake up. You have to fight."

I'm at the bottom of a ravine, my legs twisted beneath me, a boulder pushed uncomfortably between my shoulder blades. A stream laps against my thigh. I can't see anything because my eyes are closed, and I can't open my eyes because I don't have the strength.

But to be honest, I don't want to open my eyes. I want to give up, to let go.

Opening my eyes means facing the truth.

It means realizing that I have been washed onto a dry riverbank. That the wet I feel on my legs is no river.

It's blood, from a compound fracture of my right leg, the bone now jutting out of my shin.

It means knowing that I've been left for dead by my own father, some seven thousand miles from home. That the closest thing I have to a brother, Ivanick, is the one who nearly killed me, pushing me brutally off the edge of the steep ravine.

It means facing the fact that I am a Mogadorian, a member of an alien race bent on the extermination of the Loric people and the eventual domination of Earth.

I clench my eyes shut, desperately trying to hide from the truth.

With my eyes still closed, I can drift off to a sweeter place: a California beach, my bare feet digging into the sand. One sits beside me, looking at me with a smile. This is One's memory of California, a place I've never been. But we've shared the memory for so long during that three-year twilight that it feels as much mine as hers.

"I could stay here all day," I say, the sun warm on my skin.

She looks at me with a soft smile, like she couldn't agree more. But when she opens her mouth to speak, her words don't match her expression: they're harsh, stern, commanding.

"You can't stay," she says. "You have to get up. *Now.*"

My eyes open. I'm in my bed in the volunteers' sleeping quarters at the aid camp. One stands at the end of the bed.

As in my dream, she's smiling, but now it isn't a sweet smile. It's a teasing smirk.

"God," she says, rolling her eyes. "You sleep a lot."

I laugh, sitting up in bed. I *do* sleep a lot lately. It's been seven weeks since I pulled myself out of the ravine and other than some residual weakness in my right leg, I've made a full recovery. But my sleep schedule hasn't adjusted: I'm still sleeping ten hours a night.

I look around the hut and see that all the other beds are empty. My fellow aid-workers have already risen for morning chores. I get to my feet, wobbling briefly on my right leg. One smirks again at my clumsiness.

Ignoring her, I slip into my sandals, throw on a shirt, and exit the hut.

Outside, the sun and humidity hit me like a wall. I'm still sticky from sleep and I'd kill for a shower, but Marco and the other workers are already elbow-deep in morning chores. I missed my chance.

The first hour of the day is devoted to housekeeping around camp: cooking breakfast, doing laundry, cleaning dishes. After that, a jeep will pick some of us up and take us deeper into the village. We're currently working on a water project there, modernizing the town's antiquated well. The others will stay behind in the classroom next to camp, teaching the village children. I've been trying to learn Swahili, but I've got a ways to go before I'll be ready to teach.

I bust my ass at the camp. It gives me great pleasure to help the villagers. But mostly I work as hard as I do out of gratitude.

After dragging my busted body out of the ravine and a quarter mile through the jungle, I was eventually discovered by an elderly villager. She mistook me for an aid-worker, my cover while tracking down Hannu, Number Three. She went to the camp and returned an hour later with Marco and a visiting doctor. I was brought back to camp on a makeshift stretcher; the doctor reset my leg, stitched it up, and put me in a cast I've only recently shed.

Marco gave me a place here, first to recover and now to volunteer, without asking any questions. All he expects in return is that I do my chores and that I fulfill the same labor requirements as the other aid-workers.

I have no idea what story he's constructed in his head to account for my condition. I can only figure that Marco must have guessed correctly that Ivan was the one who did this to me, based on the fact that Ivan disappeared on the day of my accident without a word to anybody at camp. Perhaps Marco's generosity is motivated by pity. He may not know exactly what happened, but he knows I was forsaken by family. And since Marco is more or less right, I don't mind him pitying me.

Besides, the funny thing about being forsaken by my family, by my entire race?

I've never been happier.

Renovating the village's well is sweaty, tedious work, but I have an advantage the other workers don't. I have One. I talk to her throughout my work, and though my muscles get sore and my back aches, the hours fly.

Mostly, she motivates me by teasing me. "You're doing that wrong." "You call *that* trowelling?" "If I had a body, I'd be done with that by now." She mocks my efforts, reclining like a sunbathing lady of leisure at the edge of the work site.

You wanna try this? I bark back in my mind.

"Couldn't," she'll say. "Don't want to break a nail."

Of course I have to be careful not to actually *speak* to her while I work, not in front of the others. I'd developed a reputation as a bit of a weirdo, for talking to myself in my first few weeks here. Then I learned to silence my side of the conversation with One, to merely think *at* her, instead of actually speaking. Thankfully my reputation has recovered, and the others no longer look at me like I might be a total lunatic.

That night I have kitchen duty with Elswit, the camp's most recent addition. We cook *githeri*, a simple dish of corn and beans. Elswit shucks and scrapes the cobs of corn while I soak and rinse the beans.

I like Elswit. He asks a lot of questions about where I come from and what brought me here, questions I know better than to answer with the truth. Fortunately he doesn't seem to mind that my replies are either vague or nonexistent. He's a big talker, always racing ahead to the next question without noticing my silence, always interjecting tidbits about his own life and upbringing instead. From what I've gathered, he's the son of a very wealthy American banker, a man who does not approve of Elswit's humanitarian pursuits.

Living up to my father's standards was difficult enough when I was a child, but after my experiences in One's mind, it became impossible. I had grown soft, had developed sympathies and concerns that I knew would be impossible for my father to understand, let alone tolerate. Elswit and I have a certain amount in common. We're both disappointments to our fathers.

But I quickly realized the similarities between us don't stretch that far. Despite Elswit's claims of "estrangement" from his family, he's still in touch with his wealthy parents, and still has unlimited access to their wealth. Apparently his father has even arranged for a private plane to pick him up in Nairobi in a few weeks just so Elswit can be back home for his birthday. Meanwhile my dad thinks I'm dead and I can only guess he's happy about it.

After dinner I have a well-earned shower and get into bed. One's curled up in a rattan chair in the corner. "Bed? *Already?*" she teases.

I give the room a once-over. No one's around, so it's safe to talk out loud, as long as I keep my voice down. Talking out loud feels more natural than communicating silently.

"I want to get up with the others from here on out."

One shoots me a look.

"What? My cast's off, my limp's almost gone . . . I'm recovered. It's time for me to pull equal weight around here."

One frowns and picks at her shirt. Of course I know what's bothering her.

Her people are out there, earmarked for extinction by my race. And here she is, stuck in Kenya. Moreover, she's stuck inside my consciousness, disembodied, with no will or agency of her own. If she had her wish, I know she'd be somewhere else—*anywhere* else—taking up the fight.

"How long are we going to stay here?" she asks, somberly.

I play dumb, pretending I don't know how she feels,

and shrug as I pull up the covers and turn over on my side. "I don't have anywhere else to be."

I'm dreaming.

It's the night I tried to save Hannu. I'm running from the aid camp into the jungle, towards Hannu's hut, desperate to get there before Ivan and my father do. I know how this ends—Hannu killed, me left for dead—but in this dream all of the naïve urgency of that night comes back to me, propelling me forward through the vines and brush, the shadows, the animal sounds.

The communicator I swiped from the hut crackles at my hip, an ominous sound. I know the other Mogadorians are closing in.

I have to get there first. I *have* to.

I arrive at a clearing in the jungle. The hut where Hannu and his Cêpan lived stands right where I remembered it. My eyes struggle to adjust to the darkness.

Then I see the difference.

The hut and the clearing itself are completely overgrown with vines and foliage. Half of the hut's façade has been blown out, and the roof sags heavily over the missing section of wall. The obstacle course at the edge of the grounds that Hannu must have used for training is so overgrown I can barely tell what it is anymore.

"I'm sorry," comes a voice from the jungle.

I whip around. "Who's there?"

One emerges from the trees.

"You're sorry for what?" I'm confused, out of breath. And my feet hurt from running.

That's when it clicks. "I'm not dreaming," I say.

One shakes her head. "Nope."

"You took over." The words escape my lips before I even understand what I'm saying. But I can tell from her face I'm right: she took over my consciousness while I slept, leading me out here to the site of Hannu's death. She's never done this before. I had no idea she even *could* do this. But her being is so intimately enmeshed with my own at this point, I shouldn't be surprised. "You hijacked me."

"I'm sorry, Adam," she says. "But I needed you to come here, to remind you . . ."

"Well, it didn't work!" I'm confused, angered by One's manipulation of my will.

But as soon as I say it, I know it's a lie. It *did* work.

My adrenaline's up, my heart is racing, and I feel it: the crushing importance of what I tried and failed to do months ago. The threat my people still pose to the Garde and to the rest of the world.

They must be stopped.

I turn away, so One can't see the doubt on my face. But we share a mind. There's no hiding from her.

"I know you feel it too," she says.

She's right, but I push it away, that nagging sense

that I have a calling I'm ignoring out here in Kenya. Things were just starting to get good again. I like my life in Kenya, I like that I'm making a difference, and until One dragged me out here to rub my nose in the site of Hannu's murder, it had gotten easy for me to forget about the coming war.

I shake my head. "I'm doing good work, One. I'm helping people."

"Yeah," she says. "What about doing *great*? You could be helping the Garde to save the planet! Besides, do you really think the Mogadorians will spare this place when their ultimate plan takes form? Don't you realize that any work you do in the village is just building on quicksand unless you join the fight to stop your people?"

Sensing that she's getting through to me, she steps closer. "Adam, you could be so much more."

"I'm not a hero!" I cry, my voice catching in my throat. "I'm a weakling. A defector!"

"Adam," she begs, her voice catching now too. "You know I like to tease you, and I'd really hate for you to get a big head or something. But you are one in a million. One in *ten* million. You are the only Mogadorian who has ever defied Mogadorian authority. You have no idea how special you are, how useful to the cause you could be!"

All I've ever wanted is for One to see me as special,

as a hero. I wish I could believe her now. But I know she's wrong. .

"No. The only thing that's special about me is you. If Dr. Anu hadn't hooked me up to your brain, if I hadn't spent three years living inside your memories . . . I'd have been the one who killed Hannu. And I'd probably have been proud of it."

I see One flinch.

Good, I think. I'm getting through to her.

"You were a member of the Garde. You had powers," I say. "I'm just a skinny, powerless ex-Mogadorian. The best I can do is survive. I'm sorry."

I turn around and begin my long walk back to camp.

One doesn't follow.

CHAPTER
TWO

DESPITE MY EXHAUSTING MIDDLE-OF-THE-NIGHT run to Hannu's hut, I manage to wake up with the other aid-workers the following morning.

"Look at you, getting up early," jokes Elswit. "Sure you want to cut into your beauty sleep?"

I almost retaliate by teasing Elswit, calling him the prince like the other workers sometimes do. He earned the nickname when he arrived here with a bunch of expensive nonessentials, none more ridiculous than a luxurious pair of shiny silk pajamas. Nobody makes fun of him to his face, though: he also brought a top-of-the-line laptop with high-tech global wireless, a device he lets us all use and that no one wants to jeopardize their access to.

As I get dressed, I notice that One is nowhere to be seen. She's usually up before I am, hanging around. I figure she's sulking from our fight in the jungle.

That, or she's just disappeared for a while. She does that sometimes. Once I asked her about it. "Where do you go when you're not here?" She gave me a cryptic look. "Nowhere" was all she said.

We step outside to begin our chores, only to find a light rain is starting. It's good for the village, but it means the water project will be suspended for the day: the soil is too difficult to work with when it's raining. So after our chores, me, Marco, and Elswit are free to loaf around, and to read or write letters.

I ask Elswit if I can have an hour with his computer. He's quick to say yes. Elswit might be a spoiled prince, but he's a generous one.

I take the laptop to the hut and begin poking around on news sites. When I get time with Elswit's laptop, I always research possible Loric or Mogadorian activities. I may have removed myself from the battle, but I'm still curious about the fate of the Garde.

It's a slow news day. I double-check to make sure that I'm alone, then open up a program I've created and installed on Elswit's laptop. I've hacked into the wireless signals from Ashwood Estates, my former home, and created a shadow directory that caches Ashwood IM and email chatter.

I wish I could claim I was motivated by some heroic agenda. But the truth is my motive is so pathetic I'd rather die than discuss it with One: I just want to find out if my family misses me.

My family. They think I'm dead. The truth is, they're probably happy about it.

I spent most of my life on earth in a gated community in Virginia called Ashwood Estates, where trueborn Mogadorians live in normal suburban houses, wearing normal American clothes, living under normal American names, hiding in plain sight. But below the granite countertops and walk-in closets and faux-marble flooring, unseen by the mortals of earth, spreads a massive network of laboratories and training facilities where trueborns and vatborn Mogs work and plot together to bring about the destruction and subjugation of the entire universe.

As the son of the legendary Mogadorian warrior Andrakkus Sutekh, I was expected to be a faithful soldier in this shadowy war. I was enlisted as a subject in an experiment to extract the memories of the first fallen Loric, the girl known as One. The plan was to use the information from those memories against her people, to help us track and exterminate the rest of her kind.

The mind-transfer experiment worked only too well: I spent three years in a coma, locked inside the memories of the dead Loric, living through her happiest and most painful moments as if they were my own.

Eventually I woke from the coma. But I came back to

my Mogadorian life different, with an abiding distaste for bloodshed, a queasy but consuming sympathy for the hunted Loric, and with the ghost of One as my constant companion.

In the first of my betrayals, I lied to my people, claiming the experiment had failed and that I had no memory of my encounter with One's consciousness. I tried to change back, to be a normal, bloodthirsty Mogadorian. But with One always around me, whether as a voice in my head or a vision at my side, it became impossible to assist my people in their attacks on the Loric.

As if led by some inexorable force, I became a traitor, working against my people's efforts. I attempted to save the third Loric marked for death.

This Loric died anyway, gleefully murdered by my father right before my eyes. Despite my pathetic efforts, I failed to save him. Exposed as a traitor, I was thrown from a ravine by Ivanick, and left for dead.

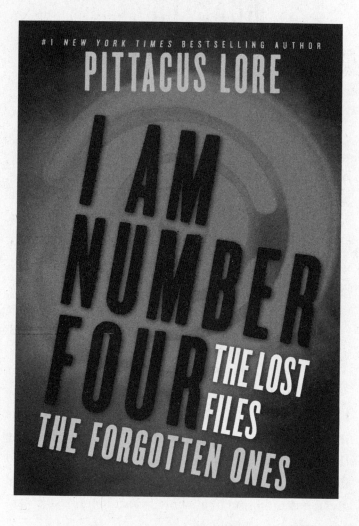

CHAPTER
ONE

MY EYES FLY OPEN, BUT I DON'T SEE ANYTHING.
Just darkness. My lungs feel weak and heavy, like they're
coated in a thick layer of grime, and when I cough, a
cloud of dust swirls around me, making me cough more
until I'm about to hack up a lung. My head is throbbing,
foggy and immobile. My arms are pinned to my sides.

Where am I?

As the dust settles, my coughing finally subsides
and I begin to remember.

New Mexico. Dulce. Wait—did all that really happen?

I want to believe it was all just a dream. But by now
I know enough to realize that there's no such thing as
just a dream anyway. And this was no dream. I was
the one who brought this place down. Without even
knowing how I did it, I took the power that One had
given me and brought a whole government base crashing down to its foundations.

Next time I pull a stunt like that, I'll wait till I'm not *in* the place before I tear it apart. It made sense at the time. I guess I have some things to learn about having a Legacy.

Now everything around me is silent. I'll take that as a good sign. It means that nobody's trying to kill me anymore. Which means that they're either just as buried as I am, or they're dead. For now, I'm alone. One is dead. Malcolm and Sam are gone—they probably think I'm dead too. As for my family, they'd prefer it if I *was* dead.

No one would even know if I gave up here, right now, and there's part of me that wants to. I've fought so hard. Isn't it enough that I came this far?

It would be so easy just to stop struggling here, to stay buried. To stay forgotten.

If One were still here, she would toss her hair impatiently and tell me to snap out of it, to get over myself. She'd tell me that I'm not even halfway finished with the job she left me with and that there are bigger things to worry about than myself. She'd remind me that it's not just my life that hangs in the balance.

But One isn't here anymore, and so it's up to me to tell myself those things.

I'm alive. That in itself is amazing. I'd triggered the explosives in the armory with the full knowledge that it might be the last thing I did. I'd done it so Malcolm

Goode, the man who'd started to feel like some kind of dad to me, could escape with his real son, Sam. I figured that if they got away, at least I would have died doing one good thing.

But I didn't die. For now, at least. And I figure that if I'm still alive despite everything, there has to be a reason for it. There's still something I need to do.

So I try to slow my racing heart, breathe steadily, and assess the situation. I'm buried, yes. But there's air here, and I can move my head, my shoulders, even my arms a little. Good. My breathing stirs up more dust and that shows me which way is up, and also that there's a little light seeping in from somewhere. And if there's any light at all, it means I can't be too far from the surface.

There's no room for me to move my arms, but I struggle anyway, trying to push against the shattered stone and concrete I'm trapped under. It doesn't do any good, of course. I'm not a vatborn with genetically enhanced strength or even a natural powerhouse like my adoptive brother, Ivan. I'm tall but slight and built like a regular human, with only moderately more physical ability. I'm not even sure if the most highly trained of the vatborn would be able to dig his way out of here; there's no way *I* have any shot at all.

But then One's face enters my mind again—her wry, affectionate eye roll, the way she would look at me like,

Really? That's all you've got? And something occurs to me. It's *not* all I've got. Not anymore. I may not have strength, but I *do* have power.

I focus on the rocks around me, knowing that, with my Legacy—the Legacy that One gave me—I can shake all this debris clear. I close my eyes and focus on it, picturing the rubble shaking and splitting, moving away from me until I'm free.

Nothing happens. It doesn't budge. *Move, dammit,* I think, and then I realize that I've actually said the words aloud without meaning to. Either way, the rocks don't pay any attention.

Suddenly I'm angry. First I'm angry at myself: for being so stupid, for being so weak, for not having mastered the gift that One gave me. For getting myself to this place at all.

But it isn't my fault. I was only trying to do what was right. It's not myself I should be angry at—it's my people, the Mogadorians who got me here. The Mogadorians, who worship brute force and believe that war is a way of life.

Soon I can feel my rage coursing through my body. Nothing in my life has ever been fair. I never had a shot at all. I think about Ivan, who was a best friend to me. We grew up together, and then he betrayed me. He tried to kill me—more than once.

I think about my father, who didn't think twice

about letting the Mogadorian scientists experiment on me with machines that had been completely untested and came close to frying my brain. It was nothing to him to risk sacrificing me for *the cause*.

And what cause was that? The cause of creating more destruction, of killing more people and gaining more power for himself. But power over what? When we'd conquered Lorien, we'd left it a lifeless, destroyed husk of a planet. There was nothing left on Lorien to rule. Was that what we were going to do to Earth too?

For people like my father, that's not the point. The point is war. The point is winning. To him, I was just another potential weapon to be used and discarded. That's all anyone's ever been worth to him.

The more I think about it, the more I feel my mind racing with rage. I hate him. I hate Ivan. I hate Setrákus Ra and the Good Book for teaching them all that this is the right way to live. I hate them all.

My fingers and toes start to tingle. I feel the rocks around me start to tremble. I'm doing it. My Legacy is working. You can let your anger destroy you, or you can use it for something. I close my eyes again, clench my fists and scream as loud as I can, letting all my fury out in one big burst. And with a massive whoosh, the dirt and stone and rubble begin to crumble. My body is shaking all over, and the ground is shaking too. Before long, it's all slid away, and I'm free again. It's as if a giant shovel has scooped me out.

But someone else isn't as lucky. Not ten feet away from me, a Mogadorian soldier is wedged beneath what looks like part of a shattered steel doorframe.

He groans and stirs now that the weight's been lifted.

He's as alive as I am. Awesome.

CHAPTER TWO

I PULL MYSELF TO MY FEET, STAGGERING A bit. My whole body aches like I've just been squeezed in a giant vise, but I don't think anything's broken. I'm covered in dirt and dust and sweat and, yes, some blood, but not a lot of that either. Somehow, I've managed to avoid any serious injury. I don't know how, and I don't really care.

The other Mogadorian isn't so lucky. As I stand, he lets out a low groan, but he doesn't look up at me or move. He's so beaten up that he barely seems to realize he's not buried anymore. I don't even think he realizes I'm here.

He must have gotten hit pretty hard, because this guy doesn't look like the type who would be easy to take out. He's as big as Ivan and built like a pro linebacker, with a thick neck and bulging muscles, but I can tell even from here that he's not vatborn—his facial features are too clean lined and too even to be one of the genetically altered warriors who make up the majority of the Mogadorians' army.

This one is a trueborn, like me. Like my father. From the tattoo on his skull I can tell that he's an officer, not a grunt. It figures. The vatborn are bred to be cannon fodder, while the trueborn give the orders. Maybe that's why I don't remember seeing him while I was holding back the troops. Unlike Ivan, who charged after me and got himself killed as a result, this guy must've been leading from the rear.

I actually feel a stab of disgust at the thought. A good commander leads by example, not by cowering behind his men. Not that it did him much good. Anyway, none of it matters much. I need to figure out what I'm going to do with him.

First things first: I check him over for any weapons. He grunts a little as I pat him down, and his eyes flutter for a moment, but he doesn't resist my search. Not that I find anything useful on him—if he had a blaster it's long gone, and he doesn't seem to have a knife on him either. I don't find so much as a breath mint in his pockets. Which, from the foul stench of the air emitting from his mouth in wheezing bursts, would probably do him more good than a weapon right about now.

The one thing that I can't help but notice is the blood. This guy's practically covered in it. It's seeping out from under the dust and dirt that coat his pale skin, and staining through the torn-up clothes he still has on. I don't see any one big injury, but he's a mess for sure.

When I'm satisfied that he's not going to jump to his feet and take me down the moment I turn my back on him, I look around the area I'm standing in and try to get my bearings. The bulk of Dulce Base was built underground to keep it away from prying eyes, but I guess my little stunt changed all that. I'm standing in a giant crater at least a hundred feet across at the top, and there's a clear blue sky above. The only problem is, I'm at least twenty feet down from where rock ends and sky begins.

The wreckage is everywhere—rocks and cement and toppled columns, busted computers and equipment with their exposed electrical wires sparking dangerously. When I smell the familiar stench of gasoline, I realize that I'm basically standing in the middle of a huge powder keg. This place could go up in flames at any second. It's sort of a miracle there haven't been any more explosions yet.

I have to get out of here quick. Luckily, despite the fact that we're so far down, there's so much debris piled high in every direction that I figure it won't be too hard to climb my way to the surface.

I figure out which direction will be the easiest to negotiate, and start to head that way—and then stop. I look behind me, at the guy lying there on the ground—the Mogadorian who still hasn't stirred beyond a groan.

I could leave him here to die alone. I have myself to worry about, and besides, one more dead Mogadorian is a good thing. But something stops me.

It's not that I'm just being nice. It's way too late to start having moral qualms now. After all, I've killed more than my share of Mogs since all this started.

For a moment I wonder if my dad ever would have guessed that I had it in me. I wonder if it would give him even a tiny bit of pride if he knew.

Of course, my dad's pride is the last thing I'm looking for now. That's not why I decide to turn back, though. Instead, it's because I know that a single, unarmed Mogadorian officer can do me more good alive than he can dead. For one thing, if he was stationed here he'll know his way around the surrounding area and any nearby towns. Deep in the middle of the desert, without even a compass to guide me, that stuff matters if I want to get out alive.

So I head back to the guy, grab him under the arms and start hauling him along.

This guy's really heavy, and it's all I can do to drag him over the craggy piles of junk and rocks as we make our way across the vast expanse of the base's ruins towards the edge of the crater. The sun is higher in the sky now and we're completely exposed to it. I feel a bead of sweat forming at my brow and making its way down my face and then, before I know it, I'm completely drenched. I try to clear a path as I move, kicking aside dusty monitors and crushed aluminum piping and whatever else is blocking the way.

Not that it does much good. Within minutes, my arms feel like noodles, my legs hurt and my back is killing me. We're not even halfway to where we need to be. This isn't going to work. Finally, when I drop the Mogadorian to the ground to catch my breath, he stirs.

"Hey," I say. "Can you hear me?"

"Uhhhrm," he replies. Well, it's not that helpful, but it's better than nothing, I figure.

"Hey, listen," I try again. "We've got to get out of here. Can you walk?"

He peers up at me, his heavy brow furrowed, and I can guess why. He's trying to figure out who I am and what I'm doing here. I'm covered in grime, so he probably can't tell that I don't have the skull tattoo that denotes Mogadorian rank, and he looks up at me in confusion.

I don't have time for him to be confused, or time for him to come to his senses—assuming he ever will. We have to get out of here *now*. I have no idea whether there are any others still alive elsewhere on the base, or if reinforcements are on the way. Plus, I'm half expecting the whole place to go up flames at any second. That's *if* I don't die of thirst before it happened.

I try a different tack. I speak to him in our native Mogadorian tongue, the language that's mostly only ever used now for ceremonial purposes. I quote the Good Book. *"Strength is sacred,"* I say. It's one of the most important tenets in Mogadorian society. His eyes come into focus.

"On your feet, soldier!" I snap. I'm only half surprised when it does the trick and he slowly levers himself up onto one knee and raises himself to his feet. Typical Mogadorian—there's nothing my people respond to more enthusiastically than empty authority. He's swaying a bit as he comes to a standing position. His left arm is hanging funny, and he's pale, sweat popping out across his forehead and along his upper lip, but he's up. For now.

"Let's go," I tell him, pointing towards the opening high above. "March." Without a word, he lumbers past me.

I follow him, realizing that I'm not in much better shape than he is. As we scramble over the heaps of rubble, I find myself thinking of Sam and Malcolm. I hope they made it out of here okay. My cell phone got crushed when I brought down the base, so I can't call Malcolm to find out what happened, arrange somewhere to meet up or even ask for help. All I can do is have some hope.

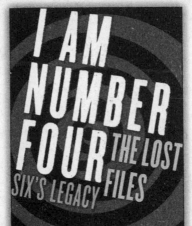
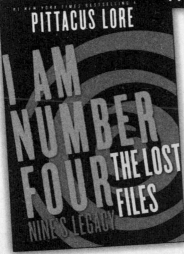
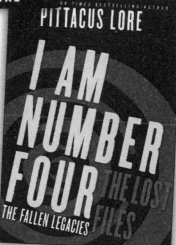

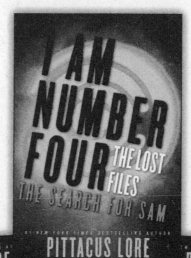
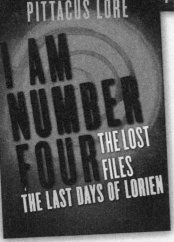

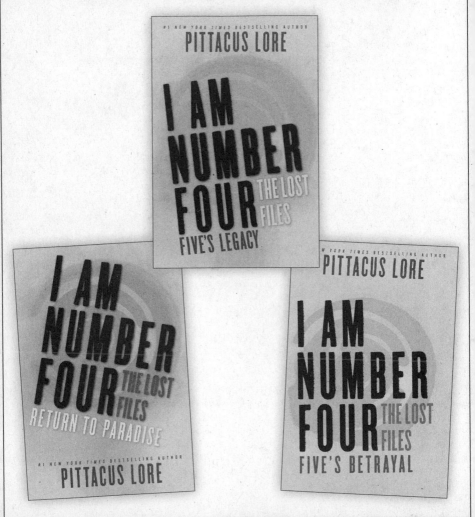